A Claim to Murder

ALSO BY JEAN G. GOODHIND

A CLAIM TO MURDER

JEAN G. GOODHIND

JOFFE BOOKS

Joffe Books, London
www.joffebooks.com

First published in Great Britain in 2025

© Jean G. Goodhind

Cover art by Dee Dee Book Covers

ISBN: 978-1-80573-165-8

PROLOGUE

Norman Glendower deserved to die. And he would.

Two in the morning, dark and damp and as silent as the grave — only this was no graveyard. This was Regency Gardens, an exclusive gated community situated in Bath's World Heritage heart, afforded only by those with an income that also allowed them to afford a top-of-the-range four by four and six holidays a year plus weekend breaks. Inside its stout walls and electric gates stood pseudo-Georgian houses that cost as much — sometimes more — than the originals constructed some two hundred years before.

Although of heavy build, the man who kept to the shadows was light on his feet. The night's silence was like a cloak, not even pierced by the sound of distant traffic. The select development was adjacent to woodland and beyond that a valley of open fields.

The cry of something wild and free made him pause for a moment and take stock. The eerie noise was far from human. An owl was out hunting, a corresponding response coming from out of the darkness.

The cry of the owl was followed by the rustling of leaves disturbed by another nighttime predator.

The fox was more surprised than the intruder he met halfway along the path next to the house. Surprised to see another living creature at this unearthly hour, it slunk away. Once it had attained a relatively safe distance its nose reconnected to the ground, sniffing for its supper.

The intruder didn't break step. He'd sneaked in the back way. There were no security lights at the rear entrance, the developers having cut costs with a view to maintaining a healthy balance sheet. He knew he would not be seen.

The night was dark, dry and warm enough not to wear a coat. Ideal. The Victorian reproduction streetlights outside the cavalcade of houses were decorative, pretty and the Birmingham-based architect's idea of planned nostalgia, but they had gone out. From experience, he guessed the council had been told of the problem. But knowing them, they wouldn't hurry; passing the buck was part of their remit. Blame someone else — in this case, the management company. It was them who also employed the road sweepers, a part-time janitor and the security guard who was presently asleep at his post, television flickering, a half-empty bottle of Johnny Walker on his desk. He'd reconnoitred. Drunk security guard. No security lights. No streetlights. Perfect.

Killing a fellow human being had not been an easy decision, but in this case the need to carry out this foul deed was driven by a great wrong that demanded revenge — one that, like creeping ivy, had become even bigger and as toxic as the intended victim.

Over the top of the laurel hedge to the rear of the house, the lights of further residential crescents, squares, major roads and minor roads trailed spangled patterns in the darkness.

From somewhere down on the main road heading from the city to Warminster and all things south of there, an ambulance siren wailed mournfully. The headlights of passing cars flashed momentarily beyond the wrought-iron gates and were gone, the road reclaimed by the darkness.

Keeping close to the back of the house, prying fingers followed the joints between the bricks until there were no more, only the door frame and the back door. The door frame was made of the best sapele — 'guaranteed to last for many years', as it had said on the sales blurb. Guaranteed to last for the same amount of time as the other elegant terraces and closes in Bath on which these usurpers, these newly built houses, had been based. Whether it would turn out to be true was another matter.

The key fitted easily into the lock, although as it turned out, no key was needed. The door was not locked. Big surprise. A quick downward thrust, a tug and it was open. Careless. Arrogant. His victim was both of those things.

The smell that came out was nondescript, as though nothing of any consequence had been cooked in the kitchen for ages and washing up was an ad hoc affair, eating and drinking taking priority. Certainly not a proper meal, an oven roast, grilled steaks or even a hearty vegetable soup. A row of empty wine bottles cluttered the window ledge. The dishes and dirty glasses piled in the sink and scattered along the marble-topped work surfaces seemed of no importance to the person who lived here — either that or they'd ran out of washing-up liquid.

Unlike real Georgian houses these newbuilds had open-plan kitchen-diners No self-respecting IT professional or lawyer would countenance anything else. They'd been the market the building firm had been after. It may have come as a very pleasant surprise indeed that their sales pitch had proved right. The first few houses had sold like hot cakes. Those built later were a little slower going out the door — in a manner of speaking. But it didn't matter. They sold. The firm had made a fat profit. Money was all that counted in their world, just as it was in his. It was just the means of getting it that differed.

His meaty fingers grasped the cricket bat more firmly, like a guy about to hit one hell of a boundary. But it wasn't a boundary he was about to hit. Norman Glendower had not played ball.

CHAPTER ONE

Blue sky and blue Mediterranean Sea and the sailing yacht they'd named *Footloose* bobbing up and down in a gentle swell. Heaven on earth — or heaven and earth, depending which way you looked at it.

'This is the life.'

Honey Driver had muttered the same sentiment dozens of times since she and Steve Doherty had set sail to live the dream. They had considered marrying but decided to take a leave of absence — from running a hotel in Honey's case, and, for Steve, it was a two-year sabbatical from the police.

'Then we can decide what next.'

'We could keep on sailing for ever. Retirement with knobs on.'

They agreed on that. In the meantime, they were liveaboard yachties. They'd bought the sailing yacht in Ipswich, where they'd done work on it, then sailed out and around the east coast and generally became more adept at the sailing lark. After nearly two years of browsing around home waters they'd decided to take the plunge. It had everything they needed, and once May had arrived, they'd left England and headed south across the Bay of Biscay, down the Portuguese coast then due east into the Bay of Cadiz, past Gibraltar and into the warm blue waters of the Mediterranean.

There was no way she was going to miss a chance like this. Left miles behind was the Green River Hotel, where she'd installed a manager to keep the place going and cope with the likes of Smudger Smith, her slightly eccentric chef, and Mary Jane, her even more eccentric permanent resident. Plus her mother, who, although in her mid-seventies, could give *Vogue* models a run for their money.

Even her allegiance to the Bath Hotels Association was no more, and gone was her position as Crime Liaison Officer for the Association. The World Heritage city of Bath was jealous of its reputation and crime was something they wished to keep far from their door — hence Honey becoming its Crime Liaison Officer. At first she'd been reluctant, but the promise of a full hotel in the shoulder and winter months had influenced her judgement.

At present her feet were trailing in the water and she was lying full stretch across the deck. Steve was on the helm. Before he'd left to pursue his dream, the police had warned him that due to financial constraints they might very well drag him back at some point before he drew his pension.

Like Honey, he was wearing a pair of cut-off jeans, the ragged edges fluttering around his knees. The day was hot and there wasn't a soul or land to be seen, so she hadn't bothered to don a top, though an overlarge T-shirt was close at hand just in case the Italian coastguard happened by. They had powerful binoculars, so wouldn't fail to notice her state of dress. Like any good boy or girl scout, it was always best to be prepared.

Steve was humming to himself, his dark hair, in need of cutting, blowing across the white creases at the corners of his eyes and getting caught on his designer stubble, which wasn't really designer — he just couldn't be bothered to shave.

His hands, brown and strong, were applying steady pressure to the steering wheel, though thanks to a lack of ocean current and only a force-three breeze, it needed only the gentlest touch to keep it on course.

'I wonder what's happening back in Bath,' said Honey, leaning back and closing her eyes behind her overly large sunglasses.

'It's July.'

'Then it's raining.'

'Probably.'

'Wonderful!'

Honey applied more sun cream — the more, the better. Burning could be ten times more severe out on the sea thanks to sunlight reflecting off the water.

'Is there anything you truly miss?' he asked her.

It didn't take Honey long to answer. 'Lindsey. And the baby.'

'She's off living her dream . . . as much as you and me.'

'I know.'

Honey's daughter, Lindsey, with only minimal luggage and her nine-month-old daughter strapped into a front-loading papoose, was travelling the world with Grant, Lindsey's partner and the father of her child. Although he and Lindsey had discussed getting married, they'd decided to take their time. 'Just in case we get fed up with each other.'

Lindsey, Grant and baby were now in New Zealand working for a film studio that made such films as *Lord of the Rings* — in fact, anything that leaned towards fantasy or dystopian. Lindsey oversaw the catering and had stated with bemusement that she quite liked serving elves and goblins hot dogs, beefburgers and vegan sausages.

'Like us. Sailing the world before our knees go and we're relegated to a mobility scooter. You can't travel the world in one of them,' he declared with a doleful shake of his head.

They both adopted smugly satisfied expressions at the thought of what they had done. Lots of people talked about escaping the rat race and sailing the world. It took a lot of guts to do it and there were no regrets. They'd marvelled at seeing the world from a different angle. Life couldn't be more different, but self-sufficiency had beckoned. They had solar panels, a wind generator, a water maker and most of the comforts of home.

'Up and down, up and down,' sang Steve in time with the movement of the hull. 'Living the life indeed. Can't beat it!'

Honey sighed and leaned back against a cushion.

Steve sang 'A Life on the Ocean Waves', badly out of tune. Honey put her fingers in her ears. He switched to 'I Am Sailing'. Honey put a pillow over her head. Rod Stewart he was not!

She came out from behind the cushion to find that all was peaceful, not a ripple in the sea and a nice force three, almost complete calm.

It was perfect — though not for long.

A sudden bang against the hull sent the boat shuddering from bow to stern.

Steve's face paled and he uttered a loud expletive.

Honey matched it. The looks they gave each other matched too. The wheel was impossible to steer and water was already washing over the decks as the boat heeled to one side.

'Get the grab bag! Now!'

He left the wheel and scrambled to the stern to launch the life raft from beneath the shadow of the solar panels.

Honey almost fell down the ladder into the saloon. Items left loose on the kitchen tops were rolling over the floor. The microwave slammed against the countertop edging. The doors of the TV cupboard swung open. DVDs and books left out rattled and skidded across the floor.

The grab bag containing items needed in an emergency was tucked behind the ladder leading from deck to saloon.

She checked everything off in her mind. Life jackets, EPIRB — the precious device that emitted a signal back to a radio station, usually Portishead in Somerset — plus a chart of the locale. Mobile phones, of course, not that they would work this far out. Fifteen miles was about the limit of reception from a land-based mast. A bottle of water, a handheld compass, blanket, emergency food ration . . . chocolate would be good. A quick search revealed there was none in there. She'd eaten it the night before while watching a DVD. Oranges and dates would have to do.

When she got back up on deck, the boat was sinking fast and Steve was waiting to help her into the life raft, his hands folded over the guardrail, his feet in the life raft, legs in the water. He reached out a hand. 'Come on. Hurry up!'

Life rafts are not stable. This one was no exception. Once inflated, it bobbed about like a ping pong ball, one second sitting close to the hull before playfully bobbing away the next.

Jumping into it was not an option. The boat was sinking fast and Steve's hand wavered close to the boat before the distance increased and his fingers seemed too far away to grab.

'Keep her out,' she shouted to him.

The last thing they wanted was for the life raft to get caught beneath the mast or anything else on the deck as the boat turned over. There was no option but to leap into the water, dragging the grab bag behind her.

Salt water rushed into her throat and her hair trailed out behind her like a clutch of dark seaweed.

A strong hand reached out, the very sight of it like a lighthouse on a rock, though this one was to be welcomed not avoided.

Steve took the bag from her before pulling her up beside him just as the boat turned over and the mast and boom came crashing into the water.

Shocked beyond belief, they stared out of the opening in the life raft at an empty sea. Not a wave in sight. Not even a seagull or curious dolphin. The boat had disappeared. It had been that quick. All that remained was an ominous oblong shape floating just beneath the surface, the sea barely covering it. The nemesis of their ordeal floated beside it, a huge container belonging to a major shipping company.

Honey groaned. 'Of all the water covering the earth why did that container fall off a ship just here? Why when WE were in the vicinity?'

They looked around them as if for some giant finger pointing down at them but there was nothing but an expanse of empty sea, sparkling diamonds dancing on the surface against a backdrop of crystal blue. It was so vast, they may as well have been in outer space.

'Now what?'

'Take a page out of ET's book and phone home.'

'Fat chance,' muttered Steve.

They were way too far out to use a mobile phone. There were no masts at sea — well, not mobile phone masts anyway, only the ones on sailing vessels. There wasn't one of them in sight either.

There was no alternative but to activate the emergency positioning beacon, which would send out a distress signal that hopefully would be picked up in Portishead, a famed and very efficient receiving station. Not that they could let it stop there. They needed to take readings with the handheld compass and use a pencil to mark the paper chart they'd had the foresight to place inside the bag.

'Shouldn't take too long,' said Honey. 'It's not as though we're thousands of miles from land.'

'That's it,' said Steve nodding in agreement. 'It shouldn't be too long. Did you think to put the chart inside a plastic folder?'

Honey pulled a face. 'Ah!'

'What does "ah" mean?' said Steve, sounding as though he was prepared for the worst.

'Sorry.' She pulled the chart from the plastic folder then burst into laughter. 'You should have seen your face . . .'

Steve was not amused. 'That's not funny.'

'Oh, come on, Doherty. Look on the bright side.'

The glower on Steve's face deepened. 'What bright side?'

Smiling as though all was well with their world, Honey cocked her head to one side. 'We need to keep our spirits up. And before you say we can sing to keep ourselves amused, may I remind you that I have a voice like an earwig. And yours isn't much better.'

9

Steve frowned. 'Earwigs don't sing.'

'Right. And neither do I. Now, then. Let's get serious.' She unfolded the chart and spread it between them. 'We marked this chart with our position as of first thing this morning. We know where we are and that we're not far from land. We're bound to bump into another vessel.'

Steve spread his hands, indicating the massive expanse of blue they were in. Not a boat in sight.

'There's nothing out there,' he exclaimed with feeling. 'Nothing for miles.'

'I beg to differ. We've just been holed and sunk by a container that fell from a cargo ship. So, you can't say there's nothing out here.'

Steve was not reassured. Whereas Honey was eking out every ounce of humour she had, his expression remained glum.

It's because he's a man, Honey told herself. *Men are like badgers. They set out a plan and stick to it*. Not that badgers made plans — well, she didn't think they did. But badgers did tread the same track every night, even if it happened to cross the M4 between London and Cardiff.

'Look,' she said, doing her best to send out the most positive vibes she could. 'According to the last mark we made on this chart, I reckon we're less than a hundred miles from Sicily, a very small distance in the great scheme of things.'

Seeing that his chin looked in danger of sinking onto his chest, she cupped her hand over his cheek. 'We still have each other, and out here we can speak our minds and share secrets and inner thoughts like we've never done before.'

She knew immediately that she'd said the wrong thing when his look of despair was replaced by one of suspicion.

'What secrets? Is there anything I should know?'

'Nothing,' said Honey, working out how best she could backtrack. 'I was just talking about intimate moments.'

'With who?'

'With whom,' she responded, willing to argue about grammar if she had to rather than declare old secrets, of which Steve already had the lowdown, unless she made up something.

'I wonder how long it will be before the message is relayed from the emergency beacon to the UK and back again?'

She said this as she refolded the chart so that the bit showing their location was uppermost. She had entered their latest position garnered as best as possible from the compass. It was about as accurate as it could be. She peered at it accusingly. You could never be too careful. All seemed in order.

She looked out through the gap in the life raft covering. Hypnotised by sunlight blinking on water, she wondered how it would be back in Bath.

'It won't be the same,' she said out loud. 'Back in Bath. It won't be the same as when we left. That life we had, the hotel and your career have all changed.'

'We lived the life. I thought we'd go on for a few years yet.' Steve sighed. 'I've missed some things about it.' He shook his head. 'Can't say I missed it as much as I'm going to miss *Footloose*.'

Honey hugged her bare knees. Her chin sank onto the comfortable platform of her kneecaps. 'Sad about the boat. I'll miss the old girl too.'

Steve agreed. 'Rest in peace, *SY Footloose and Fancy-Free*.'

Honey echoed the sentiment.

The boat's name had been *Footloose* but they'd always tended to add the rest of the soubriquet. It seemed doubly fitting now, just as people spelled out someone's full name in an obituary or declared it at a funeral.

'Amen,' they both said. Their home was gone and so was the wandering life they'd lived.

After a period of respectful silence, Honey said, 'Oh, well. Bath it must be. Not that we have any choice. Thank goodness we're insured. After we've seen how the land lies, perhaps we could buy another one with the insurance money.'

'Not the same though. I loved that boat. She was mother, wife and lover to me.'

'Was she, now?' Honey said with a glimmer of mischief. 'And where do I fit in?'

'Just a figure of speech,' he carped back. 'Like you and that nonsense about sharing secrets.'

'Quite right. We don't have any.' She raised her hand. 'Let's make a list. First things first, get rescued. Second thing, the moment we're back in the good old UK, we make an insurance claim. Then—' she bent back her third finger — 'once the claim's settled, we can decide what's next.'

'Let's hope the insurers don't make us jump through hoops. They can be right—' His expletive was taken by the wind and only half heard. Not that Honey needed to have it shouted in her face. Insurance had never been one of her stronger points. She'd always hated paying for something that was unlikely to happen. The insurance companies were like bookies. The odds were in their favour, though on this occasion she was certain they would pay out without quibbling. The accident was genuine and not their fault.

Steve was thoughtful and his mood had improved. 'You're right. We have to plan what to do next. I wonder how much we'll get,' he said dreamily. 'Enough for a bigger boat?'

'We'll get what she was insured for and no more.'

'I might win the lottery.'

'I doubt it, seeing as you don't do the lottery. You're hard-pressed to buy a raffle ticket without a big question and answer session regarding your chances.'

'It's the waiting I hate.'

Honey suggested that they had little choice in the matter. For the foreseeable future they would reside back at the Green River Hotel in Bath while the insurance company was sorting things out. That was the plan. Little did they know at that moment in time that things wouldn't quite work out the way they wanted them to. The sky and Mediterranean Sea were still blue, but dark clouds were gathering on the horizon in England and they were sailing straight into it. On top of that, she'd left her T-shirt behind. So much for being a boy scout and adequately prepared.

Everything seemed pretty straightforward once they were rescued and their phones were working. That was when Steve mentioned he'd rung the insurance broker but got no reply.

A sudden sickly feeling in her stomach, Honey eyed him suspiciously. 'Phone? Why didn't you contact him through his website?'

Steve looked peevish. 'Good old Norman believes in personal contact.' He hesitated before declaring something she hadn't wanted to hear. 'Norman Glendower doesn't have a website.'

'A broker who prefers personal contact. That's downright archaic.'

'I told you, he believes in the personal touch.' Acute embarrassment flickered on Steve's face.

'You really did that?'

He nodded. 'It seemed a good idea at the time. He's a good bloke, Norman Glendower.'

Honey's eyes narrowed and her jawline hardened. 'Steve, there are times when you're too trusting for your own good.'

'The other guys said . . .'

'Yeah, yeah, yeah. Then they're as daft as you are!'

CHAPTER TWO

Nigel Bracket, who had once worked for Jaspar St John Gervais, one-time chairman of the Bath Hotels Association, had been running the Green River Hotel in Honey's absence, and although Honey found it hard to admit, he appeared to be doing a very good job of it.

His friend Eddie Makepeace had been helping him, the two living in the coach house at the back of the property where Honey and her daughter had once lived.

Honey had phoned them, texted them and emailed them, so they wouldn't be in any doubt that they were coming back.

And they were most of the way home now, brown-skinned, hair streaked with gold and wearing second-hand clothes that a kind friend of the Italian coast guard had given them. The clothes had been left behind by holidaymakers who had either quite forgotten to pack them or decided that they'd had their fill of wearing creased linen and flip-flops. Good common sense, seeing as such items were obsolete for feet winging it to colder climes.

Once they'd landed at Heathrow and the wind was whistling through their duds, Honey made a beeline for Marks and Spencer to buy blazers, long trousers and a pair of loafers for each of them.

'Ten out of ten for feeling warmer. Good old Marks and Spencer,' Steve said with a shiver as he buttoned up the blazer.

'Four out of ten for presentation,' murmured Honey on catching a glimpse of herself in a shop window. 'My hair looks a mess.'

As they emerged from the London Underground escalators, an announcement came over the loudspeaker: 'Bath Spa from platform four.'

Honey and Steve bolted for the comfort of the twelve thirty train. A first-class seat would have been sublime luxury, but anything was better than sitting on the cold metal seats at Paddington station. Once installed on comfortable seats, they slept most of the way, tired and dispirited, keen to get home but regretful that the dream of sailing the wide blue yonder had come to an end.

They came out of Bath Spa station with something akin to relief, then stopped in their tracks. The old buildings were unchanged, taxis still lined up outside, buses trundling in and out of the terminus next door, and tourists fixated on an overabundance of history getting in the way of ordinary Bathonians shopping, going to work or simply wandering about their city. The visitors plodded the pavements, armed with guidebooks detailing where Jane Austen used to live and the history of the Roman Baths, plus listing the best places to eat — in the author's opinion.

Both Honey and Steve stopped dead outside the Green River Hotel and stared up at the frontage with mixed feelings. It was home but they had not expected to be back for a very long time. This was where they as a couple had begun.

They might never have been thrown together if Honey hadn't been pressurised into accepting the position of Crime Liaison Officer on behalf of the Bath Hotels Association. She'd been the representative for the Association; Steve Doherty had been her opposite number on behalf of the police. From then on there was no holding them back. They'd clicked in a big way, enjoyed life in Bath and then, ditching the idea of marriage, had opted instead to sail the seven seas. Their idea had been to venture into the Pacific and sample life on the other side of the world. The container left floating in the sea had scuppered their plans.

The tragedy, the unfairness, the downright bad luck of it all was still hard to swallow. 'I can't believe we're back here.'

'Ditto.'

Honey's bottom lip curled outwards, and despite the urge to scream, cry and stamp her foot like a spoilt child, she made a stab at being positive.

'Oh well. There's no point in crying over spilled milk.'

'I'd prefer that to crying over *Footloose and Fancy-Free*. I can buy a bottle of milk anywhere.'

Steve, it seemed, was in the doldrums, a real place in sailor jargon where Samuel Taylor Coleridge's description of a painted ship on a painted ocean had true meaning. Describing Steve as an ancient mariner would be unfair. He wasn't ancient, but he was most definitely in the doldrums.

'Come on.' Honey jabbed at his side with an elbow that was far leaner than when they'd first set sail. 'Let's grit our teeth and bear it. It's all we can bloody do!'

Steve did his best to sound positive. 'Once the insurance pays out, we can buy another one.'

Honey made a grumpy sound. Heart heavy but determined to dust herself off and sort things out, she sighed and pushed open the double doors of the Green River Hotel. A mix of beeswax furniture polish and perfume from the tasteful flower arrangements displayed in mock-classical urns filled the air. So did the aroma of freshly brewed coffee.

Nigel threw his arms wide and came out from behind the reception counter, a yellow silk waistcoat stretching across his expanding girth.

'Welcome, welcome,' he cried, arms enfolding each of them in turn. His warm welcome was echoed by his partner, Eddie, although the latter, a more sensitive soul than Nigel, spoke with a trembling voice.

'Poor you,' he exclaimed. 'What awfully bad luck.'

They both proclaimed how sorry they were that their boat had come to such a sticky end, shaking their heads sadly and wiping away invisible tears.

'So sad,' said Nigel.

'So sad,' echoed Eddie.

'If there's anything we can do . . .'

Honey spread her hands and shrugged. 'There's nothing.'

A slightly tight look came to Nigel's face. 'Do you plan to stay?'

There was heaps of meaning in the question. Honey went straight in with her interpretation. 'If you mean am I going to take the reins from you, the answer is no. Please carry on as you are.'

Steve piped up. 'We hope in time to have another boat — but it could take some time for the insurance company to sort out the details.'

Honey threw him a disparaging look. He'd phoned the broker when they were waiting at Paddington station. Nobody had answered.

She turned back to Nigel. 'Nigel, darling, please carry on as usual. Pretend we're not here.'

'Will you be moving back into the coach house?' asked Eddie, glancing from them to Nigel. 'Only, it would take us a bit of time to clear out our stuff. We've kept our flat, of course, but would need to give three months' notice to our tenants that we're moving back in.'

Honey reassured them. 'We hope we won't be back for too long. *I must go down to the sea again, to the lonely sea and the sky*", and all that.' She sighed wistfully, thinking how meaningful the words of the poet John Masefield were. 'Hopefully it will be a swift process,' she added, determined not to dwell on what had happened but motor on, get the paperwork sorted, the money in the bank and seek out a new yacht to take the two of them around the world. However, she couldn't help the nervous niggle gyrating like a hula dancer inside.

Nigel and Eddie exchanged looks of relief before Nigel explained, 'Right. Well, please don't get this wrong. We were willing to move out if that's what you wanted. But, just in case, we allowed for all eventualities and made you up a bed in the honeymoon suite.'

'A bed in one of the standard rooms would have done,' said Honey, aching to get into some of the clothes she'd left behind — especially a cowl-necked pure-wool jumper with sleeves that covered her hands and so negated the wearing of gloves. It would be a while before she got used to the cooler climes.

Nigel clapped his hands and cooed, 'No, no, no, dar-lings. Mary Jane did a feng shui session in each and every room so we could be sure that you would get an uninter-rupted good night's sleep without being bothered by bad memories. Karma, darling. It's all about karma.'

'Ah! Mary Jane. I know I'm home for sure when I see her,' said Honey with a deep sigh.

Steve, who was a total sceptic when it came to Mary Jane's adherence to the occult, ancient wisdom and life after death, groaned as though he'd been punched in the stomach. As far as he could see, Mary Jane's contacts in the afterlife seemed to mainly consist of her relatives, one of whom lived in the wardrobe in her room.

'Much appreciated,' he muttered with more sarcasm than gratefulness.

Honey restrained herself from giving him a kick on the ankle. She smiled in the genuine way that these two would appreciate.

'That was very kind of you — and Mary Jane,' Honey added, at the same time throwing a warning look in Steve's direction. Mary Jane was very kind. She was also a little eccentric. Most people could cope with that, telling them-selves that it was just a little add-on to normal. Steve wasn't one of them.

Honey pronounced that she could murder a coffee.

'A Courvoisier chaser for me,' grumbled Steve.

Nigel shook his head in forlorn agreement. 'I should think you could do with it. And while we drink, darlings, tell me all about this terrible tragedy. Would that be all right?'

'Yes.' Honey answered for them both, which resulted in more applause from Nigel and an instruction fired off to Eddie for coffee, shortbread and a large brandy. Steve looked as though all he wanted to do was crawl beneath the bed-clothes and not come out until the bad dream was over.

Nigel made one last order to the slim-hipped, pony-tailed Eddie. 'Can you hold the fort for half an hour, Eddie, darling?'

Eddie waved one hand dismissively. 'Certainly, Nigel.'

Nigel cupped Honey's elbow. 'Let us repair to the sitting room and you can tell me all about it.'

Honey allowed herself to be led, aware that Steve was following. She couldn't see the expression on his face but guessed he was wearing a look like a burst football.

The sitting room smelled of roses. Once the tray arrived, it would smell of coffee. The chairs and sofas were of a soft blue velvet. Chromium-framed side and coffee tables were dotted about. A large Venetian mirror hung above the mantelpiece.

Nothing has changed, she thought to herself, until she caught sight of herself in the mirror and saw that she had.

Back in the days before sailing away, her face had had a comfortable, rounded look, a description she preferred to the more depressing 'middle-aged'. Her reflection today showed a taut, brown complexion and there were lighter streaks in hair that had once been deep brown.

Fingering the largest streak, she gasped, wound it around her finger and pulled it close to her eyes.

'Are those sun streaks or am I going grey more quickly now?' She'd said it mostly to herself, but Nigel remarked that it was nothing a visit to the hairdresser and a little dye couldn't fix.

Refreshments arrived, Nigel pouring while Honey told him the bare bones of what had happened.

'A container, you say.'

Steve confirmed it was so. 'And the boat went straight down to Davy Jones.'

'Here. Get this coffee down you. And a brandy. A few shortbreads too.'

Honey tucked in, putting three away in quick succession. Food was a great comfort when you were wearing clothes bought out of necessity and still suffering in the aftermath of an accident.

'At least we survived. Steve launched the life raft and I dived into the water and swam to it. Quite an ordeal.'

With great aplomb, as though captain of a four-masted barque, not a forty-six-foot sloop, Steve took up the story, telling Nigel how they'd just left Sicily and were on their way across the Ionian. 'The weather was fine. It's always fine — mostly.' He downed one half of the brandy and washed it down with the other half. The coffee and shortbreads were ignored. Judging by the faraway look in his eyes, his thoughts were still back there on that sunny day when the sky was as blue as the sea.

Honey took it upon herself to fill in the gaps.

Nigel continued to listen with rapt attention interspersed with sighs of 'dreadful', 'how alarming' and 'what an awful thing to happen'.

Steve sat morosely eyeing his empty brandy glass.

Nigel seemed genuinely concerned and asked about what would happen next. 'Once the insurance pays out, you can set off again. Filled in the claim form, have ya?'

Steve fingered the brandy glass. 'Not exactly . . .'

Honey rested her chin on her hand. 'We haven't heard anything yet,' she said somewhat despondently.

'These things take time. I've phoned the broker, but—'

'A broker?' Nigel raised a querulous eyebrow. 'So, you mean an online comparison site, or did you do it the old-fashioned way? A shop? A person?' He eyed Steve expectantly.

Honey glanced at Steve's gloomy expression and said, 'An old friend of someone in the police force that Steve knew.'

'Norman Glendower came highly recommended. A broker of the old school.'

'That's novel,' Nigel remarked, a wary disbelief in his voice — surprise, even. 'Didn't think they still existed.'

Honey hid her worried lips behind the rim of the coffee cup. Lindsey had pointed that out too, but then Lindsey was very computer savvy. Steve had assured her that everything would be all right and to leave the arrangements to him. 'I've got seagoing blood. I know about stuff like this.'

And so the die was cast. 'We're kind of old-fashioned,' Honey said. It sounded like an excuse because it was. Gritting her teeth, she resolved not to blame Steve for their decision to go to a broker. Everything would be fine — because it had to be.

'You can't beat getting advice face to face,' he'd said to her. She'd accepted that, though she'd presumed Norman Glendower would still have had a proper website. Now she wished she'd kept a tighter rein on things and not left it all to Steve.

Lindsey had been against the idea, whereas Honey's mother, Gloria Cross, had agreed with the advice given by Steve's police colleague.

'You shouldn't use those online sites. They're scammers and likely to run off with your money. You'll never see any of it again. Go to this broker, get whatever insurance you need, then sail away south.'

'Until the butter melts,' Steve had once said wistfully when they were navigating the Bay of Cadiz. The weather had been warm and getting warmer. Everything back then had been so much fun.

'Yep,' said Honey, who had shared Steve's high spirits and, to prove the point, really had left the butter out from the fridge. 'It's melted.'

But that was then and this was now.

'And this broker. He's local?'

Honey nodded. Her morale was taking a nosedive, and some pretty worrying negatives were taking root and not going away.

CHAPTER THREE

It wasn't exactly a match made in heaven, but there'd always been a strong bond between her and Steve. They'd always seemed to know what the other was thinking. At present neither were having good vibes about this situation. Honey was trying hard to look on the bright side of things — if she could find it within her. She could tell by Steve's manner that his reservations matched hers.

Looking worried, he got out his phone and stabbed angrily at the keyboard. There he was, not daring to tell Honey that he feared the worst. 'I'll give them another ring.'

He held the phone to his ear, trying to cover the worried look with one that clung to hope.

Honey wasn't fooled. She understood that doubt was beginning to creep in. Normally she might be supportive, tell him not to worry, but she too was beginning to entertain doubts. They were back in Bath, a city they knew well. Everything should have been straightforward. But it wasn't.

'No response from the broker. Perhaps the office is busy.'

The phone joined the coffee cups and empty brandy glass. A dash of brandy in coffee was becoming a habit. So was Nigel joining them in an effort to boost their failing spirits.

'How about going direct to the insurance company rather than through the broker?'

Honey agreed that Nigel's suggestion seemed sensible.

'Goodenough Marine. That's the name isn't it?' She looked at Steve for confirmation.

He nodded. 'Yes, though I haven't got the paperwork. It went down with the boat.'

'And their phone number?'

Steve shook his head.

'No worries.' After setting out the coffee cups and the now daily splash of brandy, Nigel pointed out that he could get the details online. 'Mind if I take a look?'

He reached for the phone.

Steve brushed him aside. 'I can do it. The good yacht *Footloose* bristled with technology, navigation and all that. If I can find my way through the Straits of Gibraltar, I'm sure I can find the company who insured my boat.'

Honey gritted her teeth. It wasn't the first time Steve had referred to the boat they'd both had a share in as 'his' boat. His alone. It rankled but, in the circumstances, and just for now, she'd let it go.

Tap, tap, tap went Steve's fingers as he tapped 'Goodenough Marine' into Google. Then he stared at the screen.

Honey asked if anything was happening.

Steve frowned. 'It can't find it.'

Honey caught the deep dive of Nigel's eyebrows, though even without seeing his expression, she'd have known this wasn't good.

Steve shrugged, non-committal but still looking worried. 'It's just a temporary glitch.'

Honey wasn't so sure.

Nigel stepped in. 'Do you mind if I have a go?'

Steve handed him the phone. 'Be my guest.'

Nigel's long, fine fingers, the nails enhanced with pale pink varnish, skipped lightly over the keys.

The phone delivered the same response.

Nigel pursed his lips. 'This is not good. It can't find any such company.' He looked at Steve. 'Are you sure this is the company name? Goodenough Marine?' He went on to spell it just in case he'd got it wrong.

Steve nodded. 'Yes. Absolutely. Try it on Honey's phone.'

'Why should the search engine find it on my phone and not yours? Phones don't have phobias.'

'No.' Steve took his phone back from Nigel and tried again. The result was the same.

'Looks like you might have got it wrong. Phone the broker. He should know.'

'I've already told you, that's what I've been doing since getting back — and before then for that matter. Nobody's answering.'

Honey chewed her bottom lip as she considered what was happening. The broker hadn't answered. Why? Why couldn't they locate a website for the insurance company?

'There has to be a logical explanation,' offered Steve, who'd obviously been thinking the same thing and, like her, was getting more worried by the minute.

The unspoken truth was that there wouldn't be a logical explanation, and perhaps no explanation at all. Horror of horrors, perhaps neither of them existed.

No, Honey told herself. *Don't go there. Steve is probably right. There must be a logical explanation.* It was little reassurance but currently all she had.

All the same, she couldn't help but glare at him. 'Doherty, what was the name of the broker?'

Steve winced because she hadn't called him Steve, she'd called him by his surname, which she only did when she was annoyed with him, or teasing him.

'Glendower. Norman Glendower.'

'A friend of yours?'

'He was a mate of a mate . . .'

She took a deep breath. 'Right. Then phone this mate of yours. Ask him to confirm the phone number and address of the office.'

Steve squirmed. 'I don't want to sound stupid.'

'Tell him you've lost this chap Norman's details and are desperate to get in touch with him. Mention what's happened. What's wrong with that?'

'I did a lot of boasting and teasing before we left. He's likely to pull my leg about it.'

'Doherty! We must take steps. I'll pull your leg off if you don't do something. So be it if it makes you sound stupid. We need confirmation that we've got the details correct or the insurance money will be joining the boat down in Davy Jones's locker. Beyond reach, anyway.'

'I did meet the insurance broker, you know.'

'With your police force mates?'

'That's right.'

'At his office?'

Again that squirming Steve did when it seemed he was going to be found out. 'Not exactly.'

Honey's look was piercing. 'What does that mean?'

Steve looked up at the ceiling then side to side.

He cleared his throat. 'In the pub.'

'The pub!'

She tried not to sound judgemental, but failed spectacularly.

Steve was well aware that she could keep up the cold glare she was giving him now for half an hour if she had to. Her persistence finally produced a result. He caved in. 'OK. I think I know the number.'

Fingers crossed for luck behind her back, she watched his expression as he waited for this old mate to answer.

Finally, not without a little surprise on her part, he did.

'Reggie! Long time no see. It's Steve Doherty.' He sounded jolly and, without giving the chap on the other end a chance to tease, he went straight into an abbreviated description of what had happened.

'Sheer bad luck,' he said. 'Of course, the insurance money will be enough to replace the boat, but it seems I've lost Norman's contact details.'

Judging by the relief etched on Steve's granite features, the leg pulling wasn't so bad. In fact, it looked as though he was enjoying it. The old sparkle shone in his eyes, the one she remembered from when they'd first met and he'd been far from keen to work with the representative of the Hotels Association.

A bit more banter, a brief discussion of old times and then Steve pushing to ask what he wanted to know.

The confidence that had momentarily lit up his face wavered.

'You don't know anything about a firm called Goodenough Marine?'

Honey could see from Steve's face that this man Reggie — surname Wolfson, if she remembered rightly — had no knowledge of such a firm.

'And the broker? Norman Glendower.'

It seemed a guffaw of laughter and their remembered meeting cheered the conversation from the other end of the phone. Memories of nights spent with other blokes in the pub tended to do that.

'Yeah. Yeah. Quite a night.'

Steve's face tensed. All trace of confidence crashed.

'He had an office in St Margaret's Buildings, you say?' Steve looked at Honey. 'And as far as you know he's still there.'

Honey breathed a sigh of relief and wafted the air in front of her face with her hand.

Something was said on the other end.

'Yeah. Great. I remember it well. Happy times,' said Steve.

A few short but well-chosen anecdotes of their days in the police force together, of nights in the Pulteney Arms with the rugby crowd, were swiftly exchanged before goodbyes were said and Steve severed the connection.

'He doesn't know anything about the companies Norman dealt with and never went to his office. He always saw him in some pub or other.'

Honey opened her mouth to say a pub was not conducive to conducting serious business — pints of bitter and strong lager would always precedence.

Steve held up his hand, palm facing her. 'Before you point out that a pub is not an office, Reggie assures me that Norman worked out of St Margaret's Buildings and as far as he's aware, still does.'

'Well, that's something. But not being able to trace the insurance company that issued the policy is a bit worrying.' Great. So, they had a way forward, except . . . 'It seems strange that there's nothing on Google. Makes me feel it might not exist.'

'Hmm.' He looked accusingly at his phone screen. 'Perhaps I got the name wrong.' He tried it again on Honey's phone with the same result.

'Nothing.'

Honey clamped her jaw tight. She wanted to say he should have checked Norman out, but Steve had been obsessed with the idea of following his dream. He'd wanted everything done in double-quick time. Living the dream had become an obsession and she too had felt a frisson of excitement at the prospect of living off-grid.

They were going round in circles. She found herself wishing that Mary Jane was here — she would consult the ancestors and tell them if they were barking up the wrong tree, and she would consult with the spirit world to see if he was hanging out with them. It was a long shot, and she'd seldom engaged Mary Jane in any of the crime cases she'd solved. That's how desperate this was.

Steve would call it clutching at straws. Mary Jane would tell her to trust her instinct. Her instinct was telling her that something wasn't quite right. It was like walking across a grassy lawn and then suddenly a mist lifts and you find yourself on a cliff edge.

Without needing to look in the mirror again, she knew beyond doubt that her face had turned a whiter shade of pale — if there was such a thing. 'I'm worried.'

Judging by Steve's face, so was he, the old 'suspicious detective' expression resurging after a long absence.

Honey was thinking, which led in turn to her pointing out, 'No "press one for enquiries, two for claims . . ." Even if the office is closed, you'd still get some kind of messaging service.'

Clever and cool-headed, Nigel offered a solution. 'Might I suggest that you search Companies House. That should tell you something.'

Honey Googled on her phone, her fingers trembling despite flying over the keys like a spider doing a tap dance.

She stared at the screen. 'Nothing.' As per search engine advice, she tried a few alternatives but still drew a blank.

At last she had to admit in words what was already in her mind.

'It seems Goodenough Marine Insurance does not exist.'

Steve groaned and hung his head in his hands.

Nigel remarked that seeing as most physical offices were closed by now and they had no phone messaging service, they might have to leave phoning Norman Glendower again — or visiting his office — until tomorrow.

Honey was already aware of the time from her phone. She shook her head. 'You're right, Nigel. Norman's office will be closed by now. We'll have to pay him a visit tomorrow. Let's hope he really does have an office that isn't in the Pulteney Arms, the Boater or the Zodiac Club.'

Steve seemed to crumple onto his knees.

Nigel added helpfully that there wasn't much they could do until then but was convinced that it was the right way forward. He began to collect everything on the tea tray.

Steve looked up to see his empty brandy glass being taken.

'There is one thing you can do for me, Nigel. Get me another brandy.'

'Me too,' said Honey while throwing an accusing look at Steve. 'With lots of ice.'

'To water it down?' asked Nigel.

'No. There's a chance I might burst into flames.'

CHAPTER FOUR

Neither of them recalled how many brandies they'd got through the night before, enough to enable them to sleep without dreaming of lynching bowler-hatted insurance agents or stabbing them with the point of their rolled-up umbrella. Perhaps in an unmentionable place.

'I raised an extra bit of money on this place to buy that boat,' Honey said glumly, slumped at a table in the corner of the dining room. She was under no illusion that the more one owed on a home or business — and the Green River Hotel was both for her — the harder you had to work to pay it back.

Steve reminded her that he was in the same boat — in a manner of speaking. Honey had mortgaged the hotel to escape from the cold, the rain and the unending drudgery of the hospitality trade. In his case he had taken a sabbatical and escaped policing the mean streets of Bath, but in so doing had mortgaged his flat. Every spare penny had gone into purchasing *Footloose*.

Breakfast consisted mostly of black coffee and buttered toast, only half a slice in Honey's case.

Sitting either side of the breakfast table, they exchanged few words but only the same worried looks they'd got out of bed with.

Once the time read nine o'clock, the average time most offices opened, they headed for reception and the landline.

'Is your mobile not working?' asked Eddie.

'We're just making sure,' replied Honey with a weak smile that barely moved her lips. 'Modern technology can be so hit and miss.'

Eddie looked as though he didn't really believe that but nodded in agreement anyway. After all, his and Nigel's livelihood depended on her. They wanted her to sail away again, leaving them here to run the Green River Hotel in their own way and to their own high standards.

'Your mother phoned earlier,' he said. 'At least that's who she said she was. She asked for Hannah.'

'That's me,' muttered Honey. Her given name was Hannah, though nobody called her that except for her mother.

'Any message?'

He looked reluctant to say anything. 'Well . . .'

Honey sighed. 'Go on. Hit me.'

Eddie rolled his shoulders and jumped in. 'She said that your judgement has always been somewhat amiss and that it was time you planted your feet on the ground and didn't go through life with your head in the air.'

Steve watched her, his arms folded on the reception desk. 'I presume she's suggesting you become a permanent landlubber.'

'Lubber, blubber,' she grunted and added that the broker's phone was ringing.

Every so often, out of exasperation more so than impatience, Steve buried his face on his forearms only daring to raise his head when Honey said, 'Ah,' which he thought meant somebody had answered.

Honey quickly quashed that idea. 'There's no reply. Not even *sorry, we cannot answer the phone at present . . .* or *press this or that.* Looks like a surprise visit is in order.'

Steve stopped falling onto his arms, straightened and showed a bit more fortitude. 'Norman Glendower, here we come.'

'Hold the fort, Eddie, if you please.'

'Against all comers,' he replied.

She thought she saw him clench his jaw as though he envisaged having a tussle with the Incredible Hulk or an official from the local council. Admittedly both could be challenging.

Grabbing her shoulder bag, she followed Steve as he strode on, head hunched into his shoulders. Former Detective Sergeant Steve Doherty was barely holding onto his anger, which might explode once in the presence of Norman Glendower.

Honey readied herself for whatever transpired.

Steve suggested getting a taxi.

Honey reminded him that they might need every penny they had. 'We'll walk.'

CHAPTER FIVE

The lower floors of St Margaret's Buildings had long been converted into shops, cafés and offices. One of these buildings had reputedly occupied Norman Glendower, specialist insurance broker. There was no trace of it now. Everything had changed. The shop had changed.

Honey stared.

Steve Doherty, him of the designer stubble and shrewd judge of human character except when it came to insurance brokers, also stared.

'Is this definitely the right place?'

Steve gathered up all the resolve — and excuses — he could muster.

'He said the name was etched in gold letters on the window.'

Swallowing her misgivings, Honey pointed at each word in turn as she read it out.

'Pampered Pooches. Dog grooming parlour. Methinks a change of use has occurred.' Honey eyed him accusingly. 'Are you sure about the address?'

'Absolutely. You heard me on the phone to Reggie. And before you ask, he wasn't in the pub. Coppers don't do all their business in the pub.'

Her shrug was neither here nor there. Basically, she had to admit Steve was right. She'd been there when he'd called so had to accept this was so. Nevertheless, she looked up and down the street in case they'd got it wrong and Norman Glendower had moved along the street to a different premises. The search proved fruitless. There was no sign whatsoever of the name they were looking for.

Steve was immovable from disbelief, jerking his chin at the plate glass window with adamant conviction. 'This is it. Reggie always had a good memory.'

'Even after a few pints?' Plagued by the possibility of everything having gone tits up, she couldn't help the sarcasm.

Without another word, she pushed open the door of the dog grooming parlour. Judging by the outside alone, it was a business that catered for only the most discerning of dog owners. Whether their dogs were of the same mind was another matter. Recalling the dogs she'd known brought the vision — and smell — of rolling in fox's dung vividly to mind. Her nostrils winced at the thought of it. If it was left to the dogs, they wouldn't be in here being pampered and perfumed with essence of roses.

Fully expecting the interior to be carpeted with dog hair and the air filled with the yapping of privileged pooches, Honey was pleasantly surprised. The pale mauve of the walls and the tasteful grey ceiling was matched by the smart overall of the receptionist. The name Pampered Pooches was embroidered on her chest just above an identity badge detailing her name as Melanie Stokes. Her Barbie-pink lips stretched into a welcoming smile and her false eyelashes fluttered onto her cheeks like two black bats looking for a place to land.

'Good morning. How wonderful to see you here at Pampered Pooches.'

To Honey's ears the welcoming tone made her look around just in case she'd walked into a hairdressing salon by mistake. The patter was the same. She found she had not.

'Good morning. Quite a place you have here.'

'Thank you.' The pink-lipped pouty smile, perhaps with the aid of one or two Botox treatments, broadened. 'Can I help you with the creature you love most in your life? A trim, nail cutting, dentistry or other—' her voice dropped to a whisper — 'more intimate attention. Anal glands cleared. Neutering. We do have a vet on call.'

Honey looked Steve up and down. 'No. All things considered, I think I would prefer to leave everything au naturel.'

The pink lips sagged open before she realised that Honey was joking. 'Very funny,' she said, quietly chuckling into her hand.

Steve grimaced. He disliked being the butt of a joke — any joke. Adopting his old professional manner, he kept to the brief. 'We're not here about a dog. We were looking for the insurance broker who used to do business here, a Mr Norman Glendower.'

'Before my time.'

'How long is that time? Can you tell me when he went?'

Melanie shook her head. 'He's been gone a while, but I can't say for sure. I've only been working here for six months.'

Like a dog with a bone — and he was certainly in the right place for that — Steve persisted. 'How long has he been gone?'

Honey heard the desperation in his voice.

The blonde-haired woman placed a pink fingernail on her pink lips and rolled her eyes skywards. 'Now let me see . . .' Suddenly she stopped, the smile vanished, and she frowned. 'Can I ask why you want to know? We're not supposed to give out personal information.'

'Personal? Are you saying that Mr Glendower was a customer here? He brought his dog in?'

'Yes. His name was Growler.' She looked skyward again. 'At least, I think it was.'

'A bulldog? A Staffie?'

'No.' Melanie looked quite miffed. 'We don't cater for that kind of breed. I would need to check the records. If you could just wait here a moment, please.'

With a flouncy, wiggly walk, she went straight to the computer, tapped a few keys and got back to them. 'A Bichon Frise. It looks a bit like a poodle but isn't a poodle,' she explained in response to Steve's puzzled expression.

Meanwhile a troubled frown creased Melanie's Botoxed brow. 'Oh dear,' she said, suddenly slipping the end of her pink-painted fingernail into her mouth. 'I shouldn't have told you that. It's personal.'

Out of patience, Steve threw back his head. 'Give me strength. Look, Melanie. I'm a policeman and the reason I'm here asking questions about Norman Glendower is that it must have slipped his mind to tell us he was moving. I need to find him pronto. Now, what else do you know about him? When did he leave and where is he now?'

Honey noticed that he had avoided explaining that this too was personal, and that Norman Glendower had taken their insurance premium and now they needed to make a claim. The problem was there was nobody to make a claim to. No insurance broker. No team of Lloyds Underwriters hovering in the background waiting to process said claim and give them their money.

It seemed from Melanie's relieved expression that her parents had always told her to trust a policeman. Ready compliance returned along /with the pink-lipped smile. 'Pampered Pooches opened about two years ago, so he might well have been here up until then.' She seemed to reconsider suddenly. 'But then I've only been here eighteen months, so it might possibly have been a bit longer than that.'

'I thought you said you'd only been here six months.' Honey's correction seemed to take Melanie off guard.

'Oh. Silly me. Yes. Of course. Six months. My mind was wandering,' she said with a silly smirk.

'Now, look here, if I don't get the truth from you, I'm going to—'

Steve looked close to exploding, so Honey dragged him away. Once outside, he swore under his breath, though it was still loud enough for a young man with a nose-ring and dreadlocks to say, 'Mind someone don't call the police, mate.'

At one time he would have glibly responded, 'I am the police,' but he wasn't — not strictly speaking. He was on sabbatical, given leave to sail into the sunset. But now he was back, and the sun had gone from his life.

'Keep your cool. Hear me, Steve? Keep your cool.'

'I loved that boat,' he said softly, his bottom lip close to trembling and eyes liquid with tears.

Honey shook her head and was ready to give him a slap if he turned hysterical. Which he wouldn't. Or she didn't think he would.

She patted his shoulder in a motherly fashion. 'Calm down. We're not going to get anywhere if you go into meltdown.'

His moment of weakness was suddenly vaporised in the hot heat of barely contained anger. 'I'm not in meltdown. I'm in murdering mode.'

'You're not murdering anyone.'

'Not anyone. Just Norman Glendower.'

'You're a policeman. It's not allowed.'

'Unless he can give me a good excuse as to why he's gone AWOL, I might ignore that.'

'Let's find him first before you plan murder most foul, shall we? And that, my dear Steve, is our priority.'

The dark clouds returned to sit on his head. His mood gave way to unfettered exasperation, which made Honey even more determined to get some kind of lead to the insurance broker's whereabouts.

She turned on her heel. Steve stared at her. 'Where are you going?'

She wagged a warning finger. 'Stay there. I'll be right back.'

He shoved his hands in his pockets and stood there like a chastised schoolboy. Honey went back into the poodle parlour.

Melanie was dealing with a Pampered Pooch customer, a particularly tiny Yorkshire Terrier that was showing needle-fine teeth at the overalled operative, who was sniffing its coat and telling the uncaring creature how lovely it smelled now it had had a shampoo and special conditioning treatment.

Having satisfied customers in this trade did not necessarily give any indication of the level of success. The acts of reassurance were not working. It yapped at the operative and, on spotting Honey, yapped at her. It saved its fiercest yapping and a threatening snap of its jaws for Melanie, who had dared to reach out to stroke it. She retrieved her hand quickly before her beautifully manicured nails were mangled in the little dog's very sharp teeth — along with her fingers.

Melanie looked surprised to see her again before adopting her professional and slightly sickly smile. 'Back again?' she asked in a lilting manner that was more professional than sincere.

Now it was Honey who did the smiling. 'Sorry to trouble you again, Melanie, but you don't happen to know where Mr Glendower moved to, do you? Or where he lived?'

Melanie shook her head before exchanging a bland, unknowing look with her colleague, who continued to tussle with the incalcitrant Yorkie. The tiny teeth latched onto her finger. 'Ouch!'

'How about you, Ellie? Do you know the whereabouts of the business that was here before Pampered Pooches?'

The girl shrugged, still gripping her injured finger. 'I'm not sure, but I think he took to doing all his business online. That would be the sensible option, wouldn't it? I mean, that's where everyone buys insurance nowadays, don't they?'

There was no way that Honey was going to admit that they weren't everyone. The fact that Steve had done otherwise made her bristle. They were the numpties who'd bought insurance the old-fashioned way by meeting their broker face to face. Kind of. In a pub. Not all scams were done online — besides which, it made them sound stupidly out of touch.

Adopting an air of confidence she didn't feel, she smiled. 'Yes, of course he would do that.' It made sense. Of course it made sense! And some though not all small businesses who set up online did so from the box room or kitchen of the house they lived in. 'You don't happen to know his home address, do you?'

She guessed the answer but needed to stay positive.

'No. Afraid not. I could phone the owner of Pampered Pooches and ask her.'

'That would be helpful — if it's not inconvenient.'

Melanie, who Honey now considered extremely helpful to their enquiries, picked up her phone. It wasn't long before her syrupy voice was trickling down the phone to the parlour's owner.

'I have some people here asking about the business who was here before Pampered Pooches. They'd like to know how they might get in touch with him.'

Although they couldn't hear the other side of the conversation, it was obvious that whoever was on the other end was asking what right they had to ask.

'They're police,' returned Melanie.

Honey did not correct her. Strictly speaking they were not. At least, she was not. But Steve was, so it wasn't lying because one half of the questioning duo was a policeman.

Whatever was next said on the other end of the call brought a red flush to the previously peachy face. Poor Melanie looked abashed when the call ended. 'Mrs Hunter doesn't know. She said she only had dealings with the owner of the property, not the previous tenant.'

'But surely there would have been some correspondence — bills, letters, even advertising bumf dropping through the door.'

Melanie shrugged. 'I don't know. I suppose there might have been, but Mrs Hunter is a very orderly person. If it's not for her it goes in the bin.' She said it as though it was a stock phrase, one of many that had been drummed into her by an employer who wanted everything neat and tidy.

'Does Mrs Hunter have dogs of her own?' asked Honey. She knew the answer even before she heard it.

'Yes. She's big in the dog world. Trains dogs. Shows them, you know, at Crufts and stuff like that.' She pointed a highly manicured finger at a photograph. 'That's a picture of her there winning first in post-graduate Afghan Hound. His name was Allerby's Diamonds Are Forever.'

Honey took in the details of the coloured photograph. The dog was quite beautiful, its blonde hair trailing down the sides of its pointy face. Mrs Hunter was also blonde, her hairstyle seeming to purposely replicate that of the dog.

'Very beautiful. Both of them. They look very good together.' She thought the dog was more dramatic, but a cliché would be a better fit.

She bid adieu just as the Yorkshire Terrier, still snapping and snarling, was stuffed into his woven willow carrier and the wire door slammed shut.

Outside, the air was fresh and lacking in the drama going on inside Pampered Pooches. Steve was slumped against a drainpipe, hands in pockets. He straightened on seeing her come out. 'Any joy?'

'Nothing, except I suspect that the owner of Pampered Pooches trains her employees in the same manner as she does her dogs.'

'Sounds barking mad.'

The joke barely brought a smile to either of their faces. Exasperated, they left St Margaret's Buildings and headed for a bar close to the Circus, which, because of its location in the tourist belt, charged a heavy price for one double vodka and one double gin — without a mixer.

Steve phoned Reggie and got him to verify they had the address right — which it turned out they had. He also asked him if he knew where Norman Glendower lived.

'Sorry, mate. Can't help you there. I'm in Bournemouth at present. The wife and I want to retire here. We're looking at a few bungalows. My knees aren't quite what they were. Why don't you give Frances Bates a call? She'll track it down.'

'I don't know her.'

'No matter. She's a dab hand with computer systems down at the nick. Ask her to check the electoral register. She won't mind, seeing as you're a boy in blue — or was. Still got that old black leather jacket, have you?'

'I haven't chucked it yet. Anyway, what's that got to do with it?'

'Trademark — so to speak. Holmes wore a deerstalker, Columbo wore a raincoat and Miss Marple did a lot of knitting.'

'Yeah, yeah. And Kojak sucked a lollipop.'

'Yep. You got it. When are you getting back in harness?'

'Not sure.'

'Oh, come on. You're not the sort who retires. That's my sort with a wife who insists.' He sounded reluctant. 'Truth is, I'm worried I might get bored. Got bored on that boat, did you?'

'Something like that.'

There was no way Steve intended to explain what had happened in detail. The incident was still an open wound, and even after they'd received the insurance money, it would take some time to heal. If they ever received it, that is.

CHAPTER SIX

Hildegard Hunter had a sharp face and a sharper disposition.

Clive Hunter, twelve years her junior and sitting comfortably in the leather armchair in front of the window, looked up from the text messages he was reading. His tanned skin positively glowed against the crisp whiteness of his short-sleeved linen Ralph Lauren shirt.

'You sound a little snappy, my darling.' His voice was a long-exhaled drawl, warm and sweet as molasses, the voice he always used to placate her sharp moods.

Hildegard glared at him. 'Someone's at the shop — a policeman according to Melanie — asking for Norman Glendower's address.'

Clive raised his eyebrows at the same time as letting the paper fold into his lap. 'So why not tell them?'

'I don't want to make things easy for them. He never made things easy for us.'

Shaking his head, Clive turned his attention back to the text messages that kept pinging in at a steady rate. 'It's all over now, darling. Done and dusted. Now, if you'll excuse me, I need to send off a few emails.'

'Can't they wait?'

'The world is our oyster and if we want to harvest pearls, well . . . it takes a great deal of money to maintain this crumbling ruin.'

Twyford Manor was far from a ruin. It had its origins back in the seventeenth century, built by a man who had had a knack of backing the right side at the right time in the English Civil War. Loyalty was not a word or creed he entertained — except to himself.

The house, with its twenty bedrooms, banqueting hall and white-framed orangery, added on in the early eighteenth century, was set in parklands of over fifty acres. At one time there had been one hundred and fifty acres. There was less now but still enough to warrant a contractor to cut the grass and garden. The whole estate was bounded by a high wall and a formidable set of decorative iron gates.

Hildegard's loving gaze loitered on his body as he unfolded his legs and got to his feet. There were trophy wives, but Hildegard had a trophy husband. There he stood, lean and beautiful, his dark hair gleaming, his eyes like deep blue lakes in an ocean of honeyed bronze.

She fully accepted that he had married her for her money. Still, better to curl up in bed with a firm bolster of a man than one of her own age with sagging muscles and flagging libido.

He held her chin between finger and thumb while giving her a kiss — just a short one. 'Excuse me, darling. Let's get this show on the road, shall we? Why don't you go for a walk?'

'I will.'

He clicked his tongue against the inside of his mouth and winked.

Little things meant a lot. He knew it and so did she. A little kiss was a promise of more delights to come later.

Smile fixed on her face, Hildegard made her way to the boot room, opened the back door and let the dogs in. Yapping excitedly, they followed her to the outhouse, where the innards of a dead horse waited to be cut into manageable pieces.

She chose her favourite knife for the task from a rank of them fixed to a magnetic rail above the deep freezer. Not without pleasure, she ran her finger along the blade, testing for sharpness. Once chosen, she sawed into the rich meat. Blood dripped to the floor when she sliced into the liver, heart and kidneys. She shared a little of each between the three bowls and the dogs dived in.

The dishes were cleared in no time, and she reopened the door to let them out. They went yapping with tails wagging out into the waving grass.

Blood still dripped from the carcass, and knife in hand, she went to where a bag of sawdust used to soak up spilled fluids hung in the corner. A smile came to her face on imagining that it was Norman Glendower.

'Take that.'

She plunged the knife into the sack. A little sawdust trickled out. She imagined it was blood. Norman Glendower's blood.

CHAPTER SEVEN

The large executive-style houses at Regency Gardens vaguely aped the traditional Georgian terraces of Bath, but without the draughty windows or lack of parking. These houses were well insulated and had garages and tarmacked drives with enough room for at least three SUVs and possibly a small runabout like a Mini or a fashionable Fiat 800.

There was only one privately owned SUV parked out front at present, plus four police cars, and the vehicle belonging to the pathologist, who was sweating profusely in a white suit of protective clothing and mumbling under his breath at the sheer awkwardness of the gloves he was forced to wear.

The usual police incident tape had been festooned around the crime scene to keep the public out. Not that it was needed. The neighbours in Regency Gardens didn't seem too bothered about venturing into police territory. In fact, it seemed to Detective Inspector Paul Marchant that they were totally uninterested, either that or there was nobody at home in these grandiose houses that overlooked the Avon and Kennet Canal and were by preference isolated from the world at large. Too busy out making money. Or they simply didn't wish to get involved. He also surmised that was the way the residents wanted it, even when the world had dared bring a crime more familiar to the outside world within its protective gates, walls and hedges.

The medical examiner, one Charlene Oxbridge, approached to give him the basics of her findings. 'The man inside is dead. I'll let you know fuller details when I have him spread on a slab of marble back at the ranch.'

Paul Marchant didn't push her to tell him how long the man had been dead — a bloody long time, by the looks of him. Suspicions that something wasn't right had been conveyed via a phone call from the next-door neighbour.

'I take it the neighbour smelled something a bit off,' said Paul.

'No. They noticed that the cat flap was closed, and the cat was mooching around to their place mewing for food. Top cat,' said Charlene without bothering to suppress a grin. 'I take it we know who he is?'

'A Mr Norman Glendower. A businessman who had his finger in a lot of pies, according to the neighbours.'

'Did they say this in a disapproving manner?'

He sniffed. 'Don't think they liked him much.'

'Imagine,' she said, looking at the neat terraces and elegant detached residences. 'Gated against all they disliked in the outside world but finding there was something they didn't like inside either.'

* * *

They were at breakfast when Lindsey phoned. Honey almost leaped on the phone when she saw her daughter's name come up.

'Hi, Mum. Just thought I'd call to see how things are.'

'Darling, I've missed you.' It was the first thing that entered her head, nothing about her own troubles. She was just glad to hear her daughter's voice. Her own was trembling slightly.

'I miss you too. I miss Bath. I even miss my grandmother, but don't tell her that. She hates being reminded that she is a grandmother.'

The sound of a chuckling baby sounded.

'She knows what a phone is for,' Lindsey explained. 'That's her saying hi to you. Grant's just dashed in to say hi too.'

'Hi,' sounded in the background, short and swift, a bit like Grant himself.

Honey returned the greeting. 'Hi, Grant.'

'Too late, Mum. He's dashed out. One of the drones has gone a bit out of control. He thinks its gyro mechanism is a bit giddy. He's got to get it right asap. There's a pop festival in Dresden this weekend and he's the official photographer.'

'Are you all going?'

'Of course. Minnie loves it. She sits in her papoose on my back and takes it all in.'

'Isn't the music a bit loud for her?'

'She's got a pair of furry ear defenders. They're pink.'

Of course they are, thought Honey. She bit her bottom lip to stop from crying. 'When are you coming home?'

She hadn't planned to ask the question, but suddenly overcome with emotion, she couldn't help herself.

'That depends how long you're there,' Lindsey responded.

Was that sad hesitancy Honey detected?

'It looks like I could be here indefinitely.' She flashed a look at Steve.

'We'll get the money,' he hissed. 'Honest we will.'

Honey glared at him, her attention turning back to the phone and her daughter. 'I'm missing you. And Minnie.'

'Me too. Oh, wait a minute . . .' She seemed suddenly distracted before finally saying, 'Sorry, Mum. Got to go. I'll be in touch.'

Honey put down the phone and met the look Steve was giving her.

'You will come away with me again, won't you?'

She shrugged. 'We'll see. 'It was a big adventure, but at times . . .'

'You were missing home.'

'Home is where the heart is.'

Steve looked downhearted, his finger drawing circles on the tablecloth, eyelids flickering as he sought words he didn't really mean.

'If you don't want to buy another boat . . . I'll understand.' He sounded desolate.

In that moment she felt sorry for him and managed a weak smile. 'We might not be buying one anyway if we don't get the payout. But that doesn't mean we shouldn't find out what Norman Glen-bloody-dower was up to. That's still our next step, isn't it?' She spat the words out forcefully.

As suggested by Reggie, Steve Doherty contacted Frances Bates, one of those people who hovered in the background but knew everything that many of the higher-up detectives only thought they knew.

As Reggie had suggested, Steve explained that he'd been on a sabbatical and that he was investigating a possible insurance fraud. He didn't go on to explain that this was a personal thing. *No point in complicating matters*, he thought with grim determination.

Frances was instantly helpful and sounded quite jovial when she began to outline what she knew. 'I don't need to trawl through the electoral register. I know where he lives — or where he did live, not that he'll answer when you ring the doorbell.'

Catching the tone of amusement, Steve couldn't help himself. 'If he's not dead, I might do the job myself.'

'You're too late. Someone got to him before you.'

Steve listened in grim silence, brow furrowed and the corners of his mouth turned down as she went on to explain that the man he was after had been found murdered in his executive house within a gated community. 'At least we think he was murdered. It seems the most likely. We await further details from Forensics.'

'When did this happen?'

'At least a week ago, perhaps more. His body has only just been discovered.'

'Nobody noticed he wasn't around?'

'That's the way it seems.'

'Nobody noticed until now.' He shook his head incredulously. 'I take it that everyone minds their own business in Regency Gardens.'

'It was the cat that led to his discovery. One of the neighbours saw that it was hanging around looking hungry. It was an expensive cat and never normally allowed to wander. The neighbour found its cat flap was shut and it couldn't get in. Then they looked through the patio doors at the back of the property and there he was. As I said, nobody noticed.'

Steve had never been much of a poetry fan, but it came out anyway. 'Some men are islands, after all.'

'You could say that. When are you coming back on duty by the way?'

'As of now, I think.'

'You're the go-to man, from what I've been hearing.'

'Good to know that Manvers nick can't operate without me. My ways are famous — or should that be infamous?'

'Could be either. Doherty, Prince of Darkness. Or the Man in Black — our very own Johnny Cash.'

'Yeah. Just don't ask me to sing. It'll scratch at your eardrums.'

'Wish I'd phoned sooner,' he said once the call was over. He was sitting back in his chair experiencing loss of appetite and a feeling that he'd been done out of the revenge he'd been thirsting for ever since finding out he'd been taken for a ride. It was clear now why Norman hadn't been answering the phone, but it didn't clear him of taking their money to pay a premium to an insurance company that didn't exist. Now all he had to do was share the information with his nearest and dearest.

Honey was eyeing him nervously. 'I overheard. Something's happened to our Mr Glendower?'

Steve pushed aside the portion of smashed avocado on toast he'd ordered. 'Someone got to our wayward insurance broker before us. He's been murdered.'

48

Honey almost choked on her coffee. 'Dead! Norman Glendower has been found dead? There's no possibility of suicide?'

He shook his head. 'I don't know all the details yet, except the circumstances of his discovery and the probability that he's been dead a while. It seems that it was down to his pet cat.' He wrinkled his nose. 'He must have ponged something awful by the time the neighbours decided the poor thing was starving.'

Honey leaped from her chair. 'Come on.'

'I haven't finished my coffee.'

'No time for that. We need to know what's going on pronto.'

CHAPTER EIGHT

The local police station had been downsized recently due to technical advances — at least, that was the official line. As Steve said to Honey, cutting budgets, which in turn led to cutting corners, had more to do with it. Parts of the old station had been sold off to the university for student accommodation. Not everyone was happy about it.

There were only three police cars parked outside of the small building that now constituted the main police station. If extra resources were required, they came from the larger station in a nearby suburb of Bristol.

Honey took all this in. She would have liked to add a few positive comments herself but on this occasion had to leave it to Steve. This was his world, the one he'd refused to permanently retire from but just take a two-year break. The old dog still knew the tricks; he was the man who knew the procedures and had left his beloved career to sail away with her on the good ship *Footloose*.one.

It was Paul Marchant who heard they had entered the hallowed ground of the police station he regarded as his own. He immediately asked that they come to his office.

'Welcome to the rabbit hutch,' he said.

Even though Honey had never been a member of the police force, she could see he was what Steve called a career man, the sort whose endeavour was to rise to the top with all due speed and ride a desk until retirement came calling.

No matter about that; she considered it very courteous of him to invite them into his office and call for coffee or tea, whichever they wanted.

'I see you're back in uniform,' Paul said with a laugh, pointedly looking at Steve's leather jacket, which had become a bit crumpled while packed away.

'Part of the armoury,' returned Steve.

Paul was a new broom that was meant to sweep clean and had not been in Bath when Steve had been here. They had mostly been acquainted over the phone or at conventions when they were required to sit and learn — usually they both itched to be elsewhere, Steve at the sharp end and Paul at the best desk he could take a seat at.

It was hard to tell whether the liquid that arrived in the plastic cups was tea or coffee, and it was warm rather than hot. Honey studied the man Steve had described rather scathingly. He'd instigated a mufti day, which had gone down well in younger quarters but not particularly well with the traditional hierarchy.

Paul Marchant was over six feet tall, baby-faced and wore red chinos and a blue suede jacket. His hair was close-cropped and he wore a stud in his left ear. Honey found herself wondering if he knew Caspar, though that was unlikely given the age difference, and Caspar did not frequent gay clubs. From what Steve had told her, neither did Paul Marchant, but he did have the air of a nighthawk about him.

They outlined what they knew about Glendower and what had happened to them.

He exuded genuine sympathy. 'What a tragedy. Miles from land. That must have been frightening.'

'Yes. We were miles from land when we sank but managed to send out a signal.'

51

Honey added that she'd had to swim to the life raft. 'It was not a good experience.'

Paul clasped his hairy hands in front of him on the desk. The look of sympathy on his face seemed genuine. 'My, but I admire you. There's not many that can say they lived the dream.'

'And lived to tell the tale. We were counting on the insurance money enabling us to buy another boat,' Steve explained.

Paul's eyebrows rose. 'You would put yourself through that all over again?'

Honey said it was very likely that they would go sailing again. 'We won't make a final decision until the money is in the bank — if it should ever get there.'

Steve knew her late husband had been a keen sailor who loved boats with a passion that might not have been purely nautical. He'd gone out of his way to recruit an all-female crew and had drowned at sea on a voyage across the Atlantic. The crew had survived. She'd never quite known why.

'They'll do anything you ask of them,' her husband had said to her.

'That's the problem,' she'd growled back.

No matter. Water under the bridge. She turned to the job in hand. Steve was asking more questions about the murder of Norman Glendower. 'I suppose you don't know the weapon of choice as yet.'

Paul shook his head. 'It's an open book at present until the pathology report is finalised. If he was involved in insurance fraud and there was more than one victim, then we're likely to be spoilt for choice when it comes to suspects. We'll have to wait and see. If there's rich and influential people involved, there is the possibility of a hired hitman tasked to take him out — depending on the wealth of whoever he's fleeced. Money talks. Especially if you've nicked somebody's life savings.'

'You're right there. I felt like wringing his neck myself.'

Honey noted that Steve's jaw and fists were clenched in unison.

Paul eyed him almost suspiciously — for obvious reasons. 'Anything you want to go on the record, Doherty?'

Honey noted a definite glitter in the eyes of the man who now held the position Steve had once held.

'Yes, I'm a prime suspect.' He shoved his hands deep into his pockets. 'Here's my statement and I know from experience that it's incriminating, but here goes — for what it's worth. The boat went down, and it seems Glendower faked the insurance company he said we were with.'

Marchant's eyebrows arched high on his forehead. 'Well, if that follows through, it could make my job very much easier. "Man murdered, suspect charged."' He frowned. 'Except "police officer arrested on suspicion of murder" doesn't do the police public image much good.'

'You can't consider me a suspect until the medical examiner gives you the lowdown, and that won't be for a few days. You don't know yet how long Glendower's been dead.'

'So?'

Honey jumped in. 'How long makes a big difference — we haven't long returned to this country. I'm assuming we are indeed innocent until you can prove us guilty. Anyway, we're fully admitting our desire to kill him — aren't we, Steve?'

Steve shrugged. 'That's about it.'

The boot-button eyes of the man in front of them rolled around like a series of fruits on a fairground slot machine, blinking around on the drum to bring up a trio of matching cherries.

It finally happened. 'Point taken,' said Marchant. 'You're not a suspect.'

'Good.'

'But just in case there's any change in circumstances, don't leave town.'

'I won't,' Steve replied. 'But I wouldn't mind following this up. Once I'm regarded as returned from my sabbatical.'

Paul Marchant frowned down at his desk. 'Well, why wait? You never did the full retirement passage. I'll sign the paperwork now — you're back on the force.' There was a tightness around his eyes. 'I'm doing this for a good reason. You could always be relied on to do a good job.'

'Thank you, sir.'

Paul eyeballed him from beneath bushy eyebrows. 'You might not thank me if I don't see some progress. I want results.'

'You'll get progress, Paul — sir — I promise.'

It was a hollow promise that Paul Marchant wanted but Honey needed nobody to tell her that there were no guarantees. It all depended on logic, thorough investigation and, not to be discounted, a dose of good luck. That was police work. Catch me if you can — or not.

* * *

They were in the process of walking back to the Green River Hotel and Honey's mind was whirling with possibilities. What if this, what if that, what if there were others as annoyed with Norman Glendower as they were? All surface stuff that had to be first port of call. If that failed to yield a solution, then at least they could let it go and look elsewhere.

She made up her mind, grabbed his arm and swerved their footsteps to the car park where she kept her old Citroen. 'I'm not leaving things like this!'

'Oh no,' said Steve, slamming to a halt. 'You're not thinking what I think you're thinking, are you?'

'I'm doing a lot of thinking.' She fluttered her eyelashes like Betty Boo.

He grimaced. 'And I'm reading your mind.'

'Be careful. You might send your blood pressure soaring.'

'I can think of a lot of things that will do that.' His grin was fragile, his heart not really in repartee. Yes, he loved Honey, but he'd also loved *Footloose*, his pride and joy. He also hated being taken for a mug, and although the death of Norman Glendower had brought him back into police action, he half wished he'd bashed Glendower over the head himself. That charlatan had caused him grief and plenty of it.

Honey stopped at the entrance to the car park, chewing her bottom lip as she tried to nail down her whirring thoughts, which were scooting round like slices of Victoria sponge on a lazy Susan. And boy, did she like cakes!

'How long will it take the police to follow the insurance scam lead?'

Steve shrugged. He wouldn't admit it, but this whole thing had taken the wind out of his sails — in more ways than one. 'We don't know there's a scam, though I get your drift. For some reason we were the ones who lost. Nobody else has come forward.'

'Why pick on us? That so-called trusted insurance broker stole from us without bothering to get us insured — or at least that's the way it seems. No office and an insurance company that doesn't exist. That's scam enough for me, but I get what you're saying. Surprising though, don't you think?'

'And highly criminal.' Steve looked up at the overcast sky, only half concentrating. His heart and mind were elsewhere. 'I bet the temperature's around twenty-six just south of Sicily.' He sighed heavily. 'I miss it.'

There were pluses and minuses to their current situation. Honey tugged at her skirt. She'd lost weight while sailing — a definite plus. It meant she could indulge her enjoyment of food and wine for a while without worrying too much about putting on the pounds.

She stroked his arm in the hope it would help soothe his dour thoughts.

'I did like blue skies and bright sunshine . . .' Sunshine was preferable to the grey clouds currently frowning above them, ready to let loose with a downpour and them get soaked. But other thoughts took hold, pushing such triviality to the back of her mind. 'The name of the insurance company rankles. Goodenough. Was he being sarcastic, do you think?'

'*Goodenough.* Good enough for the purpose of scamming people.'

'And it doesn't exist. We would have got through by now if it existed.'

Steve came back down to earth. Grey sky. Cold wind. 'True.'

Honey's expression was one of serious contemplation. 'It's still odd that we haven't heard of anyone else being fleeced.'

'I can assure you our best internet investigators have been on it. The police don't run around blowing a whistle and riding a bicycle like they used to. We have moved on, you know.'

Honey was still musing. 'Perhaps he had a dodgy finger in other dodgy pies.'

'It's being investigated. Whispers from informers and all that. Rumour in the underworld takes longer to track down than hard facts.'

'I can understand that. I'm also aware that criminals have short tempers. If he diddled them, he wouldn't last long. Am I right?'

'True. Which begs the question how many people, other than me, might have wanted to kill him?' Judging by his expression he meant every word. 'Cause of death will be top priority.'

'And once that's confirmed, they'll be investigating motives. The probability that Norman Glendower took money on false pretences is likely to be one of them. The net will spread. And we'll be involved.'

Steve nodded slowly as though he was chewing it over prior to letting it slide down his throat — or into his brain. He was the one who'd insisted on using a broker and had been adamant that this bloke was a good one. If the word of his police mates who drank at the same watering hole wasn't good enough recommendation, he didn't know what was.

He looked at her, looked at the entrance to the car park and waited for her to confirm what it was she had in mind.

'Why are we standing here? Where are we going that needs a car?'

'Oh, come on, Steve. I can see it in your face. You're thinking along the same lines as me.'

He wasn't. He was away in warmer climes. At least in his mind.

'We should work on our own behalf, take a look at Glendower's house and talk to the neighbours. Don't you agree? Anyway, Mr Marchant's more or less given you the go-ahead, hasn't he?'

His face took on the old law-and-order look that all policemen adopt when they're standing one side of the fence and a civilian's on the other. 'It's a crime scene. We'd get in serious trouble if I jumped the gun.'

'But you wouldn't be. Marchant seems keen to have you involved.'

'Hmm.' Steve didn't look too convinced. 'The alternative is that he wants me to incriminate myself.'

'That depends on the date of the murder. We've only been back in the country a short time.'

'Crimes cleared up in double-quick fashion look good on a career man's CV. My old boss would have thrown the book at us — or at least at me. It's a heavy book. Could do a lot of damage.'

'But Steve — darling . . .'

'Uh oh.'

'What do you mean, "uh oh"?'

'That wheedling tone means you want something that I might not be able to give. Or to do something I might not want to do.'

She purposefully tickled his chin in a lovey-dovey way and smiled up at him. 'Oh, come on, Steve.' It was her best cajoling voice. 'We need to get in there to ask questions. The sooner we get this wrapped up, the sooner we can sail back to the sunshine. If that's still what you want to do.'

A smile came a little bit faster than it had of late. Steve Doherty was returning to form, though only so far. He needed extra encouragement.

Steve threw back his head in exasperation. 'Honey, it's a gated community. Marchant wants me to investigate, but I do need some reason to barge in at this stage. There's another officer in charge at present. It wouldn't be polite to show up unannounced.'

Her eyebrows rose questioningly. 'It's never stopped you before.'

'I could be shut out — in more ways than one.'

'You mean the police won't let you in because you haven't been around for a while?'

'They might not.'

Honey's brow furrowed in thought. 'What if we say that we're visiting someone we know?'

'I don't know anyone there. Do you?'

Honey chewed this over. He was right, she personally didn't know anyone in Regency Gardens. But from experience she did know that besides well-heeled people who drove BMWs or SUVs, such places were favoured by older folk who appreciated the security that gated communities offered. She knew one senior who might very well have the key — at least metaphorically speaking.

She gave him a coquettish smile that in less fraught times would have led to an early night but had to readily concede that there was no chance of that at present. However, she had a maverick ace up her sleeve. 'No. You're right. I don't anyone who lives there, but what's the bet my mother does?'

Steve threw back his head and closed his eyes. She knew without asking that he was revisiting the carefree lifestyle they'd only recently enjoyed. It was just the two of them out on the boat, all the old acquaintances who vexed him left far behind. Honey's mother, Gloria Cross, was one of them.

She could see the nostalgia lingering on Steve's face. Oh, how he wished to turn the clock back. His only solace was that, if they did get their money, at least he could buy another. Unfortunately, the possibility of that happening was getting less and less likely.

For her part, Honey was asking herself whether she would willingly go back to living the dream simply because she wasn't sure it was still her dream. The conversation with Lindsey today, the chuckle of baby Minnie in the background, had made an impression. Not that she would tell Steve she was having reservations. Let sleeping dogs lie for now and wait until things were clearer.

Steve stayed silently chewing over the option she'd given him.

'Your mother.' That was all he said. It was followed by a jerk of his ever so square and solid chin. Permission enough.

'I'll give her a call.'

Tap, tap, tap on the keypad. The voice on the other end was so loud that Honey had to put distance between it and her ear.

Steve winced. He could hear every word.

'Don't know why she bothers with a phone. She's got a voice like a foghorn,' he grumbled.

Gloria didn't hear, of course. Honey continued to hold the phone an inch from her ear or risk going deaf.

'Darling, I heard you were back. I'll come over when I can and have a chat. Not for a few weeks though. I have a very full social calendar, you know.'

Visibly brightening, Steve opened his eyes but kept his mouth shut. Honey knew how he felt about her mother. However, she did have a point. Gloria knew everyone who was worth knowing, some seniors who'd lived in Bath for aeons and some newcomers who she delighted in introducing to her own particular social whirl. The fact was that Gloria Cross knew everyone of her age who lived in Bath — those she liked and those she didn't. She immediately gave her a name.

'Gladys Faversham. She lives at number sixteen.'

'Thanks. How are you keeping?'

'Actually, I'm busy packing for a cruise, which is why I haven't been in touch, but I'm sure everything will be fine. You and he will settle back in in no time.'

Steve balked at her referring to him as 'he'.

Unperturbed, Gloria carried on. 'So, hello and goodbye, darling. I really do have to go.'

'Of course. Have a good time and don't lumber yourself with too much luggage.'

'I can take as much as I like. It's a ship, not an aircraft. The chauffeur picks us up here and drops us at the terminal. And anyway, darling, you know me — I don't believe in travelling light.'

This was indeed true. Her mother, a shining example of expertly coiffured hair, immaculate nails and quality clothes that made her look as if she'd come straight off the catwalk, liked to take her whole wardrobe with her. She was one of those rarities who still wore heels sharp enough to put out jealous eyes.

'No,' Honey responded with a knowing smile. 'You never did travel light.'

Once the connection was cut — from her mother's end as it turned out — Honey turned to Steve.

'She's given me a name we can use that will give us a credible reason to get us through the gates. Are you game to go there?'

Steve chewed his mouth from side to side. 'I don't know if it will do much good. Give me a reason for giving it a try.'

'OK, you're edging back into the old routine. But think of the money we paid and lost. Isn't that a good enough excuse for doing our utmost to find out what's going on?'

He repeated the sideways motion of his mouth and gave up without a fight.

'Good enough — sorry to use those words again.' Honey fixed him a wry smile. 'Let's get on our way to Regency Gardens, then.'

Steve frowned. 'Regency Gardens. Ever since I first heard the name, it's rung a bell. But I can't place it . . .'

'Ding-a-ling.'

'Ah!' Steve clicked his fingers, and enlightenment came to his face. 'Ace of Hearts.'

'Is that a name?'

'Yes. That's what we called him. Ace of Hearts, though this particular Hart is spelt without an 'e'. Warren Hart. Ace of Hearts, get it?'

'I couldn't fail,' returned Honey with a hint of mockery.

Steve didn't seem to notice. He was back from the blue yonder and ploughing coppers' trivia and nostalgia.

'Sergeant: Avon and Somerset Police. Or used to be. I remember him telling me just before he retired, he had a job lined up as security at a gated community and the word at the station was that he ended up there. Come on. Get the car.'

He stopped when she didn't follow him but instead stood there stroking her chin, her brow crumpled in thought.

'What is it now?'

'I've had second thoughts about the Citroen. We need to make an impression that we mean business and look as though we belong there. What with you in your black gear and me looking . . .' She looked down at her jeans. They were new. So were her trainers and the long-sleeved top she was wearing. 'OK, this isn't a top-notch outfit, but my earrings look good.' She tugged each earlobe and beamed as though they were switches that turned on the sunlight.

'Hmm. This isn't a fashion show. This is serious business. The Citroen will have to do. My car went to the scrapyard in the sky yonks ago.'

A Cheshire Cat grin transformed Honey's face to something he could only interpret as conniving. 'Mary Jane is away and I've got the keys to her car.'

He thought about it, then with a jerk of his chin made a decision. 'I'm game to use it, as long as she's not driving it.'

'She won't be. I am.'

CHAPTER NINE

Warren Hart considered himself a lucky son of a gun. He'd stayed in the police service just long enough to collect his pension and without letting the grass grow under his feet had landed a security job at the gated community of Regency Gardens. It was almost a home from home, though with a far grander exterior than the semi-detached he lived in at Batheaston on the outskirts of the city.

The outside of the gatehouse aped the classical designs of Rome and Greece, a Dorian column either side of a six-panel Georgian door. The plastic-framed double-glazed windows looked authentic and thankfully lacked the rattles and draughts of the real McCoy.

Inside he shared his space with a bank of security screens, a microwave, a fridge just large enough to make ice and keep a few bottles of beer cool, and a thirty-two-inch television screen with access to a plethora of TV channels.

Every so often, after he'd smoothed down the jacket of his uniform, he'd make his way out onto the stair-lined ramp in front of the door. The police contingent was still moseying around the front garden and the street immediately in front of Norman Glendower's house.

Warren was enjoying the attention. He'd even given an interview to a journalist from the local press who wanted to know the name of the dead man and if he'd seen anything of interest. She'd also asked if anything like it had ever happened before.

'Oh no,' he'd responded, shaking his head sagely as though he was the source of all things interesting that happened here. 'This has always been a quiet, upstanding place. Nothing untoward has ever happened here. The residents are very respectable — all smart cars and suits and what have you.'

'What sort of cars?' the daft little thing had asked him.

He'd been more than willing to oblige. 'BMWs, Mercedes, Jaguars, Range Rovers . . .'

His bland acceptance vanished the moment he saw a pink car of classic American mould pull up on the other side of the security gates.

'What the—' Luckily the journalist had gone by then.

On the other side of the gates, Mary Jane's bubblegum-coloured Cadillac coupe pulled up, the chrome gleaming, its pinkness assaulting the eyeballs.

It was hardly a limousine, but did have an old-style Hollywood, in-your-face luxury look about it.

'Here goes,' Honey murmured to Steve.

Luckily for them, Mary Jane, professor of the paranormal and long-time friend, had gone on holiday to a haunted house with a group of people who were as enthusiastic as she was about the 'other side'. Steve had mischievously pointed out that as Mary Jane and her friends were all over seventy, they had a vested interest in finding out where they were soon heading.

Feeling extremely thankful that the journalist had gone, Warren Hart raised his eyebrows at the pink vehicle that had stopped outside the gates. The sight of it reminded him of a psychedelic experience he'd once had when he was younger and had never repeated. His head had felt as though the world in front of him was coated in candyfloss — a big, bulging pink cloud of it.

Still, he had a job to do. He couldn't help but investigate. Eyebrows that had been arched dived into a deep V above his purple-veined nose. Feeling deeply officious, which in no slight means had been brought on by the offensive colour, he stepped out of his office onto the narrow area at the front from where he could scrutinise this alien vehicle up close.

Honey and Steve watched him come to a halt immediately in front of his door and the electronically controlled security gates.

'Judging by his body language, I don't think he's as impressed by Mary Jane's car as we hoped,' said a bemused Steve.

Warren stood with twitching thumbs hooked in his belt looking at Mary Jane's car as if it had landed from Mars. Not the type for Regency Gardens, surely. Too brash. Too pink. If they were visiting a resident, he had no alternative but to let them in. If not . . .

A smirk came to his face once he'd made up his mind to make them squirm and effectively put them in their place. He was up for giving the new arrivals a bit of grilling and leg pulling — until he spotted Steve Doherty.

At the sight of a fellow ex-cop his face lit up. He unhooked his thumbs from his belt and his tough demeanour gave way to one of unfettered welcome. It wasn't often he got to meet up with his old mates nowadays. The younger lot rummaging around in the murder scene had been offhand to say the least. It never entered his head that he hadn't been the most popular of coppers. They were just young. That's what he told himself. Wet behind the ears.

His pink face glowed like a blood orange. 'Well, I'll be blowed. Steve Doherty. The man in black. Ain't seen you for yonks!'

The windows on both sides of the car wound down, and Steve raised a hand in greeting before getting out. Arms folded, he leaned on the car roof, grinning across at his one-time brother in uniform. Not that they'd ever been that close. Warren was a man who was tolerated rather than liked.

He turned amiable anyway. 'Well, if it isn't Warren Hart. Long time no see.'

'Long time indeed.' Warren stepped forward. 'What you doin' 'ere?'

'I'm visiting an aged aunt. You may know her. Gladys Faversham. She lives at number sixteen.'

An aunt! Honey kept her head down, admiring how easily the necessary lies could roll off Steve's tongue. It struck her that the old Steve Doherty was back on form, more than willing to twist the truth a bit if it got him what he wanted.

Steve had always been like a hound on the scent of the fox. Get a sniff where and when you could, and he was away. It was a tried and tested routine that would hopefully result in some inside information that the police already here on the case might not have. He could imagine the younger set being a bit snotty towards the former police officer who had the job of gatekeeper. Security blokes weren't always on the ball, but you never know, Warren might be the exception. Anything was better than nothing.

Just as Honey expected, old policemen never die. They just trade stories of past exploits.

'Good to see you.' They shook hands.

'Well, well. Do you remember when . . .'

'Well, well. How could I forget? And then there was that incident . . .'

Honey rested her chin on a clenched fist. This could go on for some time. Might as well be patient.

Steve looked the grey uniform up and down but didn't remark that it made Warren look like a hotel doorman.

All was exuberant chumminess. 'Warren Hart. I won't ask what you're doing here.'

'Topping up the pension. Hard times, Steve, hard times.' He shook his head mournfully as though it was the honest truth, and he was very hard done by. In his mind

Steve added up his likely pension, plus what he was making here, and concluded he wasn't doing bad.

Honey held in a groan and fixed her downward gaze on the car dashboard. When retired coppers met up, they could talk the socks off any woman.

Warren jerked his head to the door behind him with a look of pure pride on his face. 'Come on in. I'll show you around.' He glanced at Honey, who was sitting behind the wheel of the left-hand drive car. 'Your little lady all right to wait?'

Honey didn't wait for Steve to answer but pushed the door open and was out.

'I'd like to come in too. I've visited my aunt a few times but never got the opportunity to look into the security office.'

Warren eyed her suspiciously. 'I don't recall seeing this car before . . .'

Honey was quick off the mark with a viable excuse. 'I came in my Citroen before. It's nowhere near as glamorous as this and not nearly as noticeable.'

Warren made a so-so face as he conceded that a Citroen would go almost unnoticed.

Steve opted to talk business, their business being the sort that only the boys in blue could possibly understand. Mutual ground.

'You'd better come in. I don't let anyone in here, you know. Consider yourself privileged.'

Barely attracting the briefest glance, Honey followed on feeling a bit like a pageboy at a wedding — kind of needed but not really that important.

The interior of the gatehouse was extremely warm, as though an electric fire had been left on all day. Honey conceded it was more likely due to the plethora of security screens and the large TV monitor that was presently airing some drivel from daytime television, the sort of stuff designed for those with nothing else to do. Retirees mostly. The two men almost filled the space without her tagging on behind.

Steve stood in front of her, eyeing the screens. 'The security cameras are going to be crucial to the investigation, though you already know that.'

'Bound to be. Not that there's much on them. I've had a look meself, but unless someone knows who or what they're looking for, well . . .' He shrugged. 'Diddly squat.'

'Still, it's a preamble to getting the juices flowing. Shadows in the dark. Who's doing what at late hours. It's amazing what people get up to in the dark.' Steve kept up the amiable old mate routine.

Warren sat himself down in the broad-beamed chair placed in front of the monitors. His wide rear was as well upholstered as his seat. He was in his stride, a man no longer of the profession suddenly of some importance again.

Steve could ask anything he liked and Warren would answer without a moment's hesitation.

'They've taken what they wanted and downloaded the record of the last two months. I keep copies, of course, and it's on the hard drive and cloud, et cetera. It's certainly livened things up around here.'

'Usually quiet, is it?' asked Steve.

Warren shook his head. 'As the grave — or almost,' he added, recalling the events going on. 'Peace and quiet away from the hoi polloi is what people pay for when they buy a place in Regency Gardens. They certainly don't expect murder and mayhem.'

'Did you know Norman Glendower very well?'

'No better than anyone else here.'

'Do you know much about what he did for a living?'

'A businessman. That's all I knew. I think he had something to do with insurance and finance. Heard tale he used to be something of a player in the city. Knew a lot of people there.'

'I see.'

Honey could see that Steve was on a roll. She kept silent. This was his game and he knew how to play it.

'Had a nice house, did he?'

'Yep. The Beeches is one of the biggest here. Detached. Big garden. Car in drive — used to be two cars in drive but that was a while ago. Wife ran off with a keeper from Longleat twenty years her junior. Never saw her again. His daughter used to be around a lot more than she is now. She's away working, so I understand.'

'I'll speak to her when available. We would have got in touch with her by now, informing her of her father's death.'

'Of course.' A salacious smile suddenly lit up Warren's face. 'Wait till you see her. Quite a looker.'

Steve showed no matching response, which told Honey something about the slightly off-key way he viewed his old colleague. She suspected him being a lecher was likely the reason why.

Steve asked him if he could flash over a copy of the security footage.

'I've already sent what I have to the police.'

Steve was ready with a reason that he too should have a recording. 'You know I like to be ahead of the game. Marchant asked me to pop in and take a shufti. He reckons I've got a nose for this.'

'My nose too,' said Warren Hart, tapping the side of his pale purple and slightly bulbous nose. 'A suspicious death according to my sources, though time of death and suchlike have not been confirmed.'

Honey was getting impatient. She felt like a third wheel. Intervention was unavoidable.

'Is that near number sixteen?' she asked, leaning between them, her hair flicking against Steve's face as she took in what was on the screen, though her aim was to break this up and get going.

'Kind of opposite,' said Warren, looking a bit put out that the old pals act was broken.

'Great. That's where my aunt lives. Time we popped in to see her,' she said pointedly, an unseen finger digging into Steve's side.

'Right opposite. Only the terraced and semi-detached houses have numbers. The detached places have names.'

Steve remarked that such a division sounded like class distinction.

Warren shrugged. 'That's the way it is, Steve. Them that got it and them that ain't got so much.'

'Heard anything about how the investigation's going? Any lines of enquiry going anywhere?'

'I'm hearing a few things. You know how it is, it takes one to know one. Even though I'm retired, the boys aren't averse to sharing a few details.'

He wasn't going to admit that he was too old to be in the loop and Steve wasn't going to go there either. He knew the score. Young blood was coming up behind, barking at their heels.

Determined not to be left out, Honey asked, 'So what happened? Stabbed, shot, poisoned or bludgeoned to death?'

Steve's ex-colleague dipped his head slightly before he answered. She recognised his reluctance to bring her in on the conversation.

On seeing nothing amiss in her looks, besides which she was in the right company, he gave her an answer. 'Nasty mess. Been lying there a while. That place will need a deep clean to get rid of the stink.'

Steve took over. 'Did you see anything to get the old vibes going? On the camera or otherwise?'

Warren tapped the side of his nose again. 'Of course. I'm the one in charge of the security around here, the cameras and all that.'

'Did anyone in this place have a grudge against him?'

'Not that I know of, though he did keep 'imself to 'imself. Not a mixer, if you know what I mean, and he was away in London a lot.' He looked thoughtful. 'I think that was something to do with insurance.'

'What kind of insurance?'

'Couldn't tell you. Don't know much about stuff like that meself. As long as the car's insured nothing much else matters. Don't own enough to. I did 'ear he arranged insurance on some valuable stuff in his time. Don't know the details though.'

'Did you have a look at the security records yourself?'

Warren adopted an officious stance, straight-backed and full of self-importance. 'I've had a quick butcher.'

'Anything of interest?'

'Not that I could see.'

Honey looked tellingly at the television screen. The programme currently showing had been on there for years. All to do with finding a new home for the right budget in the right place. A bit like these people, looking for a perfect haven — only this one had turned out not to be so perfect after all.

Steve's eyes slid to a half-empty bottle of whisky. 'This is quite a plum job, I should think. A little place all to yourself. Nobody to bother you. Just flick a switch and open the gate. Almost a home from home.'

'It's that, all right. I was lucky to get it.'

'Heard through the grapevine? Friend of a friend and all that?'

'Not really. I was hired via an agency. I'm the permanent operative and they supply temporary ones to step in when needed.'

'You don't do nights?'

'Sometimes I do.' He chuckled and his expression was crafty. 'It all depends if there's anything I want to watch on Netflix. The nights get long and boring without something to do. But now and again I like to be away from the wife.' He tapped the top of the whisky bottle. 'If you know what I mean.'

Although Steve had heard a rumour that Warren and his wife had parted, he kept it to himself. Leave the man some pride. And anyway, it paid to keep him on board.

'Let me know if you need company. I can bring you a beer or two. A takeaway too, if you fancy.'

Warren beamed. 'You're on. How do I get in touch?'

'Here's my details.' Steve handed him a Green River Hotel business card.

'Living in a hotel? That must be nice. Isn't that the one off Pulteney Street? How come you're living there, then?'

Before Steve had the chance to go into detail, Honey decided to get the subject back on course. She had no wish for her and Steve's private life to be dissected in the close confines of a security gatehouse.

'This Norman Glendower. A recluse, was he? Retired and locking himself away from the world?' She smiled sweetly as she said it although there was no doubt Norman was doing a bit on the side. The very thought of the insurance broker and what he'd done had her grinding her teeth.

Warren frowned and scratched at his stubbly chin. 'As I've already said, he wasn't retired. There's many a tale going round. That business about London and also about him being an insurance broker. Not many of them about anymore. Everyone arranges their insurance on the internet these days. Daft not to.'

Honey cringed, and although Steve gave no sign of it, she knew he also was feeling a bit of a chump. Why hadn't they bought insurance direct and online with one of the big companies? Why go through a little man? She reminded herself that Steve had got him on recommendation — from a police colleague.

Before she had a chance to pursue her questioning further, Steve voiced what she too would have asked.

'I understand he used to have a premises in town.'

'Did he? You could be right. Not got it anymore?'

'No. Gone to the dogs now — literally. It's a dog grooming parlour.'

Warren chuckled. 'Still got a nice house, a car in the garage and a load of computer equipment in an upstairs bedroom. So I hear,' he added and yet again tapped the side of his nose before frowning. 'Or I think it was him with the computer gear. Might be someone else though.'

'Someone told you that?'

He frowned. Honey got the impression he genuinely wasn't too sure.

'I let in an electrician to put in more power sockets, though for the life of me I'm not sure if it was him or another of the residents.'

'It's intriguing,' Steve responded.

It's more than that, thought Honey with a glower. *It's our money that paid for that — might have paid for it all.*

'Nice car though. I've seen that parked outside.' He frowned. 'Think somebody told me it belonged to his daughter. The old car was his. Renault, I think. Have you met his daughter?' He asked the question with what Honey could only describe as an expression of salacious interest. It was the second time he'd mentioned her. 'Right looker, she is.'

'No doubt we'll be meeting her in time.'

Warren gave a quick jerk of his stubbly chin. The salacious smile disappeared from his wide mouth but lingered in his eyes. For a moment he seemed away with the fairies until Steve gave him a verbal nudge.

'Right. Better let us in.'

Steve's demand broke through Warren's musing.

'Right away.'

Honey and Steve got back in the car. Neither bothered to wave.

'Creep,' murmured Honey.

'Always was,' returned Steve.

* * *

From inside his office, Warren Hart activated the iron gates and watched as DI Steve Doherty and his bit of fluff drove into the compound.

Bit of fluff, he thought grimly. Just like Samantha, his wife, her who'd driven him to drink. It was all her fault that he couldn't leave the booze alone and it was hard to admit that she was no more. He still referred to her in conversation as though they were still together, sharing the house, throwing the dishes, grabbing the nearest weapon and hitting each other when shouting and screaming had reached their limits. He didn't want pity and he certainly didn't wish for unwelcome questions. She was gone and that was that and it wasn't his fault. His world with her was long over. This little gatehouse offered him comfort and something to occupy his lonely days.

Certain women reminded him of her. Honey Driver, the bint with Doherty, was one of those who caused it to resurge.

'Cow,' he muttered. 'Cow, bitch, whore, slut.'

He repeated the same words on a regular basis like an act of cleansing, poured himself a double shot of whisky, knocked it back and sat down to watch the television.

He'd email or transfer the security camera records to Steve Doherty sometime this evening. Not that they'd show very much. The police had already looked over his shoulder as he'd downloaded them from the cloud and onto the main monitor.

They'd laughed when he'd said, 'Boring, aren't they? Just the people that live in Regency Gardens going in and out. That's why I watch Netflix most of the time.'

They'd laughed too and patted him on the shoulder.

'You're a good egg, Warren. The police lost a good man when you retired.' There was little sincerity in their comments. It was as if they said it by rote. Underneath it all they despised him — and he knew it.

He poured himself another double scotch after his visitors had gone. Once he was sure the coast was clear, he reached for the small Dell laptop he kept in the bottom drawer of the desk, opened it and connected it to the main system.

At first the screen lit up with the last crash-bang-wallop film he'd been watching on Netflix, the usual stuff, car chase after car chase, gunfight after gunfight. He tapped in a four-digit code and up came a channel that was like YouTube but catered for a more adult market.

And there she was, all blonde hair and naked, bronzed body. At first it was bare buttocks, then bare breasts. Writhing and twisting like a snake while purring like a contented pussycat. Sometimes there was a cat in the flick too, one he recognised. As for her . . .

She twisted into a sitting position and pouted suggestively at the camera. 'Hi there, pussycat.'

Warren smiled, and even though he knew she couldn't hear him and that he was one of many men watching this luscious beauty with her firm body and come-hither eyes, he responded.

'Hi, darling. Nice to know you'll be coming home. Drop in and see me once you are.'

Gabriella Glendower, Norman's daughter, was a right glamour puss. She'd always treated him with contempt, ignored him when he'd asked her out for a drink. She wouldn't now. He knew what her game was, how she earned her money. Her father didn't know. Neither did anyone else in Regency Gardens. Or he didn't think so. Unless someone else watched the comings and goings of the gated street.

He shook the very idea of it from his head. Just your imagination running riot, he thought. Stick to your plan. Accost Gabriella Glendower. Tell her what you know and what you plan to do about it.

He smiled as the most lascivious thoughts came into his head, thoughts he sorely wanted to act upon.

He said nothing but there were words in his head. She'll do anything you want to keep you quiet. Anything.

CHAPTER TEN

'I'm guessing he doesn't go out much,' said Honey as the electronics whirred and the gates glided open.

She glanced over her shoulder. The security guard post was behind them. The gates clanged shut. They were in.

The neo-Georgian houses had been built about five years ago, knock-offs of the real ones in the centre of the city. Terraced houses at entry-level price — a pretty penny in anyone's language — were set in crescents facing detached and semi-detached houses built for those with a bit more money in the bank and/or access to a larger mortgage. Each had a front lawn edged with ornamental bushes gathered in clusters around ornamental trees — Honey guessed magnolia. A wide driveway capable of taking two cars easily catered for the terraced houses. The more substantial houses had room for three vehicles, four at a pinch.

Mary Jane's car being a left-hand drive, it was Steve sitting in the passenger seat on the right side whose eyes followed the curving terrace looking for number sixteen.

'Found it.' He pointed. It was fairly central, a terraced house in the deep curve of a crescent. The larger houses were situated at the end of two opposing crescents.

'I feel as though I'm driving down the Mall on my way to an audience with the King,' Honey remarked. 'Houses to the left of me, houses to the right. It's as though they're funnelling me along to the ones that really count.'

As they came to a halt outside number sixteen, Steve scrutinised the police incident tape stretched around the curtilage of the house where Norman Glendower had been found stone dead.

They had a good view as they got out of the car.

True to form, a uniformed constable stood beneath a tiled canopy above the front door. The place was large, impressive — the sort of property coveted by those whose lives were ruled by status and success.

Honey pulled on the handbrake. Steve looked at the house at the end of Regency Gardens and then at number sixteen. 'Well, that's a turn-up for the books. Your mother's friend lives in the right spot.'

Honey's interest strayed from the murder scene to the house occupied by Gladys Faversham.

'Not many people gawping at us. What are they, dead or asleep?'

Steve looked at her, then at the end of the road. Nobody around. Nothing happening. 'I take your point. I've seen more activity in a graveyard.'

Honey jerked her head at number sixteen. 'Gladys must have an incredible view of the whole street from where she is. So too most of the other houses in these crescents, the one on this side of the road and the one on the other. Do you think the investigating officers have noticed that yet?'

Steve looked, looked again, and once it had sunk in was out of the car before she was, like a bloodhound on the scent. 'Mrs Faversham, here we come.'

'You're not a bloodhound,' she blurted. 'Seeing as you're dressed in black, you're more like a panther.'

He threw her a frown over his shoulder before heading over the pristine front path to the pristine front door in the pristine house. Everything about Regency Gardens was pristine.

The front door had six panels and a decorative arched window at the top. In the past it would have been made of wood — generally mahogany. This one was of plastic, aping the original but designed to last longer. The windows too were Georgian in style.

The door knocker was brass, the stay-bright kind that didn't need cleaning. There was also a doorbell, which Steve decided to press.

Gladys Faversham's appearance was not quite what Honey had expected. She might have been in the same age group as Honey's mother — mid-seventies — but was not out of the same box.

Whereas Gloria Cross was lithe, beautifully turned out and a possible fashionista for *Saga Magazine*, Gladys looked more likely to adorn the pages of *Marathon Running Today*. She was wearing jogging pants and vest in a uniform grey. Even her hair was grey.

She had angular shoulders, long limbs and an energetic charisma that made Honey think she spent more time at the gym than listening to talks or playing bingo at the Senior Citizens' Club. She was tall too, possibly around the same height as Mary Jane — about five feet eleven inches.

Her mother's words came to mind. 'She's seventy-seven but fit in mind and body. Lifts forty kilograms, whatever that means. Used to work for the government. Very hush-hush.'

Totally opposite to my mother, she thought, who never lifts anything heavier than a champagne flute.

Steve was the first to introduce himself. 'Detective Inspector Doherty. I'm making door-to-door enquiries regarding the incident at the end of the road. You have heard that Mr Glendower has been found dead?'

'Another one bites the dust.' Very forthright and said without any emotion.

Steve picked up on it. 'Excuse me?'

'We all go the same way in the end.'

Her strong face gave not the slightest indication of being perturbed by Glendower's death; she had a flippant disrespect for the man. Her tone was flat and totally without emotion.

'I would like to ask you some questions, if you don't mind.'

'What kind of questions?'

'General things. Just some idea of what it's like living here and what you might have seen. People looking out of their windows observing the day-to-day life of a place can sometimes be a goldmine of information.'

The words were music to her ears.

Gladys seemed to think about it before she finally jerked her chin. 'I can see the logic in that.' She turned to Honey. 'And where's your ID?'

Trying hard not to succumb to embarrassment, Honey hesitated. Gladys had a no-nonsense demeanour, and she wasn't the sort you could lie to or fool easily. No form of warrant card, so she had to do what she could.

'I don't have one. DI Doherty asked me along. We both have personal reasons for finding out what happened to Mr Glendower. He conned us out of some money, and we want to know what happened to it — and to him. My mother, Mrs Cross, said you wouldn't mind helping us out.'

The strong chin jutted. The deep-set eyes narrowed as she looked them up and down.

Finally, she made a decision.

'Yes.' She flung the door open wide and, turning her back, left it there swinging on its hinges inwards.

'Come in. Shut the door behind you and follow me,' she shouted over her shoulder. 'I'm halfway through my routine so you'll have to talk to me while I ride my bicycle.'

To say her tone was brisk would be putting it mildly. Her climb up to the first floor of the house was even more so. She took two stairs at a time like a springbok aiming to get to the waterhole before the rest of the herd.

They traipsed along the landing. The bedroom doors were closed. A slight tinkling electronic sound could be heard — like a digital clock gently turning over the seconds, minutes and hours.

Their feet clumped along the bare boards of the landing to a large room at the front of the house. Once a bedroom, it was now bursting at the seams with all manner of exercise equipment.

'Waiting for a new carpet?' asked Steve, who was clueless when it came to interior design. He wouldn't know bare boards were the in thing.

'No. Bare boards mean I can hear if an intruder approaches and deal with it accordingly.'

What the 'accordingly' might refer to was best blocked out. Honey reminded herself that this was an old lady, fit and spry as the first impression might be.

A treadmill, an exercise bike and a frame of overhead weights took up the length in front of the window.

'Thank you for agreeing to see us.' Steve extended his hand. Gladys ignored it and in the blink of an eye threw one leg over her exercise bike and began pedalling ferociously.

'This is a very light room,' remarked Honey as she took in the plain surroundings. Magnolia walls. White doors. White plastic Venetian blind rustling in the open window. The draught made her shiver but Gladys, already in sprint mode on her exercise bike, faced into it looking as though she was about to freewheel downhill with the wind in her hair.

There were no curtains and the view of the road was terrific. Honey exchanged a look with Steve. She could see from his expression that he too had realised that Gladys could see everything from here. It occurred to Honey that the exercise equipment had been placed there for that very purpose.

Steve stepped past the madly cycling woman and into the bay, eyes sweeping from one end of the street to the other. 'You've got a great view from here.'

Pedalling even harder, Gladys grunted what sounded like agreement. She dropped into a slower mode before she answered.

'It beats watching TV or some mindless rubbish on the internet. That's what they do at the gym, you know.' Her body dropped low over the bike again. Time for fast-forward. She pedalled like mad.

It was noticeable that the aged athlete did not pause for breath. Feeling just the tiniest bit intimidated, Honey looked at Steve, who guiltily touched the centre of his stomach and breathed in. There was the hint of a six pack but not so pronounced as it had once been.

'Did you see anything prior to the murder?' Steve asked as he fingered a dumbbell but didn't attempt to pick it up. Honey balked. It looked to be five kilos at least.

'The usual suspects,' Gladys pronounced.

'Who are?'

'Postman. Parcel deliveries.'

'During the past two weeks or so?'

'Postman. Parcel deliveries.'

'No visitors?'

Her pace slowed. She took deep breaths.

'I don't think he was that popular. He had no close friends visit. Only his daughter.'

Gladys was the second person to mention the daughter. Honey and Steve exchanged a glance. Honey, chilled to the bone, hugged herself. 'And he lived alone?'

'Except for the cat. Not your average moggy. An expensive cat.'

Honey nodded. 'Ah, yes. We did hear it was the cat that led to the discovery of the body.'

'Not surprising. It got noisy when it got hungry. The creature was pampered. He once told me that he'd mentioned it in his will.'

Eccentric, thought Honey, and nodded as though it was a perfectly normal thing to do. Still, it wasn't the cat that concerned them.

'Have the police asked you what you've seen?'

'No. And I won't offer unless they come calling.'

'And nobody's called?'

'No. Too busy sifting through the crime scene.'

Gladys suddenly swooped low over the handlebars and upped her speed. Honey thought that if she'd been on a bike with wheels she would have sped through the window, across the road and off into the sunset.

'Ask the right questions and I can tell you. You must ask the right questions.'

Steve didn't look well pleased. Before he could bridle, Honey pulled a question out of thin air that just might elicit an answer.

'Did Mr Glendower have any lady callers?'

'Yes.'

'Strangers or relatives?'

'Only the daughter. A clothes horse with bronze complexion, a blonde mane and the air of a pit pony pretending to be a thoroughbred.'

Honey hid her smile.

Recognising she'd enjoyed the description and might burst into giggles, Steve took over. 'No other women?'

'One. Always late at night.'

'Can you give us a description?'

'No. Too dark.'

'What sort of car did she drive?'

'She didn't.'

'She walked in?'

'Most likely. If she did drive, then the car must have been left outside.'

Steve frowned. Warren hadn't mentioned a woman visiting on foot. He made a mental note to ask him about it. Surely he would have seen it on the security monitors? If he was paying attention, that is.

'Do you know where Mrs Glendower lives?'

'Yes.'

Pleased to hear it, Steve got out his phone so he could record the address. 'Can you tell me where?'

'St Luke's cemetery. She's been there years.'

'So, Mrs Glendower is dead.'

'Correct.'

The exercise bike slowed to a total stop. Gladys took deep breaths, hands pushing at the handlebars as she jerked up and down in a last exercise.

'Can you tell me how she died?'

'Food poisoning. Went into hospital and never came out. That's what I heard.'

'And the daughter? I believe she lives in London. Is that correct?'

'As far as I know. Right.' She swung her leg so suddenly over the bicycle saddle that Steve had to draw back rather than risk being hit in the face with a size eight trainer, then wiped her sweaty face in a thin cotton towel. When her flushed face reappeared, Steve asked, 'Do you jog as well?'

'Yes.'

'Night owl or skylark?'

'I prefer to run at night. The pavements get too crowded during the day.'

'And the security guard lets you out and lets you back in?'

'Most of the time.'

Steve raised his eyebrows. 'Most of the time?'

'If he fails to notice me I either climb over the gates or go round to the back lane.'

Steve raised his eyebrows. 'Really? I didn't know there was a back lane. Can you tell me where it is?'

'Cross the road and follow the old footpath between The Beeches and Swallows Nest. Two detached houses. The builders wanted to block it off, but members of a footpath pressure group protested. The planners relented. It drops down at the back to the canal path.'

There was an expectant look on Steve's face. 'Do you run along the canal?'

Her response was brusque. 'Yes. I do. And, before you ask, I often run along there in the middle of the night.'

'A bit dark.'

'I take a torch.'

'Aren't you worried about muggers?' asked Honey.

'No. The torch is heavy and I'm not afraid to use it.'

Steve kept a deadpan expression as he wondered at Gladys's strength. His final analysis was that he wouldn't like to encounter her late at night. Despite her age it seemed Gladys could defend herself.

Honey offered her thanks for seeing them.

'You've been a great help, but if you think of anything that might help, please contact me,' Steve said. 'Text or phone. I don't mind which.' He gave her a card.

'The old-fashioned way,' she said, somewhat incredulously, a look of wry amusement on her face.

* * *

Leaving Honey at the steering wheel, Steve called in on the security gatehouse to say goodbye to Warren.

'Warren. I'll be off now but will pop in again.'

'Sure,' said Warren. 'It'll be great to catch up on old times.'

'Just one question before I leave. Mrs Faversham has indicated that Mr Glendower did have a lady caller who visited late at night. Have you seen her? She might have left her car outside.'

Warren shook his head. 'No, I didn't, but then if she walked in the cameras might not have picked her up.'

'And I believe there's a footpath at the end of the street. Are there no cameras there?'

Warren shook his head. 'No. If someone didn't want to be seen, then the footpath is the way to come in.' His face suddenly brightened, the salacious look from before now mapped on his face. 'A fancy woman. Well, I never knew that. Who would have thought it? Dark horse, then.'

'Yeah,' said Steve, his opinion of Warren even lower than it had been. 'Dark horse.'

Warren came out front to wave them off, his face as red and rosy as Santa Claus on an old advent calendar.

'Is he still sending you a copy of the security camera film?'

'Supposedly, but don't hold your breath. That whisky bottle was half full when we went in. It's now less than a quarter. I'll run through the copy at the station.'

'This drinking. Won't he lose his job if his employers find out?'

'Very likely, although I'm not going to tell them.'

* * *

Hot and sweaty after her exercise, Gladys Faversham headed to the airing cupboard for fresh towels and took them to the bathroom. A nice shower, a pot of Earl Grey and she was ready to make notes in the diary she kept on the computer, which she would also handwrite in a thick red journal. She opened her laptop and began to type.

> *Had visit from police in connection with murder of Mr Slippery. A policeman. Middle-aged. Wearing black.*

She always used nicknames for people mentioned in her diary. She liked those names and congratulated herself on her ingenuity.

Mr Slippery was her name for Norman Glendower. The policeman should have one too, she decided, and thought about it for a minute.

Johnny Cash. Very apt.

Now for the daughter of Gloria Cross.

> *Middle-aged accomplice. Daughter of Pussy Galore. Pussy's Kitten. I'm guessing she's the police officer's love interest. They seem well suited.*

She chuckled to herself as she read what she'd written, tickled pink by making up nicknames on the spot. Wasn't that clever? Gloria Cross was Pussy Galore and so her daughter was Pussy's Kitten. Of course, she always called Gloria by her proper name when they met — which wasn't that often, and when they did, they tiptoed around each other as they waited for the first snide aside, the first to pretend they weren't being sarcastic. It hadn't always been like that. They were convivial and had met up regularly when Gladys was still in work, a signatory to the Official Secrets Act and doing things she enjoyed — spying, listening in, watching what people were doing. All in the past now, of course.

Being retired bored her. Being objectionable filled the gap. Her attention went back to the laptop.

Mr Slippery was killed approximately two weeks ago. I understand he was bludgeoned over the head with a cricket bat.

She stopped typing today's entry and scrolled backwards. Two weeks. Ah, yes. That was roughly the night she'd been unable to sleep. Her legs were jerking. One of the daft things that happened in old age. Exercise usually calmed it down and even though it was two in the morning that's what she'd done, back in front of the window with the lights off, cycling for all she was worth.

Her eyes had scooted over the screen, finding the right date, the right time and reading what she'd written.

Podge. That's what she'd entered in the diary. She had a nickname for almost everybody. Podge, real name Warren, had been out and about but as usual had walked Regency Gardens for the shortest time possible. He'd seen nothing, but she had. It was the habit of a lifetime to be alert, a habit she couldn't shake off. Podge was hopeless.

She laughed out loud. 'Just you wait,' she chuckled. 'Just you wait.'

She had been about to turn off the computer but was distracted by the sight of the smart Jaguar purring its way into Norman Glendower's drive.

Aha! The Glendower offspring was home. She watched as first one tanned leg then another appeared. The heels were notoriously high, too high to drive in, surely. But there, Gabriella Glendower was a woman who believed in keeping up appearances. A hundred years ago she would have been a kept woman, earning her money and living in style, all expenses paid in exchange for occasionally lying on her back. Nowadays she prostituted herself from a distance via the internet. In a way, Gladys admired her and certainly understood her. Not for her the routine boredom of an office job and she wasn't selling her body — not in the accepted sense.

'What a naughty little girl you are,' she murmured. 'What would Daddy say?'

The door buzzer sounded. She flicked the switch that would show her who was at the door. The anxious face of Karen Turpin, the young woman who lived across the road with her two children came into view. The husband had once lived there too but she hadn't seen him for a while. Gone with the wind, she thought with amusement.

She pressed a button and spoke into the microphone.

'Come on in, Karen. I'm in the study.'

The study was a small room at the front of the house, only big enough for a curved work chair and a long ledge stretching from one wall to another. Her laptop sat in the centre of the workstation in front of a monitor. A pile of books sat at one end. The thick red leather journal sat to the other side of the computer. Half a dozen pens sat in a neat row beside it.

'Good day to you, Karen.' *Turnip*, thought Gladys. *It would be so easy to call you by your nickname — the one I gave you.* 'Please take a seat.'

'You wanted to see me?'

Fingers devoid of adornment twisted and turned anxiously.

Gladys sat back in her chair, her own hands folded with an air of complacent relish across her flat stomach.

'I texted you out of neighbourly concern. I can't help commenting that you're looking a bit lost these days.'

'I've got things on my mind.'

'Yeeesss,' Gladys said slowly, a slight smile on her thin lips, a look in her eyes reminiscent of a cat sharpening its claws before pouncing on a humble sparrow. 'You would do — what with your husband not being around. Away working, so you say.'

'Yes. Yes. He was offered a very good contract.'

Gladys looked up at the ceiling. 'Now, remind me what he works at. Drilling for oil off the coast of Scotland or Norway?'

Her incisive look floated back down to fix on Karen's pale and rather haggard face.

'Yes. He's in the oil industry.'

This was the moment Gladys enjoyed the most, the moment when she would spring the truth from the pack of lies Karen — and others like her — were telling.

'In London?'

Karen's face drained of what little colour it had. Once the truth had hit, she shook her head vehemently.

'I don't know what you mean. Ron isn't working in London.' She attempted a weak smile. 'He's working on the oil rigs off Aberdeen.'

Sheer bravado, thought Gladys — and totally untrue.

Gladys shook her head. 'I don't think so, my dear. I think your darling Ron is incarcerated following a drug deal that went wrong. He was the lamb led to the slaughter.'

Karen trembled like an unset jelly. 'You won't tell, will you? Please don't tell. Please. Think of my children. They don't know Ron is in jail. They wouldn't understand.'

'Of course they wouldn't. And I'm not going to tell all and sundry about the men you entertain . . .'

'It's not what you think!'

'No need to shout, my dear.'

Karen's eyes were round with fear. 'What is it you want? I don't have any money so there's no point in blackmailing me. I couldn't pay even if I wanted to.'

'You think I'm a common blackmailer,' said Gladys, her moon-shaped face beaming as if with reflected sunlight. She shook her head. 'How tawdry! Oh no. I have no need for money. Now,' she said, tilting her head to one side, a cruel curl to one side of her mouth. 'I'm writing a book.'

'A book?'

Karen sounded surprised and slightly relieved — though with the next sentence she realised a sense of relief was a bit premature.

'You see, I'm writing a book about the smug inhabitants of Regency Gardens. I watch all of you go about your little lives as though you own the entire world. With time you'll realise that it is all a fallacy. The respectable and vaguely pompous veneer is just that. A veneer. Underneath we're all just silly little apes. There's no such thing as civilisation. Not really. Do you understand what I'm saying?'

Karen frowned and shook her head. She had the look of Little Red Riding Hood about her. 'I'm not sure.'

Karen was trembling inside as well as out. She'd responded to the unexpected text, curious to find out what exactly was expected of her. The text had read, *I need to speak to you urgently about your husband.* She'd had to come. Up until now she'd kept the secret to herself and was receiving enough money to keep going, but God, it was lonely. She missed men. She had a yearning for some of her neighbours. Had gone out of her way to speak to them — was that what Gladys was going to spring on her, that she'd seen her dallying? That was all she'd done. Dallied.

'My book will blow Regency Gardens apart and all the residents with it. Shutting oneself off from the world is quite impossible nowadays. The information highway has blasted everything wide open.' She looked bemused. 'It's quite interesting. I watch a real-life soap unfold before my eyes.' She patted the thick red journal. 'And I record it all. In my book.' She patted the laptop. 'And on my computer.'

'I don't understand. What is it you want from me? I've already told you I don't have any money.'

Gladys laughed. 'Money! I don't want money.'

Her face clouded over into a devilish mask, a gloating countenance of outright cruelty.

'I want to see you squirm. I want to see all of the atrocious residents of Regency Gardens squirm when I publish my book, and all their secrets are laid bare.'

'You can't do that! Not without their permission.'

A smiling Gladys shook her head. 'I haven't mentioned their names as such. Just nicknames. The ones I've given you all.' She patted the laptop, patted the thick red journal. 'You're all in here.'

'But why?' Karen shook her head, not understanding.

'Pure devilment,' laughed Gladys. 'Pure devilment. I never wanted to retire and when I did, I had to find something to fill my time. You and everyone like you are my revenge on being put out to pasture. I enjoy teasing people, making them feel uncomfortable, diving into their lives and exposing their truths.' She leaned closer to a scared-looking Karen. 'I want you to feel my cruelty.'

Karen stared. 'You're mad.' She got up from the chair. 'You're a mad old woman.'

'But you won't want the neighbours to know about your husband, will you?' Gladys shouted as Karen ran for the front door. 'You won't want them to know that he's a jailbird, will you!'

CHAPTER ELEVEN

Back at the Green River Hotel, Nigel was looking a trifle agitated. Presuming it was something to do with him moving out of the coach house, swapping it with her and Steve's occupation of the honeymoon suite, Honey asked him what the matter was, apologising again for turfing them out. Nigel had been the one to insist, though. He'd said they needed a few home comforts after such a horrendous ordeal.

'Not a problem,' he said, flapping his hands. 'In fact, Eddie and I quite like that four-poster bed. And we won't be staying there too long now anyway.'

A friend with a posh house in Daniel Mews was working abroad for a few years and had asked them to house sit. Who wouldn't want to live in a Georgian house in Jane Austen territory and within spitting distance of Great Pulteney Street?

'We've given our tenant notice, so it won't be long before we get our flat back and our friend wants us to house sit later in the year. In the meantime, we'll be quite comfortable.'

It meant it couldn't be let to a paying guest but as they had nothing booked in, they could cope for now. Besides, it seemed they were holding out for the luxury of the townhouse. Honey was easy about it all. Nigel was a valued employee.

'That's a relief,' she said. 'So what's worrying you?'

'It's just that Mary Jane phoned. She's coming back early. Apparently, she had a falling out with the organisers of the psychic fair in Marling Buntford, the village close to the haunted house she was staying at. She reckons they were too grounded in the here and now to know what they were talking about.'

'I bet that went down well.'

'They threatened to sue her if she didn't pay for the table she broke in her workshop.'

Honey's eyebrows arched as a wild guess at the reason popped into her mind. 'A table tapping workshop by any chance?'

'I believe so.' Nigel smoothed both hands over his green brocade waistcoat. 'Apparently the table was a handsome piece with cabriole legs and a highly polished surface. She told me that the organisers were livid and that she couldn't possibly be held responsible for the legs falling off. Anyway, she reckoned a bit of wood glue would set things to rights. Unfortunately for her the organisers of the fair believed otherwise. She was accused of vandalism and ordered to leave. On top of that they're billing her for the repair.'

'Oh dear.' Honey sucked in her bottom lip. It was hard not to laugh. 'Poor Mary Jane.'

Steve smirked. Honey glared at him until the broad grin he entertained had fallen from his face.

Nigel was as nice as ninepence and a very confident young man. He capably dealt with the most awkward customer without breaking a sweat. His Achilles heel was Mary Jane. His face paled the moment she appeared — not that Mary Jane seemed to notice. Steve Doherty tolerated her and never took her seriously, whereas she made Nigel downright nervous.

'Does this mean she was bashing the table a bit too harshly?' Steve said to Honey as they made their way over to the coach house.

Honey didn't dignify this with an answer. Once she and Steve were inside, she kicked off her shoes and collapsed on the sofa. 'I think Nigel and Eddie are quite looking forward to moving.'

Steve flopped beside her, his arms outstretched along the back of the sofa. He lay his head back and closed his eyes.

'And avoiding Mary Jane. As for the broken table at this psychic fair . . .' Honey chuckled. 'I reckon it sent the ghosts running back from where they came.'

Honey snuggled down further into the deep-seated sofa, one of a pair of Chesterfield settees that had lately been reupholstered in a soft shade of champagne. However, it wasn't champagne Honey had in mind.

'Put the kettle on. I could murder a cup of tea.'

While Steve followed her orders, she made the effort to leave the settee and attend to the clothes piled on the dining table. There'd been no time to grab any decent clothes when the boat went down so she'd had to go out and buy a new selection for her wardrobe — not an unpleasant task. She listed each item she'd bought with a view to adding it to the insurance claim if it ever came to be, though things didn't look promising. Along with the boat they might as well accept that they wouldn't be getting a penny. Sad but true.

Steve passed her a mug of tea. 'Hot and sweet,' he said. 'Just like me.'

He'd hoped for a smile to lighten the moment. Losing everything at sea was bad enough, but finding out that the insurance broker supposedly acting in your interests had been acting in his own was enough to dampen anyone's spirits. And now he was dead.

'More clothes?' he asked, misconstruing a fresh outburst of scribbling.

'Actually, this one's a list regarding our very dead insurance broker, Mr Norman Glendower. There are options and, let's face it, we must be practical. We can't live on hope and fresh air.'

Steve took a large gulp of tea, though it couldn't possibly sustain him as much as a stiff drink from the bar.

'Go on.' He was holding his breath.

'Firstly, you've got your old pals in the police force. And you're back in with them now.'

He immediately corrected her. 'Service. It's now the police service. We are a service. We're not in the market to be forceful.'

Eyebrows no longer plucked at her favourite beauty parlour — she couldn't afford it — rose questioningly. 'Does that change anything?'

'I reserve judgement.'

Pen in hand, Honey nodded at the notepad, scratched something out and scribbled something in. 'But you do have mates there still, don't you? I mean, there's Warren up at Regency Gardens for a start. The security tapes should be useful.'

Steve agreed. 'I'll get Nigel to check if they've come through. Who knows, somebody might spot this mystery woman who sneaked in one dark and stormy night.'

'Or when your mate Warren Hart was off his head on whisky.'

Steve grimaced. 'He's not my mate. Just an old colleague.'

Honey turned her attention back to the list. 'Then there's Gladys Faversham. There's nothing so useful as a nosy neighbour.'

Steve buried his head in his hands. 'She wasn't that cooperative. Besides which, I think she was a bit strange — except for her mentioning a strange woman who visited him late at night.'

'Precisely. If she hadn't mentioned this woman we wouldn't have heard from your . . . Warren . . . about where people parked their cars who didn't want to be seen.'

'She's old. She could have been mistaken.'

Honey threw him an accusing look. 'Don't write her off.' She wagged her pen at him like a disapproving schoolmarm. 'Nosy parkers have nothing better to do with their time than watch their neighbours. To them it's a hobby and, let's face it, far more interesting than bridge, knitting or origami.'

Steve shook his head. 'I'd still prefer something more dependable than old ladies with nothing better to do than peering out of their windows. In a small street of terraced houses, perhaps, but a place like Regency Gardens?'

'Just because they live in posh houses doesn't mean that they're any different to anyone else. It's a gated housing estate, everything spick and span, manicured lawns and shiny BMWs, Jaguars and Mercedes. Pristine prettiness can become extremely boring. Bored people tend to seek diversions. There are no net curtains hanging at the windows, but that doesn't mean people don't get up to anything naughty.'

'Have you ever spied on your neighbours?'

Honey pulled in her chin. 'Steve, I run a hotel. I keep an eye on my guests and on my staff — oh, but don't tell them that. Not the staff, I mean. I don't want Smudger running amok with a meat cleaver.' Smudger Smith was her head chef and easily upset, especially by people who thought they knew more than he did about cooking. And he was handy with a meat cleaver. 'Besides, isn't that what coppers do? Keep an eye on people?'

He pursed his lips and nodded. 'Sometimes.'

She knew he wasn't one hundred per cent convinced. He had that lost boy look as though she was Wendy, he was Peter Pan, and they were not far from Neverland.

She made the effort to press home the point. 'The way I see it, a gated community has got to be even more boring than an ordinary street full of curtain twitchers. Nobody's allowed in unless they've got permission to be there. So, nobody interesting arrives except perhaps at night or at the weekend. During the day everyone's gone to the office or whatever, and nothing much happens. There weren't even any kids kicking a ball in the street or skateboarding over those lovely flat paths. I didn't even see a dog or a cat. So, in the absence of anything else they latch onto little things.'

'As in little things mean a lot?' he said with a grin.

Honey landed an affectionate slap on his arm. 'You're being facetious, but . . .' She took a deep breath. 'But you've got it, and as a woman . . .'

'I have noticed this.' He brought his forehead to rest against hers so that their eyes met.

She fixed him with a businesslike glare. 'Be serious.'

He straightened. 'OK. I'll be serious. In fact, I'll be very serious.'

She eyed him speculatively. 'Is it good serious?'

His grin blossomed into a full-blown smile. 'What you were saying earlier about getting back with the police. I have a confession to make.'

Honey eyed him steadily. 'Confess away.'

'Right. I've just received an interesting text.'

'How interesting?'

'Seeing as I've first-hand experience of dealing with this Norman—'

'This crook.'

'This dead man before he became dead, the powers that be suggested I come on board the case and I'm happy to oblige.'

'They obviously value you.'

'Don't sound so surprised.'

'I'm not.' She patted his arm and reassured him it just showed how much the local constabulary thought of him. 'You do what you must do. I'm sure your old buddies will appreciate your input. You working with them on the inside and me on the outside . . .'

He eyed her warily. 'Honey! Hold it right there. I know that look. You're planning something.'

'Why not? I want to know who killed the man who robbed us of our dream.' She grimaced. 'One thousand four hundred pounds a year insurance should have covered the cost of replacement when the boat went down.' She gritted her teeth. 'There should be a whole coachload of suspects. We can't have been the only ones who thought he had it coming.

'We already know he had a finger in a number of pies. What if he was involved in another scam — not necessarily to do with insurance. It's been hinted at that he spent time in

London, though not necessarily to do with insurance. What else was he involved in, I wonder?'

Steve's phone pinged and he read the text. Whatever the content, he got up from the sofa. 'Sorry, doll. I've got to take this.'

The courtyard at the back of the coach house was private. Nobody could overhear what was said even though it was surrounded by six-storey Georgian buildings, originally houses but divided into flats in the twentieth century.

The governor was on the other end.

'Guv. How can I help?'

Paul Marchant phoning him came as a bit of a surprise. From what he knew, Marchant was a face-to-face man in that he liked to read expressions and body language. Steve concluded this had to be important.

'After a bit of searching around, it seems the Met knew of our dead man, Norman Glendower. There was a suspected insurance scam, but no boats were involved. Seems you were the only one on that score. A series of valuable items were insured and stolen shortly afterwards.'

'And he didn't pay out. He kept the money?'

'No. That's just it. With one or two exceptions who do not want to speak about it, they were all paid out. None of the items stolen were recovered. The Met suspect it was a team effort. All the insurance policies were taken out in quick succession. It seemed our man had a sales drive or some such thing.'

Obvious scenarios ticked over in Steve's mind. 'There had to be other people involved.'

'Yes, I'm afraid so, but not quite in the way you were. The insurance company suspect collusion on the part of Mr Glendower and several wealthy clients.'

Paul Marchant's voice was naturally a deep bass. It deepened noticeably as he outlined what the Metropolitan Police in London had deduced from their investigations. 'He was in with some pretty tasty London gangs, not your old bash 'em and shoot 'em lot, but sophisticated — internet savvy, you could say.'

'So it's possible that our victim might have done something to upset them?'

'It's very likely.'

'And they wouldn't like being taken for a ride.'

'Correct.'

'Thanks for letting me know.'

His attitude towards the case had changed abruptly by the time he rejoined Honey, who was sprawled out on the sofa, one hand resting on her forehead. 'I take it that was he who must be obeyed.'

'Paul Marchant.'

She heaved herself up on her elbows. 'Are you going to tell me what he said?'

'No. Just that there's been a few new developments in the case that could possibly explain why our man was murdered and who wanted him dead.'

'That's exciting.' Her eyes shone with interest. 'Do we have new leads? Anything I can follow up by myself?'

'Honey, I don't want you getting involved.'

Steve did not look happy. He didn't sound it either.

Honey wasn't prepared to leave it there. She was fired up with the energy that only a wronged woman could feel. Their dream had turned to ashes, and somebody should have paid the price, i.e. the insurance company. Said insurance company was untraceable and the broker had had his head bashed in. She considered how she might further their quest without stepping on the toes of the likes of Paul Marchant.

'How about I do my own investigating? How about I make friends with the residents of Regency Gardens? I'll make them offers they can't refuse.'

Steve eyed her sceptically. 'Not the head of a horse left in a bed?'

'Don't be ridiculous. There's no godfather involved — unless you're keeping something back.'

She gave him the sheepish look she reserved for those moments when she wasn't too sure herself of her 'clever' ideas — just in case they weren't that clever.

Steve had a great urge to throw his hands over his ears and start singing 'la, la, la, la' in a very loud voice. But it was clear that she already had a plan of action. Her enthusiasm for the task was breathtaking.

'You're going to trace that footpath the old girl, Gladys, was on about.' Steve thought about it for a moment. 'It can't hurt, I suppose.' He pointed a finger. 'Just be careful.'

Honey tossed her mop of mahogany brown hair, which betrayed the fine silver threads running through it. 'I promise I will be, but you have to admit it's worth a look. However—' a sharp nod of her head sent her hair falling forwards — 'that wasn't quite what I had in mind. Rather than me go to them, I thought it might be a good idea to invite the residents of Regency Gardens to high tea at the Green River Hotel, purely as an act of sympathy to help them get over their trauma.'

Steve swallowed the last of his tea before pushing the empty mug up under his chin in a futile bid to stop his jaw from dropping any further. 'Let me think about that a minute. You're saying invite them to your place rather than banging door to door.'

'Correct. Get as many of them as possible in one place, where they're more easily observed.'

It was a good sign when Steve didn't dismiss the idea out of hand.

'It has its merits.'

'And Mary Jane will be back. You know what she's like with atmospheres and instincts.'

Steve sighed. 'Oh yes. I know all right.'

Honey pulled a face and flounced back to the job in hand — jotting down the prices on the labels from M&S, Anthropologie and Apricot, a few replacements for the items she'd lost. She peered out at him from beneath her fringe. Was he in favour of her idea or not?

His decision came quickly. 'Honey,' he said, enveloping her in his arms, 'it's a brilliant idea.'

'I'm glad you think so. Now, wasn't it a good idea for me to go with you this morning?'

'I'll reserve judgement.'

She flicked his arm playfully. 'Lucky for you that my mother knows Gladys Faversham. It's likely given you a head start on your mates from Manvers Street.'

'There's one thing I do have to say. Your mother knows some pretty eccentric characters.'

'Of course she does. She's one herself. I take it you'll be attending?'

'Tea and cakes?'

'Plus wine and nibbles.' She fixed him with a look that only softly hinted at the fact that it was him who'd suggested using a broker known to some of his police mates. He had to do his best and make it up to her somehow. Who knows what the neighbours might have seen?

'So you think it's a good idea? For sure?' She eyed him quizzically.

'There's some files regarding Glendower's contacts in London to look into. People in the insurance game, for the most part.'

'Really?' She said it with an air of disbelief. Her instinct told her that there was something he wasn't telling her. 'It wouldn't be anything to do with that call you had earlier, would it?'

A 'butter wouldn't melt' look came to his face. 'If it was, I couldn't tell you. I'm police, you're not.'

'You Tarzan, me Jane. Stick to kitchen sink time, huh?'

He patted her hand. 'Don't take it personally. Anyway, there are other places I'd prefer you to be.'

She glowered. 'Be serious.'

'Of course. I can tell you that I'm getting a computer nerd at the station to see if she can track down other disgruntled clients of Mr Norman Glendower. Any clients, in fact.'

'Seems like a good move, but . . .' Honey frowned. 'It seems strange that no one has as yet come forward.'

'Unless they've gone direct to the insurance company that issued their policies. Or nobody has made a claim.'

'Or his clients were thin on the ground. Perhaps we were the only ones.'

'He lives in a nice house. He had to be making his money some way.'

'He did indeed.' Honey grimaced. 'By fair means or foul?'

'I couldn't possibly comment.'

Narrowing her eyes, she fixed him with a hard stare. 'Is there something you're not telling me?'

He spread his arms in surrender. 'Babe!'

Honey shook her head and tutted at him like his mother might have done. She conceded defeat — at least for now. 'I'll get this Saturday afternoon get-together under way. It's a lot to do in the time I have.'

* * *

The boys — that is, Nigel, Eddie, Smudger and the kitchen staff — proved keen to help.

'We've formed a committee,' explained Nigel. 'And Eddie has made a list.'

Smudger had calmed down a lot in her absence. He'd even developed a bit of a paunch.

'I wouldn't mind a house up there,' he pronounced when she told him who was coming and where they were from. 'Way beyond my pocket though. I wonder if that bloke was murdered for not paying the mortgage.'

'No. But if he was still around now he might get murdered for not paying out on Steve's beloved *Footloose and Fancy-Free*. He loved that boat.'

'More than you,' smirked Smudger.

Honey thought about it. 'It sailed with the wind. I have a tendency to sail against it.'

CHAPTER TWELVE

Gladys Faversham completed her cycling, ran on the tread-mill for another half an hour and finished off with an hour of weightlifting.

After wiping her face with a small hand towel used purely for post-exercise perspiration, she headed for the shower. Under its steaming torrent, her body became invigorated and her brain animated.

Physical exercise completed, she placed two ginseng tablets on the tea trolley beside her favourite armchair, went to the kitchen, made a cup of green tea and then made herself comfortable.

Tablets swallowed, tea sipped, she took her notebook and pen from the lower shelf of the tea trolley.

Her eyes smiled though her thin lips remained fixed in a straight line that only vaguely passed for a smile.

After a little forethought she began to write.

> *Turnip's face was a picture. She really couldn't understand the pleasure I get at pulling people to pieces. Whether I ever publish a book on the subject is neither here nor there. It's seeing people's consternation that turns me on. I just love recording the habits of the naked ape — aka humankind.*

Scarlet Woman at number eleven has a new lover. I think he's the seventh this year. I'm sure she gets them from a dating site. Nothing wrong with that, of course, in this day and age, but surely they cannot be after her for her looks. She's not exactly a car crash but she's no spring chicken either.

Penis Pender at The Haven has a different car in his drive. He's always coming home in different cars due to him being involved in the motor trade. This one's a Rover, though, my goodness, it's nothing like the old-style Rovers. In fact, it doesn't look that much different to a Renault, which is a French car, or even a Kia or any other of those tinny-looking cars from the Far East. I've seen the Jaguar parked in a layby, a blonde in the passenger seat. His wife's dark, like the Queen of Spades. Exotic. Not brassy.

As for Podge . . . fat layabout and stinking of whisky. What a useless wreck he is, unsuitable even to be a lowly security guard. His brain is so addled an elephant could go charging down Regency Gardens and he wouldn't notice. He didn't notice the woman who visited Mr Slippery, but I did. She came up from the footpath at the back of the houses. I might not have seen her if I hadn't been out running. She pushed past me. Dead of night. Seemed surprised to see me there, but then most people are. She isn't the first I've seen creeping up that footpath — or the first person I've seen go into Mr Slippery's house. If that footpath could speak, it would tell a whole multitude of stories.

Her eyes glittered with excitement. She loved to imagine what her neighbours would say if they knew she'd given them nicknames and that she recorded their every move in her diary. Not that she kept her jottings to herself. She liked to hint what she knew about them to their faces. Podge had looked at her blankly earlier today when she'd mentioned the secret stuff on his computer. It wasn't all Netflix and Amazon Prime in that cosy little snug of his and he hadn't a clue that such things could be monitored from afar, but then most people didn't and most people had neither the training nor the equipment to do so.

Penis Pender had almost bust a gut when she'd told him she'd seen him fondling the teenage girl who was a friend of his daughter. As for Holy Joe at number ten, he'd looked as if he were going to choke when she'd mentioned him having membership of a gay bar down in the centre of town.

'Well, that's it for one day,' she said with a sigh of satisfaction, slamming the journal shut. She'd transfer the written word to her laptop later on. 'Only one more thing to do.'

She reached for her desk diary, one that had come with a pen and had a profusion of flowers on the cover. This was the 'old lady' diary as she termed it, the place where she jotted down appointments with the doctor or the dentist, theatre or social events she thought might be amusing.

Turning to the next Saturday, she entered the date of the afternoon tea at the Green River Hotel. What a wonderful idea. She could watch what everyone was up to from there. A jolly event for all and for her to observe her pathetic neighbours trying to look as though they led exemplary lives. What tosh!

The text had arrived on her phone only a few moments ago, and she felt sure she was one of the first to respond.

Everyone — or almost everyone — would gather on Saturday afternoon to help them with the trauma of having a murder happen in Regency Gardens. Not that she was feeling any trauma. The whole thing quite amused her. It was her opinion that Norman Glendower had deserved to be murdered. He only lived here and goodness knows what he got up to in London. She suspected crime. If some of her equipment could fly to London she'd know more of what he got up to.

He'd had little to do with the neighbours, little to do with anyone, and she had the impression that he hadn't cared much for anyone — with the exception of that daughter of his. Looks like hers took money to maintain. *I wonder* . . . she thought, smiling as a possibility entered her head. Give the girl a chance to move in, put the house on the market, get her feet comfortably under the table then begin watching her. She took out a tiny LED fixture. What a wonderful little gadget it was. She read the headline on the paperwork that came with it. *Undetectable security surveillance — little more than the head of a pin.*

The insinuation that it was the size of a pinhead wasn't quite correct, but it was small. *Wonderful gadgets available nowadays*, she thought to herself. *Better than when I first worked for 'the establishment'.*

Once she'd finished writing, she got up from her chair and peered through the slats in the Venetian blinds. Two children were alighting from their mother's silver-grey SUV, heaving school bags over their shoulders before ambling to the front door.

Their mother, Karen Turpin, who she'd nicknamed Turnip, the children Mustard and Cress, was flicking the electronic key at the vehicle until a quartet of orange lights flashed and confirmed it was locked. Goodness knows why she was so pedantic about locking it. They lived in a gated community with a guard in the gatehouse. Stupid woman. The woman who told everyone that her husband was working away. What fun it had been to tell her that she knew very well where her husband was presently residing. It was so easy to find things out when you came from an intelligence background. The civil service wasn't all about pen pushing and filling out forms in triplicate.

Look at her, she thought. Putting on a brave face. Pretending that nothing had been said. It wouldn't hurt to remind her, to see again the look of consternation, the fear in the fading brown eyes. She would relish seeing that same look of helplessness for a second time. What a mouse. What a pathetic little woman.

Plastering a smile on her face, she headed for the hallway, pulled open the front door and called across the road.

'Karen. I say . . .'

Looking harassed — which quite frankly was nothing new — Karen let the kids into the house before she turned round.

'Hello, Mrs Faversham. How are you today?' Her smile looked forced, born of impatience to get away, and she looked wary — not surprising after their earlier meeting.

It pleased Gladys that Karen called her Mrs Faversham rather than Gladys. It showed respect. Younger people — although Karen was at least thirty-five — should always show respect.

'I'm very well under the circumstances,' she said as she homed in on her neighbour. 'I don't know whether you're aware yet, but the whole of Regency Gardens have been invited for afternoon tea next Saturday at the Green River Hotel. It's a kindly gesture meant to alleviate our trauma following the dreadful events that happened here.' Gladys added a few tuts along with a worried look and a disapproving shake of her head. 'A terrible thing. Who would have thought something like that could happen here, although Mr Glendower did seem the sort to bring trouble to his door. He did seem a bit of a slippery character.'

She smiled at how clever she was to have used his extended nickname without betraying its origins either in her imagination or the records she kept.

'Still, who would have thought?' returned Karen, her voice trembling. 'It's a very nice gesture.' She took a step towards the front door, signalling that she really needed to tend to her children and not spend time talking to a neighbour with whom she had little in common. She was anxious to get away. One meeting with Gladys in a week was more than enough.

'This get-together should do us all good. I take it you'll be coming?'

'Only if I can take the children.'

Gladys raised her eyebrows quizzically. 'It does say that everyone is invited.'

'In that case I'll go.'

'And your husband, Ron? I take it he'll be keen to come.' She said it loudly so that any neighbours listening could hear her adhere to Karen's excuse that he was away working. Ron's nickname was AWOL — in army terms, absent without leave.

Gladys saw an apologetic expression cross a pretty face that marriage and separation was making haggard.

'I'm afraid he's working away at present, so I doubt it. Now, if you'll excuse me.' She too had said it loudly for the benefit of the neighbours.

'Have a good evening, my dear. I'm going to call around to everyone. I think this is a kindness that deserves to be accepted. Therefore, I'm off to knock on doors and drum up support. I think we could all do with it.'

With bold, confident strides, Gladys Faversham marched off while Karen Turpin took the chance to escape.

Karen's two children, Jessica and Alison, were sitting at the oak table in a designer kitchen-diner that most people would envy. The children sat there round-eyed, hands in their laps. Most children might have raided the cupboard by now, but these two wouldn't dare. In the past they might have, but that was when their father was still at home. He hadn't been around for a while now, and although in the past they'd asked when he was coming home, they no longer did so. They just sat there waiting for their mother to prepare an evening meal or order them to get something themselves.

When she continued to stare sadly out of the window, Jessica, the eldest of the two, asked if she could make some sandwiches.

Jerked back into reality, Karen said there was tinned soup in the cupboard. They could have that with bread and butter. And there were crisps. And cheap bars of chocolate.

In the past when their father was around, they'd never been allowed such things. Everything had been cooked from scratch and, young as they were, they took on board what their parents told them about healthy eating. Things had changed since he'd gone, although their mother remained in denial, telling them as well as the neighbours that he was working away and would be back in time for Christmas.

Karen took a chilled bottle from the fridge and poured herself a large glass of wine. She put a fresh one in every day. Always white and always chilled in time for her to indulge.

The small voice of her younger daughter asked if they could go to the cinema on Saturday afternoon. Just for once, the voice pierced the difficulties she was desperately trying to cope with. Money was more of a problem than her husband — and his friends — had led her to believe.

'No,' she snapped.

The girls jumped.

'No,' said Karen, a little gentler this time. The smile of the mother that used to be appeared on her face as she remembered the nicest thing that Mrs Faversham had told her. Not the nastiness, which she still had trouble taking in. How could someone live to torment and tease people who she hardly knew?

'We've been invited to afternoon tea at a lovely hotel in Bath. There'll be tasty sandwiches and gorgeous cakes. Ice cream too, I expect. It'll be quite a party and I think we should go. Don't you?'

The girls were unanimous. Of course they wanted to go. Their spirits were lifted at the prospect of an afternoon full of ice cream and cakes.

That should keep them happy for a few hours, Karen thought glumly. She drained her glass and poured herself another. The glass she used was quite large and the bottle was close to half gone. *Oh well*, she thought. *Plenty more where that came from — if I can afford it.* The thought of free wine at the Green River Hotel lifted her spirits. Karen had no idea whether the Green River was a luxury hotel. She didn't even know the address, but that didn't matter. She would book a taxi to take them there — unless some kind soul in Regency Gardens would give them a lift. It had been ages since she'd gone out and drinking home alone was a hiding to nothing. At least she'd be in company, and God knows she could certainly do with company. And having some fun, eating quality food prepared by someone else and drinking good wine, not the cheap garage stuff. *Yes*, she thought. *Saturday could be fun.*

She had half a mind to pop her head out of the front door and confirm to Mrs Faversham that yes, she would be going.

She pulled back one half of a plantation shutter to see if her neighbour was close by but couldn't see her anywhere.

A dark blue Mercedes pulled into the drive of the house next door, closely followed by a bright pink top-of-the-range Fiat. Aiden Pendle got out of the Mercedes. She waited to see if he would glance in her direction, but he didn't, not with his wife right behind him.

Night was drawing in.

Another car drove in and parked on the drive at the front of the house next door to Mrs Faversham. There were only about ten minutes now between each car arriving home from a good day's work.

During all that time Mrs Faversham did not reappear, so there was no chance to confirm that she and the children would be attending. On reflection, the thought of facing her again was distasteful. Closing the shutters, she contemplated how this impromptu party at a hotel would turn out. She found herself looking forward to it. With a bit of luck Aiden would give her and the girls a lift, which would be quite lovely — so long as his wife, Melanie, didn't go. She badly wanted him to herself. Not that it could ever come to anything. It was just a distraction. Ron would kill her if she ever so much as looked at anyone else.

With that cheering thought foremost in her mind, she poured herself another drink and raised her glass. 'Here's to Saturday.'

Aiden would probably be there with his latest flame — a redhead from Reading. Karen had given in to him just the once. It had been nothing but a fling. She'd blanked out the other more frequent trysts she'd had with Norman Glendower, who seemed to know more about her than she cared for. Thank goodness they'd kept their meetings quiet. It was Aiden she was in love with — or told herself she was.

Rumour was that it was his wife's money that had bought the house and financed his business. An estate agency. Well it would be, wouldn't it? He was suave and good-looking, not the sort to get his hands dirty for a living.

The light on her phone glowed blue. A text had arrived. Perhaps it was Aiden. Her heart skipped a beat and her face glowed with happiness — until she read the message.

> *You and Norman were lovers. I saw you. You didn't have the courage to finish the affair, so you killed him.*

Her face flushed red. 'Cow!' she screamed. 'You cow!'

The phone went flying across the room and crashed against the wall.

Gladys Faversham was playing her like a puppet on a string, or more likely a fish on a line, enjoying the wriggling, pulling her ashore and then throwing her back in to repeat the process all over again.

'I didn't kill him,' she whimpered, her legs buckling beneath her. 'I didn't kill him.'

But *they* might have. The men her husband knew. Men who brought her money as payment to her husband for not blabbing. 'Otherwise you're mincemeat.'

That's what they'd told her. 'Otherwise you're mincemeat. All of you.'

CHAPTER THIRTEEN

Visiting old haunts seemed a good idea to Honey.

'Come on. What have we got to lose?'

Steve wasn't so sure, but they decided to take the plunge and head for their favourite haunt, the Zodiac Club — or what had been the Zodiac Club.

'For old times' sake,' said Honey, excited to be visiting their old watering hole.

'For old times' sake,' Steve repeated with far less enthusiasm. In fact, the words seemed to come from a deep pit as with disbelief Steve added, 'Doesn't look like old times to me. Far from it, in fact.'

Honey stopped in her tracks and stood with her mouth open. They hadn't been for just three years and the Zodiac had changed beyond recognition.

Gone was the dungeon-like gloom and the fug of aromatic smoke rising blue and thick from sizzling platters of steak, prawns and fat-fried chips. Gone were the line of real ale pumps ranged along the bar, the brass handles gleaming, the foam from pulled pints frothing over onto the counter into the spill trays beneath each one.

This place was pristine, but since when had a proper pubby, bar atmosphere been pristine? It just wasn't done.

In the past it hadn't always been easy to pick out friends and people thanks to the subdued lighting and the blue smoke. Now it was bright as day.

The barrels that had once lined the back bar were gone too. The LED lighting, some fixed into the vaulted ceiling and some sweepingly modern as if they were part of the wall, was enough to make anyone blink. The bar staff were young and trendy, all wearing the same silver-and-black-striped waistcoats over black shirts and black trousers.

It had also been renamed. No longer was it the Zodiac Club but had metamorphosed into a new name, The Sporting Life. In a bid by the designer to emphasise its new name, cricket bats, footballs and rugby balls decorated the walls. Between sets of crossed tennis rackets were posters of past rugby, football and cricket matches.

'I hope they're made of plastic and not willow,' muttered Steve, eyeing the cricket bats with something akin to despair. Even in the hands of an eight-year-old with a mild swing, one of the bats could do damage.

Honey patted his arm. 'We're here. If you stop sounding so gloomy, I'll order the drinks. Usual?'

The young man who served her had a floppy hairstyle and three earrings in one ear. His smile was as plastic as the pseudo sporting memorabilia. 'Good evening, madam. What can I get for you?'

They had been away for so long it seemed almost alien to order a couple of shorts with a mixer. Plus they'd got into the habit of drinking wine with tons of ice, so she went with that.

'Two glasses of white wine, please.'

'Pinot Grigio, Sauvignon, French, Italian, Australian . . .'

'Chardonnay. Make it two glasses of Chardonnay.'

'125 mil, 250 mil . . .'

'Two large glasses. Two of your largest glasses. With lots of ice.'

Although even to her own ears she sounded a bit sharp, the lad behind the bar kept smiling.

'Had a bit of a refurbishment, then,' she said to him by way of conversation. Under the circumstances it was hard to smile, but she did her best.

The waiter tossed his head, giving the impression that the old place had never hit the right spot before the recent makeover.

'Oh yes. Quite frankly, it needed it. The boss reckoned it looked like an S&M dungeon, all dark and dingy with chains hanging from the walls and whips from the ceiling.'

He said it laughingly but stopped short when Honey said, 'There were no such things, if I remember rightly.'

He shrugged and eyed her almost accusingly. 'You used to come in here back then?'

'It wasn't that long ago. I . . . We . . . always liked it.'

'Well, there's no accounting for taste. Trust me, the time had come for change. Leaving it might have attracted the wrong sort — tight leather trousers and half-naked women looking a bit past their sell-by date, if you know what I mean.'

Honey was livid. She took the remark personally. 'And the boss would know that, would he? Did he dress up in leather and tap up the kind of women you describe?'

The barman's face dropped. 'No. Certainly not.'

Sorely missing the familiar old place and just a wee bit miffed — well, actually, very miffed — Honey pressed on. 'How do you know that for sure? How do you know he didn't run a downmarket knocking shop and dress up like a drag queen?'

'I just know,' he responded indignantly.

'Are you sure?'

His face flamed red. 'Of course I am. He's my dad.'

Telling herself that he was the one who started throwing insults, she didn't feel sorry for him. Tit for tat. Steve had kept aloof from the conversation. She got the impression that his mind was elsewhere.

After flashing her debit card, they took the drinks to a tall table with matching tall stools of chrome and Danish-style seats. Not the most comfortable furniture she'd ever sat on, especially when wearing a leather miniskirt she'd bought on a whim at a charity shop. It only went to prove that her wardrobe was in desperate need of replenishing. Brand new or second hand, it didn't matter a jot as long as it fitted.

'Well, that told us,' she said to Steve, who was trying to make himself comfortable on the aesthetically pleasing but physically awkward bar stools. Honey was sliding off it more so than he was but neither of them were feeling that comfortable.

'Cheers.'

They clinked glasses just like old times, but old times it most definitely was not.

Steve's searching gaze swept around the clientele. 'I don't recognise anyone here.'

Honey sighed. 'They all look so sleek and well turned out. Young too.'

Steve shook his head dolefully. 'This place used to be a fountain of knowledge for a copper hungry for information like me. Information aplenty for the price of a few pints of beer or a couple of whiskies. Now look at it. Not a crim in sight.'

Honey had to agree that he was right. Things had moved on and they'd been left behind.

Steve took a sip of his drink. 'I'd give my right arm to know who killed Norman Glendower. In fact, I'd shake his hand.'

'We need to find out more about him. Family, friends and his neighbours in Regency Gardens and any close companions further afield — this mysterious woman, for a start.'

Steve nodded in agreement.

Honey eyed him curiously. 'I get the impression that there's something you're not telling me. Cough up.'

Steve sighed and placed his glass back on the bar. 'It's a delicate matter.'

'A Metropolitan Police matter?'

Steve shifted his elbow, which until then had been resting passively on the bar. 'Let's just say there's some kind of scam involved, though not the same sort that we got taken for. It's about insuring valuable objects and the squeeze isn't local. It happened in London and Norman Glendower was involved.'

Honey gasped. 'Go on. Tell me.'

'I'm sworn to secrecy.'

Honey swept her hand from left to right, then up and down over her chest. 'Cross my heart and hope to die.'

He looked thoughtful. 'All right. I'll tell you, but you're sworn to secrecy.'

'Right. That's both of us, then.'

He repeated what Paul Marchant had told him.

'There seems to be more going on than meets the eye.'

Honey took it all in. 'No wonder you told me not to go poking my nose in.'

'I still expect you not to do that.'

'But I can hold this party and I can visit people in Regency Gardens, Gladys Faversham in particular. She was a good start and . . . I'm betting you that she sees a lot from her bedroom-cum-gym window.'

'She's an exercise freak. I thought people like that concentrate on one muscle at a time. They're dedicated — or mad — or both.'

'I think she's a gem. You have to think or do something while you're exercising. OK, she listens to music. That's her ears taken care of, but what about her eyes? I bet you she sees a lot more than she's telling us. It could be that she's looking but not seeing — if you know what I mean.'

'Enlighten me.'

'She's staring but not interpreting what she's seeing. She is old, you know. The same age as my mother, although if my mother heard me saying that, she'd tear me to ribbons.'

Steve was about to lean back before remembering that the stool didn't have a back. Honey grabbed him by his coat sleeve. 'Easy, cowboy.'

He spit out his feelings while slamming his palms down on the bar. 'It's not a bloody steer. It's a stool. Where's the common sense to have a stool without a back?'

She didn't remind him that most stools didn't have backs. It was just that he was used to the crabby old chairs with solid backs and wooden arms that the Zodiac used to have. The Sporting Life was made for fitter customers, not the more mature punter, who sought and appreciated greater comfort.

'Drink up. We're going.'

'Where are we going?'

'The bar at the Green River Hotel. Another drink or two and then it's off to bed.'

Steve knocked back his drink. 'Thank goodness for that.'

'I need to be up early in the morning. I've had a good few acceptances from the residents of Regency Gardens. Tea and cakes all round. Wine for those who want it.'

'You're being very generous if I might say so, my love.'

'I want to be. We know who ruined our yachtie life — now we want to know if there was someone else out there who was so enraged that they went out of their way to do something about it.'

'I'm warning you, be careful. These dudes in London are likely to be lethal if you dare upset them.'

She shook her head. 'Oh, I won't do that. I'll be my usual amenable self who can go overboard to be everyone's friend — if I must.'

'That's what I'm afraid of,' murmured Steve. 'That money's gone. The boat's gone. There's nothing to be gained. Not really, and besides, I don't want you gone.'

She kissed his cheek. 'I'm the limpet clinging to the rudder of your boat, the avenging angel keen to spread her wings and obtain satisfaction. That's all we can hope for.'

Steve sighed and pushed his empty glass away from him.

'I'd prefer the money, preferably enough to buy another boat.'

Deep in thought, Honey followed him out of a bar that was too pristine, too geared for the bright young things and too pricey for its own good.

* * *

If they were expecting peace and quiet at the Green River, it wasn't to be. Mary Jane had returned. Her presence resembled a multicoloured hurricane, from her dangling earrings to her luminous trainers. Within seconds of spotting them, she ran at them like a lurcher welcoming back its much-loved owners.

'Honey! Steve!' Her outstretched and very long arms enfolded them both in a fond embrace. 'You guys!' she said, leaning away, her eyes tearful and her face creased with genuine affection. 'I was there with you all the time you were drifting. You didn't see me, but you surely felt my presence — didn't you?'

As usual, Steve was loath to respond to anything referring to her belief in the other world. It was left to Honey to reassure her that of course they did. 'Your presence was very noticeable. I thought of you telling us to be strong and that all would be well.'

Mary Jane's intake of breath was big enough to suck all the oxygen out of the room. Once her lungs were full, she threw her head back and closed her eyes. 'My friends, my dearest friends.'

A trance-like expression came to her face. It might have been her imagination, but Honey was sure her complexion was glowing — either that or she'd applied too dark a tone of foundation to her sharply defined features.

'Poseidon, I thank you for your kindness to these, my wonderful friends.'

Steve whispered into Honey's ear. 'Do we know him?'

'God of the sea,' she whispered back.

Mary Jane's spindly arms and stick-like fingers reached for them again. 'Now, tell me all that's happened. Nigel gave me an outline, now I want to hear it in depth.'

For an elderly and extraordinarily thin woman, Mary Jane was surprisingly strong. Her long, thin fingers caught their elbows and, with unusual force, they found themselves being propelled to the hotel lounge.

Nigel was tiptoeing out but wasn't fast enough to get away. Grabbing his arm so fiercely he was jerked backwards,

Mary Jane demanded coffee and biscuits for Honey and Steve, rice cakes and ginger tea for herself.

She sat them together on a two-seater cane sofa and pulled up an antique yellow leather chair so she was sitting opposite, the coffee table between them.

She leaned forward, a piercing look in her eyes. 'So, tell me all about it . . . No!' She waved one of her bony hands. 'Hold it right there. Let me visualise.'

Her eyes closed and her tousled hair was flattened against the back of the chair, its curved canopy topping her head.

'I can see it all now,' she said before Honey had a chance to say anything. 'Go on. I've got the outline. You can fill in the details.'

Honey managed to outline what had happened at sea.

'And you saw lots of dolphins and flying fish,' interjected Mary Jane.

'Oh yes,' said Honey as her thoughts returned to the idyll, a world of warm sun, blue skies and the smell of lamb chops grilling in waterside tavernas.

The vision faded immediately when Steve Doherty brought the idyllic lifestyle crashing to earth. 'The boat's lost and the insurance won't be paying out, so the dream is no more.'

'And the man who was supposed to have insured our boat was found dead a few days ago. Someone hit him over the head with a cricket bat. He wasn't found until days later.'

Mary Jane's eyes flashed open. 'I smell a rat.'

'So did the cat,' said Honey. 'Or something rotten anyway.'

Mary Jane's eyes shone with fascination. 'A cat was involved?'

'It was the cat's mewing and wandering around that led to the body being discovered.'

Mary Jane looked astounded. 'You don't say.'

Honey went on to give Mary Jane a few more details. 'We were thinking the victim might have fleeced someone else out of their premiums, but as yet we've heard nothing.'

'You expected to find he'd conned other people?'

'Took the premiums and ran. It wasn't a huge amount of money but not being paid out means the sailing life is gone for ever.'

'A crook.'

Honey grimaced. All boys together, Steve had been caught off guard and trusted someone he should never have trusted. That was how much he'd yearned for the sailing life, living off-grid, soaking up the sun, sea and too much Sangria.

The coffee came. The biscuits came. So did the ginger tea and rice cakes. Once placed on the coffee table, Nigel made a quick exit.

'Delicious,' said Mary Jane as she crunched through the first rice cake.

Steve pulled a face. In his opinion, eating rice cakes was like chewing wallpaper.

Honey managed a weak smile.

'I'd like to help,' Mary Jane finally said.

The reluctance on Steve's face edged on hostile. 'I don't think there's anything constructive you can do.'

'In what way?' asked Honey, ignoring Steve's scepticism, her question aimed fair and square at Mary Jane. 'What do you think might help?'

Mary Jane's eyes looked skyward, one long finger placed on the dent in her chin. Her voice drifted upwards too. 'I could do a spiritual cleansing. It wipes the slate clean of everything that occurred there, and my senses will see the things that happened on that fateful night.'

Honey shook her head. 'No thanks. We've got the security records.'

Mary Jane's eyebrows raised along with her voice. 'And the security record tells what?'

'Who entered and exited Regency Gardens on the night in question.'

'Ah. But my visit would concentrate on the house and the people who had lately passed through there. I could feel the vibes and ask some questions.'

'That's what the police do,' mumbled a disgruntled Steve Doherty. 'Added to that, you likely wouldn't be given permission. Trampling over a crime scene can muddy the waters — interfere with the evidence. You should know that.' His last comment was directed at Honey. In his opinion, she took Mary Jane too seriously. He couldn't go there.

Honey just couldn't help herself. OK, it was a bit wild Mary Jane believing an ancestor of hers lived in the closet in her room, but the old girl was adamant that Sir Cedric, a gambler and rake by all accounts, was still with her.

'If it's of any use, I could offer my services to the police direct, then you wouldn't get the blame for trampling the crime scene.' Mary Jane's bright blue eyes fixed on Steve. 'Do you think it a possibility?'

Jaw clamped shut, Steve gathered the spent crockery and got up. 'Any more for any more?'

Without waiting for a reply, he set off in the direction of the kitchen.

Honey turned back to Mary Jane, keen to paint over what she considered to be rudeness on Steve's part. She had just the right sticky plaster to hand.

'I've invited the residents of Regency Gardens to come along on Saturday afternoon. I'm providing refreshments. Perhaps you can help calm their concerns about what happened, give them advice on how best to cope with the trauma arising from it.'

Mary Jane's face lit up like the lights on Oxford Street just before Christmas. 'I'm certainly up for that. I help them get over it and in turn they give me some idea of the atmosphere currently prevailing. Lights flickering, dogs howling, unexplained coldness on a bright summer day . . .'

'Or cats,' said Honey, on remembering the hungry cat that had raised the alarm.

'That's a very good point. That cat could be the key. Do you think I could meet it?'

'Unless someone's taken it in, it might no longer be there. I think Steve said that it's been placed in a cattery.'

When Steve came back he confirmed that it was.

'No matter! I can speak to it there. You'll have to come with me. I'm still getting over the trauma of being banned from the psychic fair.' She shook her head despairingly. 'Honestly, these people who think they're psychic and have as much insight as an earthworm.'

There was no asking, just a presumption that of course Honey would accompany her.

'Yes,' Honey said weakly, wishing she'd never opened her mouth.

CHAPTER FOURTEEN

It was six o'clock in the morning. The blinds were still drawn. It was that time of year, the muddled time between late summer and early autumn before the leaves on the trees began to change colour.

Gladys Faversham rolled onto her back in the double bed she had all to herself, sighed with satisfaction and smiled at the thought of being able to do exactly what she wanted for the rest of the day.

Her smile widened and her eyes narrowed with a hint of malice when she looked at the green alabaster urn sitting in isolation on the round glass table in its shadowy corner where daylight never reached.

'I'm going to make myself a nice cup of tea. Just for me,' she said loudly. 'And in my own good time. The day is mine. My life is mine.' She chuckled. 'Nothing for you, of course. Had me running to your schedule when you were alive. Not now, sunshine. I suit myself when I eat and drink. Not like when you were ruling the roost, strutting your stuff as though the world revolved around you. Well, it doesn't now.'

She felt smugly satisfied speaking to the urn containing her late husband's ashes, even more so when she considered that she could do as she liked without having to wait on him, have his breakfast on the table at eight o'clock sharp, make him a cup of tea or coffee whenever he demanded it. No matter that she'd held a very high-up post in the intelligence arm of the civil service. Her home life had revolved around him and his wants and desires. He'd had to go, of course. Eventually.

None of that now, she thought gleefully as she threw aside the bedclothes and gingerly placed her feet onto the dark grey carpet, searching with knobbly toes for her carpet slippers. A cup of coffee first then a shower.

She reached for a dressing gown, a nice white one that she'd brought back from a cruise. She should have paid for it but hadn't bothered. Instead she'd rolled it up and stuffed it into her suitcase, sure that the cruise line wouldn't charge her. They must get lots of guests taking them home, so what was one more?

The white disposable slippers had also come from there, but she hadn't disposed of them yet, seeing as they still had a bit of life left in them. For convenience, she kept those in the bathroom. The slippers that sat beneath her bed were thicker-soled and fur-lined with a little bunny head on the front.

As was her habit, she took the urn containing Stan's ashes down with her into the kitchen, where she related to him exactly what she was doing, relishing the fact that he could no longer dictate and control in the way he'd once done.

Some said that talking to oneself was a sign of madness. To her it was a kind of solace. Despite her high-pressure job in which she'd had a great deal of clout, once home she'd wilted. But not now. She said and did as she liked.

She winced as she recalled him calling her names, that she was fat and useless, that she had no friends and the world didn't want her in it. And she was ugly. On top of that, he'd smirked and told her that the neighbours laughed at her and that she didn't fit in and had no friends. 'Nobody loves you.' He'd burst out laughing when he'd told her that, watching gleefully as she'd crumpled with humiliation and began to sob.

'Well, I don't do that anymore. I don't sob. I don't cry. I'm in control,' she said to him as she put the kettle on. 'And nobody calls me fat. They call me fit, Stan. Far fitter than you ever were. I have my own gym equipment in the front bedroom and am fitter and leaner than I've ever been. As for the neighbours not liking me . . .' A slow smile pierced her broad face and a knowing expression bloomed. 'I really don't care whether they do or not. There they are in their superficial lives, pretending to be something they're not, all of them with secrets they keep and which I perceive and record. They don't know that I watch them when I'm working out on the equipment upstairs. I know a lot about them. It's all in here.' She tapped the side of her head. 'Gathered on little gizmos that I purloined from my job. There were so many interesting items I got from work — including the powder I mixed in with your scrambled eggs of a morning. Still, that was then and this is now. Besides my journal, everything about my neighbours is recorded on the hard drive on my computer. And on a USB. Not the cloud. I don't want anyone else seeing everything. Let's keep things personal, shall we? Just wait until they read the letters, I've sent them . . .'

The letters were a new addition to her favourite pastime — ridiculing people who tried to be something they were not.

Slippery Norman Glendower had been one of those. He'd looked upright but she'd been sure he was not. However, he kept the London half of his life hidden. Whatever he got up to in London stayed in London — or at least it did at first. Since then he'd had the odd visitor. She'd seen lights on in the kitchen window at the back and the figure of a man silhouetted against the blind. Whoever it was had not driven through the security gates or parked outside. Her conclusion had been that the car was parked out on the road and his visitor had used the footpath.

'That's at least two strangers who came in that way,' she said, directing her comment at the green alabaster urn.

She'd seen him with three other people on a cruise. She did love a cruise. So many lowly people pretending to be somebody — especially on a gala night, when everyone dressed up in evening suits and gowns. She found it quite hilarious.

It was pure coincidence that she'd booked on the same cruise as they had. The cruise liner had carried five thousand people, so it was easy to get lost in the crowd. The foursome hadn't noticed her, but she'd noticed them. Late at night when they were heavy with food and foggy with drink, she'd heard them talk through their '*lively little scheme*'.

Well, she'd noted everything she'd heard and decided to check out the passenger list when she got back. The other man sitting at Norman's table had worn a gold signet ring. His clothes had been top quality, but still a bit flash. As for his countenance . . . She smiled. A gangster. That's what he'd looked like, all thick neck, broad shoulders and brash presence.

She addressed the urn. 'Slippery has been murdered. His real name's Norman Glendower. Sounds like a stage name, don't you think? I prefer the name I gave him. Slippery by name, slippery by nature.'

She frowned as a thought came to her. 'The police asked me questions. I was quite prepared for that and for Gloria Cross — Pussy Galore — sending her daughter — Pussy's Kitten, as I call her. The boyfriend's police. He was dressed all in black, so I called him Johnny Cash.' She laughed at her cleverness. 'I didn't tell them much. I had no intention of doing so.'

She carried on making coffee.

'Gloria Cross is a silly thing. Dresses like someone half her age. And always kitten heels. That's one of the reasons I've named her Pussy Galore. Do you get it? Anyway . . .' The spout of the kettle hovered over the mug as Gladys relished the moment, the joy of being annoying to people who in her opinion justly deserved it. 'Ridiculous! I've written to her—'

Gladys didn't have the chance to say anything else. The kettle fell to the ground, spilling hot water all down the front of her towelling dressing gown. Gladys followed, blood spilling from the back of her head.

A low moan escaped through her narrow, pursed lips as her eyes fixed on a pair of feet. Her vision had become blurred, so she couldn't tell whether they were male or female feet.

Her arm shook as she reached out. Her hand clawed at something supportive that might help her to her feet but, on receiving a hard kick to the ribs, clutched at empty air. Grey ash that had once been her husband showered over her before the heavy urn smashed into her skull and the world turned black.

Stan had had his revenge.

The world went on without her as she slowly slid into death. She knew nothing of what followed, of the candle set among rags doused with petrol. Nobody in Regency Gardens would know either. They'd been invited to a jamboree that afternoon meant to help them overcome the trauma of one of their neighbours being found dead. By the time the candle had burned down and the fire had taken hold, they would be at the Green River Hotel enjoying themselves and she would already be dead. Nobody would be any the wiser — except for the person who had hit her over the head and set her house on fire.

CHAPTER FIFTEEN

'Looks as though you've got a good turnout.'

Mary Jane was eyeing the residents of Regency Gardens with interest as she chomped on her second scone in ten minutes. Honey had already informed her who they were, but she insisted on pointing at people and having Honey tell her the name and what she knew about each one — not that she knew much about them. Their names were about her limit. She repeated herself now in case Mary Jane had forgotten.

'They all live in the same street as the man who was found murdered. They've been traumatised. I still think it was a good idea to invite them here and ply—' she corrected herself quickly — 'offer them cakes, sandwiches and sympathy.'

'And tea and wine. I totally understand. And see who looks guilty.'

'If anyone.'

Honey's eyes raked over the assembled throng. Now, who could she tackle first? 'They all look pretty well turned out and none too downhearted from their ordeal. Enjoying themselves, in fact.'

'I get the impression that he wasn't a popular guy.'

Honey followed Mary Jane's line of vision. One woman had shooed her children away to where Myra, one of the waitresses, had set up a Wendy house that her own child no longer played with. They quickly installed themselves inside and, once settled, began passing round fairy cakes and chocolate biscuits.

Honey's attention fixed on the woman she knew as Karen Turpin, a slender woman with rather thin hair that would look better short — tulip style around her fragile face. She was on her third glass of white wine. Her eyes followed the movements of a man as though she would eat him for supper if she could. Unusual behaviour for a married woman, and Honey couldn't help being judgemental. Nothing catty, just that Karen had that lapdog look, as if she would roll over and let him tickle her belly if he wanted to. Whether he did or not, Karen was certainly game. A little community, people shut up together for the sake of security. It was bound to give rise to fantasies and illusions — for a lonely woman.

Said man was dressed to impress. Not a suit and tie or anything as prosaic as that, but a cashmere jumper tied nonchalantly over a purple striped shirt. His trousers were strawberry coloured, and his tan loafers looked to be Italian. In fact, she thought his overall appearance was purposely designed to look Italian. Expensive but casual. A man who had everything and was out for more.

For his part, the male neighbour was doing his best to avoid looking in her direction. Instead, he looked across at Honey and smiled.

Sensing this was an opening gambit, Honey smiled back.

'Call me Aiden,' he said, before she'd had a chance to ask his name.

Right. So, he was the forward type.

'Call me Honey. My name is Hannah, but everyone calls me Honey.'

'I bet they do,' he replied. 'The name suits you.'

There was innuendo in his expression, of course, all to her advantage.

She was straight in with the obvious question. 'So, how well did you know the victim?'

He took a small sip from his wine glass. That and his controlled expression gave Honey the impression that he was on guard.

'If he'd been a golfer I might have known him better. But he wasn't.'

'How about his daughter? Did you know her?'

Although he appeared nonchalant, Honey sensed that he'd become more wary.

'Gabriella? Everyone knows Gabriella. She always did put herself about.'

Honey raised her eyebrows. 'In what way?'

'Nightclubbing. Out on the town. That kind of thing.'

And you bumped into her there, thought Honey. *I wonder how far that relationship went.*

'And before you say it, no, we did not have a relationship. Nothing like it,' he said pointedly, his jaw setting firm. 'I'm a happily married man.'

'What was that you said, darling?'

Something like a triumphant smile came to Aiden's face. 'My wife, Melanie.'

His wife had shoulder-length red hair, and even though it was the weekend her clothes veered towards power dressing — smart rather than casual. It was unclear to Honey whether she'd noticed Karen, who looked lonely and in need of company.

'Hello. I'm Honey Driver. I own the Green River Hotel.'

'I know who you are, and I know what you do. You're Crime Liaison Officer for the Hotels Association.'

'I used to be—'

Melanie cut her off. 'And you've set this up so you can grill us about how well we knew Norman Glendower. I've heard all about you!'

Was interrogation part of her day job? Whatever it was, Honey certainly didn't care for the boot to be on the other foot.

Honey smiled sweetly and lied through her teeth. 'I set this up to relieve any stress felt by the residents of Regency Gardens.'

'Poppycock!' She slipped a silky-sleeved arm through that of her husband's and gave him a tug. 'Come along, darling. I want to go home.'

Honey pursed her lips and creased her brow. Where next?

'My name's Karen Turpin.'

It was the young woman in need of a haircut, seemingly at a loose end now that Aiden the Italiano had left the hotel with his wife.

At least someone wants to talk to me, thought Honey and smiled broadly. 'I don't think you've been here before, have you?'

Karen Turpin shook her head. 'No, I haven't.'

'Well, I'm glad you could make it. Can I get you another glass of wine?'

'Yes. That would be nice.'

Honey grabbed a fresh glass from a passing tray. 'Here you are.'

Eyes flickering towards the door where Aiden had exited, Karen accepted the glass gratefully. 'Thanks.'

'Are those your two children over there in the Wendy house?'

She nodded. 'Yes. They've got so much energy.'

'It must have been quite a shock to have a murder occur so close to where you live.'

'Yes. It was.'

'Did you know him very well?'

Karen sipped at her drink. 'Not really.'

'I believe he was an insurance broker. Is that right?'

She couldn't be sure, but she sensed a sudden hesitation, a nanosecond of surprise before she answered.

'I'm not sure.'

'I hear he did quite a lot of his work in London.'

'I wouldn't know.'

Yes. It was there. Hesitation born out of nervousness. But nervous about what?

The conversation was terminated when Karen's two children came racing over to ask if they could take some more cakes inside the Wendy house.

'Can you pass some through the window?'

Honey watched as she suddenly threw herself into what was going on at the Wendy house, immersing herself with the children rather than lingering to indulge in further conversation. Her body language had been subtle, but all the same Honey felt that something wasn't quite right.

She looked around to check whether Steve had arrived. He'd been called to the station to attend a briefing but had promised to call in when he could. Hopefully they'd made some progress in solving the crime.

She looked for Gladys Faversham but couldn't see her.

A woman she thought she recognised was standing close to the double doors leading into the function room. Now, where had she seen her before?

It might have come to her if it hadn't been for Gloria Cross, her mother, sweeping into the throng as though she was the belle of the ball. As usual she was dressed to impress, a vision in pale turquoise straight out of a Max Mara window display. She was waving half a glass of champagne in one hand that she'd demanded and got from the bar. Honey had only laid on red or white wine, tea or coffee.

Honey recalled her saying, 'Drinking champagne is like smoking a French cigarette in an ebony holder. It adds class.'

When she looked, the woman she thought she recognised had gone.

'Mother. You're here.'

'I'm here.'

Nose in the air and false eyelashes fluttering like lost butterflies, she looked around the room. 'I'm glad to say that I don't see Gladys Faversham.'

Her words and tone were surprising.

'I thought she was a friend.'

'I thought so when I first met her, but my opinion has long since changed. I gave you the connection purely to annoy her — and to help you, of course.'

Honey's gaze swept over the gathering. 'I don't see her either. Perhaps she doesn't like parties.'

Her mother scowled. 'Gladys Faversham was always mean-spirited. Not that I think she had much choice. I know she was something in intelligence, but goodness knows where that was when she married Stan Faversham. An overbearing creep who had no idea of how to treat a woman.' The corners of her mouth turned downwards in a show of disdain. 'And you did tell her about this jamboree you laid on?'

Honey frowned. 'Of course I did.'

'There you are. Exactly as I said. She's mean-spirited.'

After another quick survey of the gathered neighbours, Honey had to agree that Gladys Faversham was not there. 'I definitely don't see her.'

Her mother scowled. 'I haven't seen her and believe me, I'd have had a word with her by now if I had.'

There was something in her mother's voice and all-pervasive scowl that hinted at unfinished business between the two septuagenarians.

'I get the impression that your friendship was short-lived for a good reason.'

'It was fine until I found out she was keeping a journal on the people she knew. Not a diary, a journal — and it had pictures. Cartoons of everyone she knew. Lampoons. On the surface she was their friend. Beneath the surface she was laughing at them. Giving them ridiculous nicknames. She told me that one woman, called her Turnip, had a husband in jail. Gladys liked playing on names. Crowed about it, she did.'

Turnip, not much of a leap to get to Turpin. Honey didn't need to ask if Gladys had included her mother in the journal. She could hear the grating disapproval in her tone of voice.

'She had the nerve to ask me to afternoon tea at the Ivy. A couple of glasses of Prosecco and she was laughing and boasting about how clever she was. Such a show-off! I told her keeping dossiers on people could be viewed as libellous rather than clever.'

Her mother's scowl stayed put. When she looked like that she reminded Honey of a French bulldog, a breed that looked cute but had one hell of a bite.

Honey asked herself if it was wise to ask her mother what her nickname might have been.

Her mother got in first. 'Before you ask . . .' She took a deep breath. 'My nickname was Pussy Galore.'

'Oh. That's quite flattering — isn't it?'

'Not to me. Stupid woman. Why upset people by giving them stupid names?'

'Some people get like that if they live alone. Perhaps she had early-onset dementia.' Having met Gladys, she didn't believe it that likely. The woman was a steam train, but it was the only viable excuse she could think of.

Diamond earrings sparkled when her mother sniffed and tossed her head. 'That does not give anyone carte blanche to make fun of other people. Mind you, that husband of hers was a right tyrant if what she says is true. Controlling, I think they call it nowadays. She had to report what she'd done all day and wait on him hand, foot and finger. And he used to keep tabs on the neighbours. Trouble is, living with someone like that can rub off. It seems she started doing the same.'

Although her mother didn't seem to realise it, hearing there might be a record of the comings and goings in Regency Gardens besides the security recordings was as if a light had been switched on in a deep, dark cave.

'I wonder,' exclaimed Honey, voicing her thoughts out loud, 'do you think she still keeps a journal? I mean, there's a chance that if she did, she might have recorded something relevant to the killing of Norman Glendower.'

'There's no reason why not. She thought it was funny.'

Judging by the look on her mother's face, she most certainly did not share the feeling. Honey thought of the woman pedalling like a maniac on her exercise bike conveniently placed before the front window of the upstairs bedroom. What a view she must have had, and she probably gleaned enough information to fill her journal daily — whether written or on computer.

Ideas ploughed furrows through Honey's mind. The journal could have a bearing on the murder and it perhaps confirmed what she'd said to Steve that nosy parkers could be a mine of information. All she had to do was to get Gladys to show them the records she kept on her neighbours — the comings and goings, the secrets they didn't want anyone to know.

'I'd like to see what she wrote in that journal. See what she said about people she knew — neighbours, of course,' she added on seeing the warning look on her mother's beautifully made-up face. 'Security videos are all very well, but her notes might be more close-up and personal.'

Her mother fixed her with a look she remembered from her schooldays — when she couldn't understand why her daughter liked playing hockey. Honey had gone all out to explain that it gave one the opportunity to whack the girls who picked on you.

'Don't pry!'

'What do you mean?'

'I put some distance between me and her when she confessed what she was doing. I wish I hadn't told you that she lived there.'

'But if it helps with the murder of Norman Glendower . . .'

Gloria puckered her brow and her lips. 'That man took your money. I'm no adventurer and have to say here and now that I didn't approve of you sailing off into the sunset, but I do care that he fleeced you. Took the money and gave nothing in return, so quite frankly I think he might have got what he deserved.'

Honey surveyed the throng of people who quite honestly didn't look at all traumatised by the fact that one of their neighbours had met a bad end. With certain exceptions they were chatting, eating and drinking quite gaily. Every so often a peal of laughter rang out.

She screwed up her face and squinted — as if that might help her see the scene in more detail.

'I thought one of these people might have something to say that would have a bearing on the case.'

'You putting on this spread is all very well, darling, but who cares if Norman Glendower is dead? He's left you out of pocket. I would have clobbered him if it was me.'

'Steve had that idea in mind.'

Her mother gave her a searching look and raised her eyebrows. 'Did he? Well, darling, your policeman has certainly gone up in my estimation.' She looked suitably impressed. 'Do you think he might have done?'

'No. Of course not. He upholds the law. He doesn't go around breaking it.'

'Nobody would blame you if you had murdered him.' Her mother shook her head disdainfully, waving her champagne glass. 'I would have done the same.'

'Everything is under control — more or less. The insurers told me they're looking into things more deeply.'

It wasn't true. They'd still not been able to track down the insurance company who held their policy. No matter what they tried, Goodenough Marine Insurance was untraceable. The only conclusion they could come to was that it did not exist.

Her mother made a *humph* noise, a sure sign she didn't believe that route would lead anywhere.

'Say goodbye to the sailing life, darling. The boat's gone and so's the money. Oh my goodness. It's suddenly gone cold in here.' She shuddered and mentioned the old saying about someone having walked over her grave. The someone, it seemed, was Gladys Faversham.

'I'm off before Gladys arrives. I'm not sure I can smile sweetly and pretend we're still friends. My face might crack. The woman had the nerve to write me a letter. I wouldn't put it past her to blackmail other people. That's what she was doing to me — not indirectly — poking fun, but doing that can lead to blackmail. That's my opinion.'

Just for once Honey was crestfallen to see her mother take off. She had to admit that she might have a point. It wasn't the first time Gloria Cross had got involved in a case, but never before had she put forward a personal insight into the character of someone involved. She wondered what had been in the letter, but her mother was gone before she could ask. Gladys was certainly worth questioning. She'd confront her the moment she arrived.

In the meantime . . .

A man with a strong jaw and slick way of dressing looked over her head as she asked him what he knew of his dead neighbour.

'To tell you the truth, he wasn't my type. Never went to the country club.'

'Country club? What one might that be?'

He continued to look over her head, more interested in the women present — the waitresses in particular.

'South Stoke Country Club. Superb golf course. Good food.'

He reeled it off as though pushing the place was to his advantage.

'Yes, someone else said he wasn't a golfer.'

'Wasn't much of anything.' He turned suddenly and grinned at her. 'His daughter was a corker though. I heard she had her own business on the side, in the oldest profession on earth, if you know what I mean. Nudge nudge, wink wink.'

'Did she now?' That was the second time this afternoon it had been suggested that Miss Glendower was a bit of a looker, and Warren Hart had said the same. And if she was a prostitute, she definitely had something to hide.

No sign of her at the gathering, not that Honey would know her, but the descriptions she'd heard had given her a pretty good idea of what to look for.

The smooth-talking guy made his excuses and moved away, heading for a Swedish waitress gliding through the throng with a tray of sparkling wine.

She homed in on another resident of Regency Gardens, a small balding man clinging to a willowy woman with grey-ish blonde hair and rings on every finger.

The bald man seemed pleased to be approached. 'Ask away. I'll help all I can. I told the police what I knew about him, but I don't mind repeating myself, do I, Dawn?'

The woman wearing a handful of gold simpered and nodded. What a silly thing she was.

Honey recalled what she'd been told at Pampered Pooches about Norman bringing in a dog. It seemed a relevant topic of conversation that might lead to something.

'Did you ever see him walking the dog?'

'He didn't have a dog. Just the cat. Wandered all over the place, that cat. Fed it the best of food. Tinned salmon. Scallops, even. Free-range chicken. Fussy cat, it was. Stalked around as though it owned the place.'

She thanked the pair, figuring if they knew anything they'd have spilled the details instead of discussing cat food, though it was interesting to know Pampered Pooches had lied about Norman having a dog. What was that about?

Honey proceeded to pinpoint anyone else who looked useful. They all looked pretty drunk. Too much wine, she thought.

'I'm getting a mix of vibes from these people.' The tone of voice and Californian accent was like a ringing in her ears. Always open to meeting new people and taking a genuine interest in them, Mary Jane had gone out of her way to circulate among the gathering.

'What kind of vibes?'

'Not very friendly ones. Are you sure these people are neighbours? They don't seem very . . . well . . . neighbourly towards one another. In my opinion, it's a darn good job they don't carry guns!'

Honey did not voice her agreement but accepted that she did have a point. She poured herself another wine, not because she regretted arranging the event, but because what her mother had said hit home — like a stiletto piercing her heart. The money was lost. The monthly direct debit was one thing, but not being paid out for a legitimate claim was far larger. Two hundred and fifty thousand pounds. That's how much the boat had been worth. More than spilt milk. A huge chunk of money and their life to cry over.

The boat was lost and the effort of containing her anger wasn't always working. Like a grim-faced jack-in-the-box, it kept popping up and refusing to stay put when she tried to slam it shut. It had long legs, she decided, too long and spindly to be pushed back in.

She gulped the wine down in swift sips. 'Definitely,' she said in response to Mary Jane's earlier comment about guns. Norman Glendower hadn't been shot. Forensics were a bit behind schedule on their report but were guessing he'd been hit over the head with the cricket bat found at the scene. They didn't think it belonged to him but that the perpetrator had brought it with them.

Craning her long neck, Mary Jane turned her head slowly from right to left, her ghostly pale eyes scrutinising the crowd from her superior height. Her sharp features reminded Honey of a stork sitting atop a tall chimney.

At last she spoke. 'The vibes aren't good. There's a definite imbalance of interaction.'

Clueless of what that meant, Honey pulled a face. 'That's annoying.' She hesitated before asking, 'What do you mean by that exactly?'

Mary Jane gave her a pitying look. 'You don't feel it?'

Honey shook her head.

'Well, it's like Native American tribes used to say. Porcupines are best kept at a distance. Otherwise, you end up full of holes.'

'Very astute.'

Honey was still none the wiser. Over the years she had got used to Mary Jane and her pronouncements. Most of them referred to Sir Cedric, the supposed ancestor who occupied the wardrobe in the room she had rented since first coming to the Green River Hotel. Others were more random and picked up on a day-to-day basis. Everything was to do with the spirit world and there were certain places in Bath where she went regularly to commune with the past and the people who had lived in it. Her favourite was the Theatre Royal, where the 'Grey Lady' put in regular appearances preceded by the smell of jasmine. Her second favourite by a very close margin was the Roman legion who tramped through the cellar of a public house in Abbey Churchyard, their lower limbs hidden beneath the floor, their stalwart faces looking straight ahead, arms swinging with the rhythm of their marching.

She assured Honey that she'd observed their leather tunics very closely and such was her excitement that she told her all about it in lurid detail. 'They were nowhere near as short as Hollywood would have us believe. Those leather skirts, I mean. That length might be OK in an Italian climate, but England? Scotland? Wales?' She shook her head. 'Not a good idea.' Her face brightened suddenly. 'Good thighs though.'

Honey often giggled. Most of the time Mary Jane's pronouncements were entertaining. Today they were something else, dour expressions dominating her sharp features. Her brow was furrowed with concentration, and when she wrinkled her nose her whole face took on the appearance of a square of silk that had got overheated in the washing machine and was so wrinkled it was not worth ironing.

Honey decided to go along with it. 'So, these vibes. Is someone here who shouldn't be here — either in this world or the next? I don't mind either.'

Mary Jane's face screwed up like a crab apple long past the time for picking. 'Up until now they were a mixture, but suddenly I can smell something. Like toast.'

'Well, it's too late for that. Breakfast was over ages ago.'

'Not from your kitchen. It's from somewhere else, and you know what's so odd? I think these people here might not know it, but they've brought a trace of the smell with them.'

Honey sniffed but couldn't detect anything much except for the usual waft from the kitchen each time the swing door was pushed open.

'Smudger's been valiantly attempting to make meringues again. It could be those. They usually end up not rising and resembling sick pads.'

Smudger Smith was her long-time chef. He could produce meals at a rate of knots. His one drawback was that he was a good chef — good chefs owned the reputation of being temperamental. The thing that could really send him off his trolley was when someone asked for a fillet steak to be well done. Offering to butterfly it — that is, slice it laterally — was the best course of action, if the customer knew what was good for them.

Many a time Honey had had to throw herself across the kitchen door to keep Smudger and his meat cleaver away from a customer who insisted on having it cooked as it was.

'It's too thick,' he'd shout.

Honey was never quite sure whether he was referring to the customer or the steak. Possibly both.

Her thoughts rejoined the present and listening to Mary Jane.

Mary Jane shook her head again. 'Nothing to do with Smudger. I told you — it's not from inside this hotel, it's from outside, but I can't get the feeling out of my mind that these people gorging themselves brought it with them.' She frowned. 'At least, I think so, but there just might be . . .'

Her eyes narrowed to mere slits and her voice sounded a bit fuzzy. A faraway moment, thought Honey. Mary Jane was prone to those. A slight shiver ran down her spine. She couldn't escape the feeling that something was about to happen, though goodness knows what.

At times when she was distressed, Mary Jane, all six feet of skin and bone, adopted an adamant air that made her seem like a cardboard cutout, fixed in place yet oddly separate from everyone else. She'd landed in the Green River Hotel from California some years back. It was in San Diego that she'd qualified in all things zany — that is, psychic knowledge on the spectral front and everything else connected with it.

Honey looked around, half expecting to see a few gremlins sitting on shoulders or a ghostly spectre sharing a bottle of wine with someone who was too drunk to notice. There might be such creatures doing just that, but regardless what Steve thought, Honey didn't share Mary Jane's beliefs or claim to see creatures from another world. What with customers, staff and a bank taken over by bots and other stuff she hated, this world was enough to cope with.

'I'll take another wander,' Mary Jane stated, her piercing eyes popping out from their slits and scouring the crowded dining room as though concerned she might have missed something.

With that she wandered off, a path opening up for her between people who looked surprised by her appearance — principally her silky black outfit, its glowing stars and crescent moons teamed with a purple turban and Turkish slippers, bells hanging from the upturned toes.

If ghosts were present, Honey didn't see them. She'd leave that task to Mary Jane.

Looking around the old place was pleasant enough, but she still entertained visions of the life she'd led on the ocean waves. It had sped past in a flash. Neither she nor Steve had known it would be so brief. Back in the Green River. Who would have thought it? No more sun, sea and sundowners.

A latecomer entered the hotel, snatched a glass of wine from a tray and proceeded to eye everyone there.

Curious eyes looked in her direction. Something about her was familiar. Blonde bobbed hair. Sleek as a panther and about forty years old.

Honey couldn't work out where she'd seen her before.

Intrigued, she approached her. 'Do I know you?'

Disdainful flash of eyes.

She looked Honey up and down. 'I don't think so.'

'Do you know everyone here? Are you a neighbour of the man who was found dead — by his cat?'

'Certainly not.'

Such a superior tone.

It was hard not to bristle, so Honey let it out.

'I'm sorry, but this event is for the residents of Regency Gardens only. If you're not a resident, then I must ask you to leave.'

A slight loosening of the hard look. 'I don't live there. A friend lives there. I was expecting to see her here.' As if to confirm her answer was genuine, her heavily made-up eyes searched the room.

Now what sort of friend would this woman have in Regency Gardens? thought Honey. She hazarded a guess. 'It wouldn't be Gladys Faversham, would it?'

In one deft action, the woman replaced the empty wine glass on a tray and took a full one. A gulp of wine before she asked, 'Have you seen her? She said she'd be here.'

Manners cost nothing, thought Honey, but on this occasion, she would let it be. The woman had fired up her curiosity. 'No. She assured me she was coming, but I haven't seen her.'

The woman pursed her lips. 'Blast.'

'You're welcome to stay and wait for her. There's plenty to eat. And drink.'

Why bother to say that? Another empty glass in one hand while the other reached for a refill. The woman could certainly hold her drink.

'I may do.'

I've never met this woman but feel I should know her, thought Honey. *Think. Stir up the old grey cells! Start with the obvious question.*

'I feel I know you from somewhere, I just can't think where.'

She looked tellingly up into the other woman's silky complexion. Whatever foundation she used wasn't from No.7 at Boots. And the eyelashes were too perfect to be natural.

A crass look was followed by a crass comment. 'I can't think where.' That look up and down again.

'Might I ask your name?' Honey asked with a friendly smile.

For a moment it looked as though she wasn't about to answer. Then she came to a decision.

'Hildegard. Hildegard Hunter.'

The face rang a bell. The name more so.

'Pampered Pooches. Am I right?'

'You are.'

The wine was going fast.

'And your reason for coming here is?'

She awaited an answer, half suspecting she wasn't going to get one.

'I was hoping to meet Gladys. That's all.'

With that she spun on her heels, slammed the wine glass down on a tray so it was in danger of breaking its stem, and then she was off, the double doors slamming behind her.

Now, what should she want with Gladys Faversham? Judging by looks alone, they weren't the sort to meet socially. She really needed to have a conversation with the woman.

Her train of thought was interrupted by way of her mother waving the champagne flute in her hand and tottering on three-inch heels.

'You don't happen to have seen your friend Gladys?' Honey asked. 'Someone was looking for her.'

'No luck here, and there was me all fired up to have a go at her about that bloody journal.'

In a bid to spot the elderly athlete, Honey stood on tiptoe. She mostly saw heads, but not the tall athletic frame she hoped for.

She suggested to her mother that Gladys might be ill. 'Old people get ill more frequently than younger ones. It comes with age.'

Gloria Cross threw her a fierce look in response to what she regarded as an insult. 'Don't be ridiculous. Gladys is a keep-fit fanatic. If she doesn't become a centenarian, then the advice from the health industry to keep fit and eat sensibly is rubbish.'

CHAPTER SIXTEEN

Dwelling on the possible reasons might have persisted if a cacophony of chirping phones hadn't suddenly rung through the air. Food and wine were forgotten. People delved into pockets and handbags, gagging to get to whatever message was coming through.

As if that wasn't enough, to add more drama to the occasion, the main door to the function room flew open. Clad head-to-toe in black, Doherty — she couldn't help reverting to his surname when he was in police officer mode — dashed through the crowd like Batman about to grab the Joker. Only it wasn't the Joker he wanted to speak to. He was heading straight for Honey.

Leather jacket flying out behind him, expression closed and serious, he brushed past those who had been getting merry on the free wine. Sober now.

His locked jaw didn't unlock until he was there beside her.

The hubbub of conversation from those who'd answered their phones became more agitated, the mundane swept aside and replaced with squeals of alarm and obvious disbelief.

'No.'

'I can't believe it.'

'Oh my God.'

Honey raised her eyebrows quizzically.

Grabbing her arm, Steve took her to one side behind the leaves of a tropical palm and a folded screen that was used to divide the restaurant when reduced numbers dictated. She knew for sure this was nothing to do with grabbing a secret kiss — or the kind of embrace that was too hot to be seen in public.

Honey read his expression. 'Go on. Tell me what's happened.'

'Gladys Faversham won't be coming this afternoon.'

'Right,' she said slowly, her eyes fixed on his. 'I take it there's a valid and rather extreme reason.'

'You bet. There's been a fire at her house in Regency Gardens. A body has been found inside. No confirmation yet, of course, but we think it's her. We'll want to check what time everyone arrived and whether you noticed anyone arriving late or leaving early. Preferably the former.'

'And you want me to keep everyone here for questioning?'

'You bet I do.'

Mary Jane intervened, her head popping between them both like a parrot between two lovebirds.

'I told you it wasn't toast,' she said, almost accusingly.

Steve looked at Honey for explanation.

'She said she could smell toast and that it was a bad vibe.'

He looked puzzled.

'I pointed out that breakfast was over, but the smell of burning was Gladys, not a slice of bread!'

He took the explanation on the chin. 'As everyone was here, there's no point in checking alibis. You've given them all an alibi — unless someone did leave during the afternoon?'

His look was accusing. Hers was one of innocence, and she quickly filled him in on what she'd found out. 'Where are you off to now?'

'Back to Regency Gardens and the smouldering hovel that was Gladys Faversham's last place of abode. The fire service should be finished by now.'

'Can I come for the ride?'

Leather coat flying out behind him, Steve was already sweeping towards the double doors that would lead them out into Duke Street, Honey trailing in his wake.

'That's what I had in mind. If anyone asks, you're there on behalf of the Bath Hotels Association. OK?'

'Tourists don't stay or visit a place like Regency Gardens. It's too new.'

'That's the best excuse I can come up with for you getting in on the scene. If all else fails, lie through your back teeth.'

She nodded compliantly. 'I can do that.'

He left behind a few junior officers to ask questions and take statements just in case, although alibis had been set. The crowd that had turned so jolly earlier were now more subdued. He scanned them for any emotional response that might be of use but saw nothing.

'I'm not sure we'll get much out of them. You'd think that a relatively small community would be more friendly towards one another. Not that I got much chance to ask them anything. The incineration of Gladys Faversham put an end to that.'

'In other words, they keep themselves to themselves. Except for Gladys, who knew everything about everyone. I wonder if her journal survived the fire?'

On seeing that Steve was there and somehow sensing it was a big deal, Nigel nodded in her direction, confirmation that he would stand in to take care of things while she was off doing her amateur sleuthing thing.

'You can borrow my car,' Mary Jane called out.

Honey was about to accept when Steve shouted back, 'No problem. We're going low-key.' He whispered an aside to Honey: 'Don't want to frighten the neighbours.'

'I take it the fire was no accident.'

'That's the fire brigade's prognosis so far. There's evidence of an accelerant. They'll let me know as soon as it's one hundred per cent confirmed and the fire's manageable.'

'Will today's security footage show anything?'

'I doubt it. If it's anything like the last lot, it'll be a waste of time. These people never do anything that might look suspicious.' He wore a look of outright contempt, as though they were the most boring people he'd ever come across.

'Your old mate Warren might have seen something.'

'Doubtful,' he grumbled. 'I don't think he sees anything much unless it's out of the end of a whisky bottle. But I did take his laptop. I noticed on our earlier visit that it was connected to the security system. And before you ask, I don't know why. But my nerdy friend at the office will inspect and report back.'

'What's the betting he uses it to download pornography?'

'No question at all. I know him of old.'

Honey chewed thoughtfully at her lip.

'Are you coming or what?'

'Will your police colleagues let me in?'

'If you're with me, they will.'

The little yellow Citroen that barely had room for two people let alone the four passengers the dealer had stated it could take was ideal for driving around Bath. It needed only a small parking space. It ran on a cupful of petrol. It sped through traffic jams along the bus and taxi lane, a blue police light affixed with a magnet flashing from its roof. Occupants of other vehicles gaped. Police cars were usually big beasts, not tiny things of French origin and not much more impressive than a moped.

The blue light and the nippy little vehicle did the trick, darting in and out of the traffic all the way to their destination.

The pair of double gates were wide open. Two uniformed constables were on duty, along with firemen tugging heavy hoses.

Steve flashed his warrant card. Both the fire brigade and the police presence waved them in, Honey making herself look as small as possible in the driver's seat of the unimpressive little car.

Steve was first out. She took her time, head down, looking pensive and serious as a low-ranking female officer was likely to do. 'Feel your way, gain their confidence and then make a grab for better things.' That's what female police officers she'd known had told her. 'Keep your wits about you and your eyes open. Vault into the stratosphere while the boys are looking the other way — or at your breasts.'

She wasn't a police officer, but she had been Crime Liaison Officer for the Bath Hotels Association. It was something from the past that could be resurrected at any time. And today it was.

Several police officers held up a hand in acknowledgement on recognising DI Steve Doherty and the all-black outfit he chose to wear. One or two stopped him and said it was good to see him back in harness.

Most had heard about the unlucky termination of his life in the sun. There was lots of backslapping, and comments about piracy and having to swim for his life. Someone asked if they'd saved the parrot. More laughter.

They spared a quick nod of acknowledgement for Honey but that was about it.

One of his erstwhile colleagues brought him up to speed. 'The fire department have confirmed it was started deliberately. They're preparing a report.'

Steve grunted his understanding and crooked his index finger at Honey, a signal for her to follow.

First stop was a look at the exterior of the house. Smears of black smoke coated the double-glazed windows, which had stopped the fire from spreading. Everything they needed to know was inside.

The fire had been put out, but the acrid smell of destruction wafted out even before they'd stepped over the threshold.

A young constable with fluff on his upper lip stood in the porch of Gladys's house. He lifted the incident tape to let them in, saluting in an old-fashioned manner.

Steve nodded. Honey followed.

The walls and ceilings were blackened and still dripping with the deluge of water from firemen's hoses. Bits of glass splintered underfoot and the waterlogged carpets oozed liquid like juice squeezed from a lemon — a very dirty lemon.

'All those people at your bash and without a clue about the barbecue back home.'

Honey shook her head. 'Are you sure about that?'

'The fire didn't begin until around one this afternoon, according to a police sergeant. He was told that by the fire department. Delayed ignition of some sort?'

'A foregone conclusion. It would explain why nobody saw anything before they left.'

Brow furrowed in concentration, Steve agreed with her. 'Nobody noticed.'

A fireman, face streaked with soot and sweat, overheard. 'There's a reason for that. Somebody had drawn the curtains. That's number one. All the doors and windows were closed. That's number two. These houses are remarkably well insulated. The cold can't get in and the heat can't get out. Neither could the smoke, so nobody would see anything until the fire had taken hold in a big way. The smoke was contained for the woman who lived here to swallow. And there was something else. Accelerant was scattered all over the place, but conflagration was delayed. The perpetrator used a delaying device, a really simple one.'

'Is that so?'

'A candle was lit, the kind you might use for a dinner party — not too big but big enough to take its time to burn down. Once it did — whoosh! It ignited the accelerant-drenched rags and paper surrounding it. Went up like a Roman candle. So to speak.'

The fire officer who'd spoken checked his wristwatch, a substantial-looking affair that could cope with heat, water and the perils of a dangerous job.

Honey pulled a face as she imagined the scene inside the house. The woman was basically a stranger — still, she couldn't help feeling sorry for her.

They stood aside to let the stretcher pass.

Honey eyed the passing body in disbelief. 'Poor Gladys.'

'Where was she found?' asked Steve.

The fireman pointed. 'In the kitchen. We're guessing she'd just got up and put the kettle on.'

'But that wasn't what caused it? There wasn't a gas explosion?'

The fireman shook his head. 'The gas was out. The accelerant was confined to the kitchen table. We reckon that was the heart of the incineration.' He jerked his head at the woman from Forensics who was following the same route as the stretcher.

Steve introduced himself. The dark-eyed young woman didn't look as if she was going to stop until she looked up into his face and saw a man she hadn't seen before, one with a taciturn look on his handsome face.

'Pleased to meet you. I'm Ayesha Balin.' She extended her hand.

Steve shook it. 'Pleased to meet you too, Ayesha. Do we know yet how Mrs Faversham died? Did the fire kill her?'

She shook her head. 'I can't be sure as yet but reckon she was dead before the fire started.'

Steve raised his eyebrows. 'Is that so?'

She screwed up her face. 'It's quite yucky. She was hit over the head with a very heavy urn, one of those that contain ashes of the deceased. The ashes have got waterlogged from the fire hoses and have formed a gooey mess on the kitchen floor.'

Honey pulled a wry expression. She recalled the information her mother had offered. 'Murder from beyond the grave. I'm presuming the urn held her husband's ashes.'

'It seems most likely,' said the new girl from Forensics. 'Though we also considered it might be one of those dumbbells.' She pointed to where six multicoloured dumbbells sat in a sea of sticky plastic. 'The stand's melted, hence the mess. It could have been one of those, but my money is on the funeral urn.'

'So much for keeping fit.' Exercise had never rated high on Honey's to-do list. Even less so at present.

Taking a plastic glove from his pocket, Steve picked up a piece of the urn. 'Pretty heavy.'

'So are the dumbbells.'

'I've always thought dumbbells were dangerous,' muttered Honey.

Steve already knew this. After thanking Ayesha, he turned and commented to Honey that she was never likely to be hit over the head with one because she never went near a set of dumbbells.

Honey pretended she hadn't heard and carried on. 'No wonder all her neighbours were in a bit of a tizz at the Green River when they found out there'd been a fire. Still, at least we know they were all gathered in one place and couldn't possibly . . . Oh, damn.'

'My thinking too,' exclaimed Steve.

'Oh, damn again! I've given all of them an alibi.'

'Not with the delaying device. Any one of them could have done it before attending the function.'

Steve texted the officers taking statements at the hotel, telling them about the delaying device.

Honey weighed up the possibilities. 'So it could have been any of them. How many do you think have some pyrotechnic experience?'

'Anyone can look up how to build a bomb online. No great shakes that they could also find out how to start an inferno. And any of them could have been blackmailed by Gladys, from what you said.'

'It doesn't leave the police with much choice.'

'We only need one.'

'Have they got one?'

'No. Not for Mrs Faversham or for Norman Glendower.'

Their feet crunched on broken glass and other detritus as they made their way into what had been a pristine hallway to what had been an equally pristine kitchen. The walls were black, the ceiling was blacker and what had been white kitchen cupboards were streaked with grey soot.

Honey wrinkled her nose. 'Smells like bonfire night at the Rec.'

Her reference to Bath rugby ground brought a frown to Steve's thoughtful brow, even though he wasn't a keen follower.

Frank Club, the senior medical officer, was talking head-to-head with the chap from the fire brigade who investigated fire scenes.

'Any joy?' he asked.

The fire brigade officer brushed the dirt from his hands. 'Early days yet, but as I think you already know, there are traces of accelerant.'

'So I understand. Plus, a bump on the head then a fire to wipe out all traces.'

'It didn't quite work out like that. These houses are mostly built of stone, and although the windows look authentically Georgian, they're made of plastic not pine. There wasn't quite enough wood to really get it going or fresh air getting in, for that matter.'

Honey noticed that Steve's frown had deepened. He addressed the medical officer, who looked to be in a hurry to get away, shoving rubber gloves in his pocket, grabbing his kit bag as though it was about to make an escape.

'I understand the bump on the head was the cause of death. How soon can you confirm?'

'I don't know yet. Sorry.' He took a hurried look at his watch. 'I'll know more during the working week. Next week, in fact.'

'I thought you were on call all the time.'

'Not today. My daughter's getting married this after-noon. I'm giving her away and the au pair will disappear if I'm not back there on time, so we're under pressure this weekend. My estranged wife threatened me with kneecap-ping if I don't appear. What with her and the au pair . . .' He muttered something unintelligible before his face sud-denly brightened. 'Still, my new assistant will be covering my absence. Met her, have you?'

The look on his face was sheer lust. Honey felt like slapping it. Ayesha Balin was half his age, but Frank Club was one of those men for whom hope springs eternal — even when the mirror and his BMI said otherwise. 'Can't stop. Sorry. See you again.'

A quick wave and he was gone.

The scene-of-crime officer had been otherwise engaged with a young officer trying to get Gladys's mobile phone to work alongside her computer. For some reason both had been sitting on the kitchen table and, although they looked to be far from working order, the young man had managed to get both to light up. Unfortunately, that was as far as it went. A flicker, a pop and they both died. Honey looked around but couldn't spot Gladys's journal.

Ben Mortimer, the SOCO who'd pulled the short straw and was in on a Saturday, saw Steve and glowered. 'We've done without you for two years and have enough men on the ground without you and your girlfriend tramping around the place.'

Steve stood his ground and a hard, determined look came to his face, the kind that usually preceded grabbing somebody by the collar and laying down the law — or landing a punch.

'I would appreciate you being a bit more sympathetic, Mortimer. Gladys Faversham was a personal friend of Honey's mother.'

Honey adopted a sad countenance as though Gladys had been a family friend and not a woman her mother was going to war with.

'Poor Gladys.' Honey shook her head. 'Who would want to hurt an old woman like her? It just doesn't make sense.'

My mother for a start, she thought, but she had no intention of putting her in the frame. A show of sympathy was the right thing to do.

Well-heeled and down-at-heel old ladies alike thrived on gossip, but Gladys — well, Gladys had crossed the line. She'd spied on her neighbours and, according to her mother, had kept notes on them.

'Find any reason somebody might have wanted to do her harm?' asked Steve disarmingly.

My very own Prince Charming, thought Honey. He could really turn on the charm when he had to.

Ahmed, the young officer, looked consternated. 'Not so far. Except for a flash of what looked to be a diary. I didn't recognise any of the names. A "Mr Slippery" apparently had an affair with someone named "Turnip", but I couldn't keep it long enough on screen to get into the cloud. I think its brain got fried in the fire.'

'Can you let me know if you find anything?'

'Sure.'

Ben Mortimer was looking on, his eyes narrowed. There was no love lost between him and Steve Doherty. His expression veered on a sneer.

'Anyway, what are you doing here, Doherty? I thought you'd left the force.'

'Only temporarily. I took a sabbatical to explore the world outside Manvers Street and the city of Bath. Took time off for a while. Marchant called me in as somebody with interest in the insurance dude who got bumped off at the other house. Literally bumped — on the head — though not with a funeral urn, as far as I know. I do believe a cricket bat was the weapon of choice in that particular scenario.'

Honey took in the information, which seemed fresh from the body farm, as she mulled over who Mr Slippery might be. That was the second time 'Turnip' had turned up in Gladys's gossip. Karen Turpin was looking more and more interesting.

Mortimer was determinedly sniffy. 'Well, this is a separate incident.'

'The two could be connected.'

Mortimer let out a half-hearted guffaw. 'You'll have trouble proving that.'

'That's what coppers do, Mortimer. They wear out the shoe leather in a bid to find proof. Worn much of yours out of late, have you?'

Mortimer stiffened as aggression took hold of his face and body. 'Look here, matey, I've been holding the fort while you've been off sunning yourself. Don't accuse me of not holding my end up. You weren't here to know, so don't come back here barging in when you don't know what's been going on. As for her—' he pointed a grimy finger at Honey — 'how do I know she's telling the truth about the old girl being a personal friend?'

'I can assure you that she was. My mother's known her for years. Very well, in fact. They didn't always get on, but that's beside the point.'

'Friend' sounded better than 'acquaintance', though that was precisely all she was once Gloria Cross had found out about her habit of recording observations and gossip. Should she mention Gladys's journal and spying on her neighbours? Not now, she decided. She'd leave Steve to do that.

On their way out they found Warren Hart standing at the doorway to his post with a mug of tea in his hand, raising a hand at officers he knew and generally doing his best to look important and still part of the team. His jovial expression disappeared when he saw the yellow Citroen come to a halt in front of his post.

'Warren.'

The security officer offered only a begrudging grunt by way of reply.

'I'll get your laptop back to you as soon as we've had a look. There might be something on there the main recordings missed.'

Warren didn't look at all happy about his promise to return the laptop, nor the suggestion that the main storage system might have missed something.

'No hard feelings,' said Steve and held out his hand to be shaken. 'And just to confirm there are none . . .'

Stretching his arm out behind him was the signal for Honey to come racing over after going back to the car and fetching the brown paper carrier bag containing a bottle of Glenmorangie. She'd quelled at the sight of the bottle when

Steve had shown it to her. 'A cheap bottle of Bells or Famous Grouse blend would have done. Why a twelve-year-old malt?'

'Warren is a connoisseur of whisky. He'd think I was being a cheapskate. Anyway, remember what's at stake here. He wasn't the best copper in the world and he isn't the best security officer, but a bottle of Glenmorangie will keep him sweet — especially now I've nicked his laptop.'

'Are you really back in the firm?' Warren asked him, the sight of the whisky compensating for the laptop being taken.

'I am.'

Steve flashed the warrant card he'd been issued. A temporary one had quickly morphed into a permanent one on accepting that the life on the waves was gone and he needed to make a living. Back into the police it was. But he lived in hope.

Despite his renewed professionalism, Honey perceived the look in his eyes, the kind people have when there's been a death in the family. Oh, how he'd loved that boat.

With some reluctance Warren ushered them both inside, where he thanked Steve for the whisky and invited them to take a seat.

Honey kept her eyes peeled as she sat down. Places could change from one day to another. The main thing she deduced was that there was a fresh bottle of whisky next to a scraggy-looking spider plant. The head of the empty peeped above the rim of the wicker bin.

'Can you run through the film footage?' Steve asked.

Honey's attention snapped to Warren. His dark eyebrows formed a straight line over his nose. 'Sorry I didn't send them to you, but quite frankly I don't think you'll find anything of interest — in either murder. And they're quite extensive. After all, time of death is a bit vague.' He leaned forward, a worried look on his face. 'There's private stuff on that laptop. You won't let it go astray, will you?'

'Of course not — as long as nothing on there is illegal.'

'No. No.' Warren looked exasperated. 'It's adult stuff. Nothing illegal — honest.'

He's lying, thought Honey. Beads of sweat had collected like tiny pearls on his forehead. Plus, when they'd met before, he'd ogled her as if he could see through to her vest. Being used to assessing hotel guests, their sins, foibles and guilty expressions, she decided that he'd been thrown off balance by the question.

Whether Steve knew what he'd done was inconclusive, but he was definitely holding out. The questioning continued. 'I want to know the movements in Regency Gardens around the time of the death of Mrs Faversham.'

Warren looked bemused. Beneath the surface he was quivering like a jelly. 'I thought I'd done that.' Any excuse.

'You did for Norman Glendower. I'm talking about Mrs Faversham.'

'Oh. Yeah. I can email them to you. It'll only take a minute.' His answer was begrudging.

'Tell me some of what you know. I can marry up whatever you say with the security footage. As they used to say in *Listen with Mother*, I'm sitting comfortably, so let's begin, shall we?'

Warren gave it another try. 'I've already sent a copy. Sorry, forgot.'

For whatever reason, he was lying. Steve was having none of it. 'Call me impatient. Run it through now.'

Warren licked his lips, perhaps reminding himself that they'd brought him a decent bottle of scotch. It wasn't so much a bribe as a present — or perhaps not.

The computer screen connected to the security system flickered into life.

'This is at three this morning. You can see the guards doing their rounds,' said Warren, pointing a podgy finger at the grey figures setting off in opposite directions around the estate.

'Two of them,' Steve exclaimed. 'You weren't on duty yourself?'

'I'm not a robot,' Warren said wryly.

'And two of them? One by day and two by night,' mentioned Honey.

'The people here have got the money to pay and everyone knows you're more likely to get burgled at night than in the daytime.'

Steve agreed this was true. Both he and Honey leaned forward, peering at the screen. The only lights of any account were the streetlights, glowing in Victorian splendour from their wrought-iron posts until the morning.

'Nothing much happening though,' Honey remarked.

Cameras in various positions beamed back pictures that were remarkably clear compared to the old types in years gone by. It had sometimes been like peering through a pea-souper. This screen was in colour.

'Now, I take it we're on the same page here. This footage refers to the fire and Mrs Faversham's demise.'

'Yes.'

'Did you know her very well?'

'No more or less than any other resident.'

'Hmm,' muttered Honey. 'She struck me as a person who liked to interact with her neighbours.' She didn't mention what she knew about the view from her front bedroom and the fact that she was a nosy parker. The journal her mother mentioned should explain what she knew from spying on her neighbours. It would be a bonus if they could find the written account her mother referred to — a journal containing sarcastic comments, nicknames of the people she knew and ugly caricatures. So far there been no mention of it being found except for Ahmed's brief glimpse on the computer screen.

Honey asked again if he knew that Gladys snooped on her neighbours.

'I only work here,' Warren said somewhat guardedly. 'I'm supposed to watch over their property, not get to know them.'

'Did you know she kept a journal and gave people nicknames?' Honey asked. 'It's possible your name might have been mentioned. Would she have any reason to spy on you? Would you have anything she might like to know about?'

Warren exploded. 'I'm a professional. I would have known if she was spying on me.'

'Would you? My mother told me that Gladys used to work in intelligence. She spied on enemies of this country. It wasn't that big a step for her to spy on her neighbours — purely out of interest and to keep her hand in, so to speak.'

Warren's face turned puce. 'Her?'

'Her,' replied Honey. 'Still waters run deep and all that.'

Steve was noticeably quiet. She knew he wasn't just listening to what was being said, he was evaluating *how* it was said. A tone of voice could change markedly if someone was lying. She knew beyond doubt that he'd already noticed the earlier guarded comment. She also knew that the whisky had been given by way of loosening a thirsty tongue. Warren Hart was a prime candidate for bribery.

There was a rasping sound as Warren rubbed his hands together as though rolling his thoughts between them. 'I don't know what the silly mare got up to. Didn't know anything about her past either. Only that she kept her husband's ashes in a container and took them all around the house with her. She talked to him too.'

This was a surprise.

'How do you know that?' asked Honey.

'How indeed,' said Steve.

Warren grunted. 'I went in there on a couple of occasions. She used to have me in for a drink.'

Although he already knew the answer, Steve asked the obvious question. 'Tea or whisky?'

Warren conceded that he'd drank whisky there. He also elaborated on his comment about the funeral urn, about her taking it around the house with her as she moved from one room to another.

'She used to talk to it as though her old man was still alive.'

Both Honey and Steve accepted that such behaviour wasn't that uncommon in an elderly person. However, there was still the matter of the journal.

'Did you know about the journal?'

'No. It never came into conversation when I was in there.'

'I've looked round the place. She's got a cocktail cabinet. I bet she keeps some good stuff in there. Am I right, Warren?'

Warren's head fell into his hands. 'Yes, yes, yes. I've already said that I did go in there and, yes, she did pour me a drink.'

'And ask you questions?'

He didn't meet their eyes when he nodded. 'Yes.'

Honey played good cop while Steve played both. 'About the neighbours and their lifestyles?'

He squirmed. 'She asked me about some of them.'

'While refilling your glass?'

The wet tongue moistened his dry lips. 'Yes. I thought it was just curiosity, you know, taking an interest in the neighbours. I thought she was odd, but that was all.'

'In what way?'

He shrugged. 'Out jogging at all hours of the day and night.'

As they talked, Steve kept his eyes fixed on the screen timestamp which continued to travel forward.

Eight o'clock came up. There were comings and goings, kids mostly being driven off to Saturday morning soccer, rugby, cricket or ballet. *Could be anything*, thought Honey. She reminded herself that although they seemed to be living ordinary lives, secrets were hovering, secondary lives going on both outside and within the gated community.

People came and went. Honey peered closer, recognised people getting out of their cars, letting the cat in, dressed in nightwear, stretching and yawning on the front step. Ordinary people. Ordinary lives.

'You can't see all of the houses from here,' Honey remarked.

'Certainly not.' Warren made a hissing noise and shook his head. 'The security cameras are programmed to do a sweeping motion landing on one section for a while before travelling on. They don't stay fixed on the same address all the time. That would be an infringement of privacy,' he said pompously. 'The people that live here have no wish to be spied on. It's the people that don't live here they want to know about. People who've got no business coming in here.'

'Did Norman Glendower have many visitors?'

Giving into his weakness, Warren twisted the top off the whisky bottle and poured a drop into his coffee.

'He had a few, mostly his daughter. And some woman called on one occasion. I had to go round there and stop her trying to bash the door down. He wanted her banned from the premises. I said I wouldn't let her in again now that I knew her car registration.'

'Do you have that car registration?'

He nodded.

Steve passed him the pen and paper lying on the desk. 'Write it down.'

Warren did so. The effort necessitated him further diluting his coffee with whisky.

'Do you know who she was — this woman?'

Warren shook his head. 'No. I've never seen her before.'

'And the daughter?'

He paused and blinked as though disinclined to answer. There was something odd here, but neither Honey nor Steve cold put a finger on what it was.

'Come on, man,' urged Steve.

Warren looked uncomfortable. 'I believe she's got a flat in London.'

'Do you know where in London?'

He shook his head and took a quick swig of whisky. 'I'm not sure.'

'Norman never spoke about her — where she lived — what she did?'

He shook his head again. 'No.'

Something bugged Honey. 'How often did she come and see him?'

'She didn't visit that often. Can't recall the last time she visited before he died. She'll be down a bit more regularly now though. I mean, she's got things to do — funeral once you release the body and then sorting out the will and all that.'

Steve turned to Honey. 'She identified her father's body.'

Up until now Honey had felt no pity for the murdered man. However, the fact that his daughter had not visited very often saddened her — she reminded herself that it had been a long time since she'd seen her own daughter. Or granddaughter. She missed them both.

She looked at Steve for clarification that she'd been alone when she identified the body. What a shame that would be. Alone and suddenly an orphan. She would have mentioned it, but Steve was otherwise engaged, his eyes narrowed and concentrating on the screen.

Honey wasn't sure, but thought Warren seemed relieved not to have to answer any more questions.

The gate opening to let in cars finished at one fifteen. After that, the only movement was of a security guard ambling around the estate, flashing his torch. At one point he disappeared behind an ornamental hedge. They saw him reemerge doing up his trouser flies.

Steve grinned. 'He had a pee behind the bush.'

'And mistimed when he thought he was out of range of the camera,' added Honey.

'Returning to Norman Glendower,' Steve said, 'what sort of girl was his daughter?'

Warren licked his lips and slid into super-stud mode. Not that he had any chance of becoming that. 'A bit of a corker.'

He looked away as though disinclined to say any more. 'Is that so?'

'You can see for yourself. Seen her go in there today, in fact.'

'Really?' Steve looked almost happy. 'In that case we might as well pay her a visit.'

'She's already been interviewed.'

'Not by me.'

CHAPTER SEVENTEEN

They left Warren in a subdued mood with his bottle of whisky and walked to the house where Norman Glendower had met his end.

Despite all its allusions to a past time, Regency Gardens adhered rigidly to modern building standards. Somehow its crisp exterior, plastic windows and stone-faced blockwork — not solid stone — detracted from the pseudo-classicism it was attempting to replicate. Despite that, the price tag was still way above average for a modern semi or detached house.

The shiny bonnet of a sleek Jaguar — top of the range — nosed into the boot of Norman's rather modest Renault. Judging by the number plate, the Jaguar was this year's model, sporty and sleek but still maintaining a look of plush comfort.

'Daughter must be doing all right,' Honey remarked. 'Something in the city? IT perhaps? Or something seedier?'

'Or a car dealer?'

'Petrolhead!'

Steve rang the bell.

If they were expecting a wan-faced girl with red-rimmed eyes as a result of grieving for her dead father, they were proved instantly wrong.

Warren Hart had been telling the truth. Gabriella Glendower was a stunner. Her hair was long and blonde, smoky eye make-up accentuated the colour of her eyes and her lips were too perfect to be real.

Honey was instantly convinced that Glendower's daughter had invested in more than a little enhancement. Botox at least. Hair extensions. A fake tan straight from a bottle — or the real thing from Malaga.

Her black crop top had long sleeves but the bodice stopped well short of her pierced navel. Her trousers were black satin. Black for mourning, thought Honey. Fair enough, though the bare belly and pink mules were more Mandolin nightclub than mourning garb.

'Miss Glendower?'

'Yes.'

'Police.' Steve flashed his warrant card. 'I'm Detective Inspector Doherty. This is my partner, Hannah Driver.'

'I've already been interviewed. I know nothing about my father's death.'

'There's just a few things I need to go over. If you don't mind.' Steve smiled, turning on the charm as easily as he could take the top off a bottle of Chianti.

Gabriella Glendower very purposely took the warrant card from Steve and looked him up and down before giving it back. She turned her attention to Honey, though not with the same deliberation of looking her up and down. 'Where's yours?'

It was the question Honey had hoped Glendower's daughter would not ask. She said all she could say. 'I haven't got one, but—'

She didn't get a chance to give her the spiel about being Crime Laison Officer for the Bath Hotels Association — past tense, of course, but still worth a punt.

'You can come in,' Gabriella said, nodding to Steve. 'But not you. Not without proper ID.'

Steve didn't argue the point. 'Wait here. I won't be long.'

The door slammed in her face.

'Nice,' muttered Honey and went back to the car.

* * *

Steve knew Gabriella was playing a game and had every intention of playing one too. He'd flatter her to get what he wanted, which was any bit of information she might have.

There hadn't been much time to look around when Glendower's body was found. He found himself in a rather blandly decorated oblong living room, where Gabriella flung her arm at the settee by way of invitation to sit down.

While he curved himself into the plush upholstery of the sofa, Gabriella lowered her rounded bottom into a nursing chair that dated from the nineteenth century. Steve prided himself on knowing a bit about antiques. You couldn't live in Bath and not have some idea of period pieces. Its frame was ornate and highly polished wood, its upholstery a vibrant shade of dark pink. Like Gabriella Glendower herself, the chair stood out in a room of slate grey and white unadorned by decorative objects, the walls bereft of pictures. Odd for an upmarket residence in Bath. Everyone put pictures up, whether they were original paintings or prints. *Even me*, he thought to himself.

A bottle of champagne and a single glass sat on a small side table beside her. She looked him up and down more intimately than she had earlier while raising the glass to her lips. She took a sip, her lips leaving a pink imprint on the rim and her gaze lingering on him. He was ready to refuse a drink with the age-old comment that he was on duty, but it wasn't needed. She didn't offer.

He made the usual platitudes about being sorry for her father's death. In this instance it was hard to appear sympathetic. After all, her father was guilty of fraud and he had been the victim — he had no doubt about that now. Young Ahmed had assured him that there was no such company as Goodenough Marine Insurance. 'Good enough for mugs' was how he viewed it now. And he'd been one, so occupied with the idea of sailing into the sunset that he'd cut corners and trusted people he shouldn't have. Norman Glendower had really felt like one of the lads when he'd met him in the pub, enjoyable company and seemingly the sort you could rely on in your hour of need. How wrong he'd been.

Gabriella Glendower had the look of a woman who believed in herself and spent excessively on the better things in life. He was no expert but her clothes and general appearance screamed self-indulgence. Harvey Nicks rather than Primark. Gold earrings dangled from her ears and a series of fine gold chains cascaded over her pert breasts.

She languorously crossed one long leg over the other, a pink mule dangling from toes, the nails of which were varnished in a contrasting cerise. Pale pink and deep pink. A bit Barbie but more thought out.

'Please keep this short. I have things I need to do.'

Of course she did. Nails, make-up, hair . . .

Her tone was far from that of a grieving daughter. She had purpose. Life goes on and all that and she looked the sort to ensure that it did — on her terms.

He adopted his most sympathetic expression. 'I quite understand. It's tough losing a close relative. I'll take up as little of your time as possible.'

'Good.'

Blunt, one word. No sign of emotion on the perfect features.

'When was the last time you saw your father?'

She looked up at the ceiling. Another sip of champagne left another imprint of her lips on the glass. 'Two weeks before he died.'

'Was that here?'

She rolled her eyes. Her painted fingernails tapped against her forehead as she searched her mind.

'No. I was in London. He came there. I have a flat in Notting Hill.'

'Lucky you.' Steve chanced a smile.

She shrugged. 'It's OK, though I would prefer Chelsea or Kensington.'

Steve blanched. Notting Hill had once been downmarket. Bohemian but still far from gentrified back in the old days. It had long since up and come. There was still a good mix of people but these residents were more well-heeled than the previous incumbents. Notting Hill rents were less than the boroughs of Chelsea and Kensington, but still eyewatering.

She glanced at her wristwatch, a clear indication that he was being timed. As she did so, the sleeve of her stomach-skimming top fell back from her wrist and bunched around her elbow. The watch shouted quality. Bulgari — she had to be earning megabucks, or had inherited the money to splash around.

First impression stored for future consumption, he pressed on. 'Was there any particular reason for his visit?'

She shrugged. 'I had something I wanted to talk to him about.'

'And he was willing to come up to see you.'

'Of course he was.' Pink lips pouted as though it was only right that father should visit daughter rather than the other way round.

'Might I ask what you wanted to see him about?'

'No. You may not. It's none of your business.'

The pink lips, plumped up to make them look more kissable, froze into a grim line. They reminded him of a half-melted strawberry ice lolly.

There was also a hard look in her eyes — eyes that were blue in a sea of smoky make-up. It came to him that it wasn't a sudden hardness and wondered why he hadn't seen it before.

Because she's designed herself to be hot and not hated. Look beyond the perfect grooming, the painted features and air of desirability adopted by someone wanting to make waves and money in the modern world.

He wondered what she did for a living. Not IT. Not with those fingernails. Maybe the rumour Honey had uncovered was true. He could imagine her cruising the best nightclubs, mixing with people like her, gaining riches without having to work for them — at least not in the accepted sense.

Gabriella Glendower was the sort who craved adoration, like a marble statue of a Greek goddess, there to be adored and worshipped, her features copied by those as shallow as she was. Not loved. Not emotionally — except perhaps by her father. He therefore decided to manufacture his questions to flatter or at the very least put her at ease.

'You had a close relationship with your father?'

She tossed her head. 'Of course I did. He was my father.'

He paused. Was she a model? Somehow he didn't think so, but a little flattery might not go amiss.

'Might I ask what you do for a living? You look to me as though you might be a model, or have I seen you on TV in something?'

When her black, thick eyelashes fluttered like bats' wings, he knew that his ploy had hit the right spot. She was flattered.

'Something like that. I'm an influencer. I've got thousands of followers on social media.'

'Would I be right in thinking you use social media on a regular basis?'

'Of course I do. What kind of question is that?' She looked peeved.

What do I know? he thought to himself. Social media was best avoided. He stuck to phone calls and emails. That was more than enough for him.

One set of long pink fingernails caressed a strand of lengthy hair that had to be at least sixteen inches long. It looked too perfect to be true. His initial judgement that it wasn't real had to be right. He'd heard of hair extensions and that they cost a fortune.

He chuckled. 'I knew you were something like that — something in fashion, the way you're turned out. You're here sitting in your father's house looking better than most people do when they go to town. I understand presenting oneself on social media can be a lucrative business.'

'Only if you take care of yourself. It takes a lot of effort and I put the time in,' she said and looked smug about it. 'And money. Top-drawer accoutrements. Nothing high street. The most in-fashion houses.'

He nodded as though he understood exactly what she was on about and the look she was aiming for. Wearing black was far less hassle. 'Oh yes. That's as much as I understand.'

'I don't expect you to. It takes time and money to make traction on social media.'

Steve nodded. 'I understand from some I know that it's a full-time job, one that can achieve an incredibly high return.'

She tossed her head, sending her blonde hair showering like silk across her shoulders. 'You have to put in the hours and not spare the expense.'

'I can believe it. If I may be so bold, you certainly look as though you mean business. Would I be right in saying that you've already made your mark in the online world? You certainly look as though you might — if you don't mind me saying.'

The ice maiden melted. She positively preened. 'Hair, nails, facials, skin, clothes and restructuring treatment.' Her eyes narrowed and her smile wasn't so much Cheshire Cat as a predatory feline about to sink its teeth into her prey.

'Do you work in London — I mean anything else besides your media presence? The city perhaps? Banking? IT?'

He'd already known the answer before he'd asked it. Still, it didn't hurt to keep pressing buttons.

He fancied she flinched, but the look passed.

'I used to, but once I decided what I wanted to be, I packed it in.'

'Did you work in the beauty industry?'

'Yes. How did you guess?' She beamed.

'I'm no expert, but you look as though only the best will do as regards cosmetics, clothes and everything else a beautiful woman needs to keep on top of her game.'

'Exactly!' She rearranged herself so that her knees were slightly parted, her arms forming an arched shape along the back of the chair. 'You see,' she said, her pert breasts thrusting beneath her expensive crop top, 'I learned early on that it wasn't enough to open doors with just a smile. It's a start, but enhancing one's attributes takes time and money. So, I don't skimp. Only the best will do.'

'What did your father think of that?'

She laughed and her eyes narrowed at the corners. 'He gave me the best piece of advice he could give me. Be ruthless. Take no prisoners. Concentrate on where you want to go and who you want to be. Lie if you must.'

Her comments about her father chilled him. Was it a case of like father, like daughter — and vice versa?

His good humour vanished. His jaw set grim. 'That attitude could hurt people. It could even land you in jail — under certain circumstances.'

His comment caused a sudden change in her demeanour. Her openness shut down. The hard look returned. She looked at the face of the expensive watch.

'I've given you enough of my precious time. I think you should go.'

His look hardened. No softness now. This was his professional stance. Steve was ready to counteract. 'I haven't finished yet. There are a few more questions I must ask.'

'Isn't this a bit over the top? As far as I'm aware, everything's done that needs to be done.'

'Is that how you regard your father's murder, not worthy of further investigation? Don't you want us to catch the killer?'

'Of course I do!'

'Then please, indulge me.'

She shifted in her chair and didn't look pleased.

Steve persisted. 'How often did you see each other?'

'Often enough. It all depended on circumstances.'

'What kind of circumstances?'

He fancied she was grinding her teeth, but he wouldn't let her off the hook. Sheer bloody-mindedness craved an answer. He'd decided he didn't like her. Too vacuous.

'General things.'

He could see a chink of light opening in her armour. At the same time, he attempted to evaluate just how much all the beauty treatments, the clothes, the hair extensions amounted to. And could she really make shedloads of money purely from being an influencer? He wasn't sure. He'd ask Ahmed.

'I take it he's left the house to you.'

'Yes.'

'Will you reside here yourself?'

Her laugh was one of derision. 'Here? Locked away from the world with mummies, daddies and kids?'

'What about Gladys Faversham? She was an elderly lady. Did you ever have anything to do with her?'

She scowled. 'That old cow! I told dad she was a nasty cat and not to trust her.'

'Did he trust her?'

'I wouldn't think so.'

'But you don't know for sure.'

She didn't answer.

'So you'll sell the house?'

'You bet I will,' she replied, her chin raised and satisfaction gleaming in her eyes.

'It should make decent money when you sell it.'

'Good.'

'What will you do with the proceeds?'

For a moment he wondered whether she had heard him. She didn't exactly look thoughtful, more as though she was considering more than one option.

'Come back and ask me when I've made up my mind,' she said at last.

'I will.'

She got to her feet before he did, a sharp enough signal that this time she really did want him to leave.

He shook his head as she showed him to the door. 'I really cannot believe that you can make a living as an influencer on social media. It seems crazy. Come on, tell me the truth. What else do you do to earn money?'

She looked horribly affronted. 'Nothing!'

The door slammed behind him before he had chance to say goodbye — not that she would have cared one way or the other. She'd quite clearly had enough of his company.

A few things had rattled her cage, especially his comment about her having other means of making a living.

* * *

Honey was waiting for him in the car with her arms folded and staring down at her knees.

'You're back and virtually unscathed,' she said, not without a hint of sarcasm.

Steve frowned. 'Not once did I see any trace of grief.'

'Poor old Dad.' said Honey. 'Did you ask her about the cat?'

'The cat?'

'You told me it was his cat that led to the discovery of the body.'

'I didn't see the relevance. Anyway, it's happy enough at the cattery. Happier perhaps than it would be living with her. She'd probably have it stuffed or made into a fur coat.'

'I can see you were less than impressed. Never mind. So where next?'

Steve looked thoughtfully glum. 'I'm thinking we should take a day out shortly.'

'Anywhere nice?' Honey asked brightly.

'A funeral. Next Thursday. Norman Glendower. The coroner is releasing the body. After that, Gladys Faversham.'

'Right.' She nodded. 'I'll get out the little black dress.'

CHAPTER EIGHTEEN

It was Saturday afternoon following the funeral of Norman Glendower when Mary Jane collared Honey, a slightly manic look in her piercing eyes.

The funeral had been sparsely attended. Gabriella was there, of course, classically sleek in a black sheath of a dress. Her broad-brimmed hat wouldn't have looked out of place on the Riviera. Neither would her tanned legs, and her four-inch heels were more suited to a nightclub where the lights were low and the music loud.

Mary Jane came bounding down into reception around about teatime, her face and manner full of fertile enthusiasm.

'I had a dream last night about this murder you're investigating. There was a cat that sparkled.' She frowned. 'At least, I think it sparkled. No matter,' she said shaking her head, an intense expression on her face that sent her aged wrinkles haywire. 'Anyway, this sparkly cat. I think the cat is the key. We might learn something interesting if we can find this cat. Do you happen to know if a cat was involved, and, if so, do you know where it is? I believe cats are placed in a cattery short-term. Is that right, Steve?'

Having always regarded Mary Jane as slightly deranged, Steve confirmed that it was, rolled his eyes and bid a hasty retreat, saying he was off to the rec to watch a rugby match. As far as Honey knew, Bath Rugby Club were not playing at home, besides which Steve was a cricket rather than rugby fan.

'Which cattery would that be?' she called out after him.

He shouted something back about checking it with the on-duty officer at the station. Then changed his mind and recalled the name: Wellspring Cattery. A blast of air, a swinging of the door and he was gone.

Feeling guilty at his abrupt departure, Honey attempted to absent herself just in case Mary Jane felt slighted. It was doubtful but there was always the chance.

'Sorry, Mary Jane, but I do need to lend a hand in the dining room . . .'

Nigel overheard and assured her that everything was under control, and why didn't she take advantage of the nice weather and go for a drive?

She considered giving him a verbal warning there and then, but like Steve he found Mary Jane a bit too much to handle. The saying about killing two birds with one stone came to mind. He liked being in sole charge of the hotel and preferred to be as far away from Mary Jane as possible.

However, Nigel had experienced being a passenger in Mary Jane's car, so his encouragement was somewhat surprising. Being a non-driver himself, perhaps he was oblivious to her haphazard light-jumping and the fact that she was a natural born road hog. Perhaps he was slightly deaf or thought the horn-blowing of other drivers was some kind of fanfare celebrating the way she could weave in and out of traffic, small gaps in particular, as though she was riding a bicycle, not a pink Cadillac.

'There,' exclaimed Mary Jane with undisguised enthusiasm for Nigel's pronouncement. 'You've got no excuse. You're free for a little spin in the country. It will do you good and we haven't had a tête-à-tête since you got back. We've got a lot of catching up to do.'

Honey agreed that they hadn't spent much time together, but perhaps the alternative was to have a coffee together in the lounge.

Mary Jane was having none of it. 'No, no, no! And I need to tell you about my thoughts on the deaths at Regency Gardens. The cat is the key. Didn't you tell me that it was the cat who led them to the dead man?'

'I did, but it was already in the cattery when Gladys Faversham was killed.'

'But it all starts with the cat and with the first murder. Don't you agree?'

Honey had to agree she had a point, albeit a very negligible one. Still, anything was worth a try.

'So how do we go about questioning this cat? It's not likely to swear a statement — and even if it did, we wouldn't understand it.'

She said the last jokingly — not that Mary Jane appeared to notice.

In response, she held her hands up in front of her face. 'My hands are one hundred times more sensitive than most hands. Laying on of hands. That's what I'll do. Think of my fingers as electrodes when placed on the cat's skull. I will read its thoughts. What happened before the man's body was discovered and what happened immediately afterwards. The cat could reveal what humans might not want revealed.'

It was mad, crazy and totally illogical, but its outlandishness had whetted Honey's appetite. Not so much because she expected important results that might have a bearing on the case, but it could be quite entertaining. All she had to do was keep her nerve with Mary Jane's reckless driving.

'I'll get my things.'

Necessary things were a St Christopher hanging from the dressing table mirror and a dab of tiger balm between her eyebrows and under her nose, a weak attempt at calming her nerves, but all she could think of at short notice.

When they set off on their journey in Mary Jane's old pink Cadillac, Honey kept her eyes firmly closed. It would

174

help her cope with the journey and stop her from leaping out of the car long before they reached their destination.

As it happened, things didn't quite run to form based on past experience. Not hearing any loud honks of horns or threats from drivers waving clenched fists from behind partially opened windows, she cautiously opened one eye then the other. Mary Jane was driving more carefully than in the past. Pleasantly surprised, she began to relax.

'This is very pleasant,' she dared to say and only hoped she hadn't spoken too soon.

'It's not really me driving. It's my alter ego, Lady Caroline Lamb, and thus I have acquired a more accepting nature of this helter-skelter world.'

The name seemed familiar. 'Do I know that name from somewhere?'

Sensing her puzzlement, Mary Jane poured out a vivid explanation, her eyes shining as though her words were a vision in front of her far-seeing eyes.

'From history. She was of aristocratic breeding and totally obsessed with the poet, Lord Byron. Her love was unrequited, of course. He was what we might now call an exponent of free love. He would have gone down a storm in nineteen-seventies San Francisco — the Summer of Love would have suited him down to the ground. Including psychedelic drugs. He smoked opium, I believe. Anyway, she was still basically a lady of the highest order but was so obsessed that she once laid aside her high-born origins and accompanied him to a rather risqué social event dressed up as a harem slave. She wore a Turkish turban, billowing silk harem pants and a gold collar around her neck, her breasts were bare and she carried a long-handled fan of ostrich feathers.'

'And wafted it over Lord Byron.'

'Yes. She caused quite a stir. She was some gal, but a lady all the same. Not fiery. You might say calm and collected.'

'Yes. I might,' returned Honey. Try as she might, she couldn't quite work out the connection with the long-dead aristocrat becoming Mary Jane's alter ego and taking the wheel of the left-hand-drive Cadillac. There most likely wasn't one — not a logical one — but there, Mary Jane was not a logical person.

Immersed in her subject, Mary Jane carried on with the life of Lady Caroline Lamb. Whether the stories were true or had been elaborated by Mary Jane's imagination was neither here nor there.

'She also tried her hand at being one of the bearers carrying his sedan chair. He instructed her not to go too fast and to mind the bumps.'

The Wellspring Cattery was about five miles out of town beyond the village of Bathford.

A narrow track led up a stony lane between a colonnade of beech trees.

A single-storey portacabin abutted a stone bungalow. Both fringed a parking area that could accommodate eight cars at a push.

Here we go, thought Honey. *They're going to think we're barmy. Don't think of it as serious. Just enjoy it as a day out.*

The receptionist looked a little surprised when Mary Jane told her that they were there to question a cat about a murder.

'There were two,' Mary Jane explained, 'but Pussy Glendower was present in only one instance. No relatives were around at that time, so the police asked you to look after him. I take it he's still here?'

'She,' said the receptionist, looking no less surprised than when first told the reason they were there. 'Her name's Tassel.'

'What a lovely name,' remarked Honey.

'Yes. Tassel Glendower. She's a queen. A Bengal. A very exotic breed and quite beautiful.'

The remarks were related with breathless awe, like some people sound when in the presence of royalty.

Even though the receptionist looked totally accepting of the reason for their mission, Honey felt the need to add further explanation. 'I hope you don't mind, but my friend had a dream last night and believes the cat might help her understand what's been going on,' said Honey. It sounded bonkers to her ears, but if it made progress, all was well and good.

In a bid to bring this visit back down to earth — or at least not have it sound quite so batty, she further whispered, 'It would put my friend's mind at rest.'

Mary Jane heard her and exclaimed in a loud voice, 'Animals as well as humans can suffer from post-traumatic stress disorder.' Mary Jane sounded as though it were the most obvious thing in the world.

'Yes,' said Honey, smiling and nodding as if she too were an expert in animal behaviour — which was far from the truth. She decided to be that person and went on to say, 'The poor creature needs counselling. I'm a psychotherapist specialising in delving into the inner secrets of the mind.'

'Even of cats?' The receptionist sounded enthralled.

'Yes, indeedy,' said Mary Jane, looking incredibly smug. 'And I specialise in reading the minds of all creatures — human and otherwise. I'm helping the police with their enquiries and it's not an easy case. Your cooperation would be much appreciated.'

It wasn't strictly true, but Honey let her get on with it. What were a few white lies between friends?

Mary Jane accompanied her words with a bewitching smile — one designed to penetrate the most dyed-in-the-wool sceptic.

Perhaps it was mention of police and mind reading in the same sentence, but Honey sensed total acceptance and admiration. They would be allowed entry into the world of Wellspring Cattery. The receptionist signalled to a colleague, a person named Marion, to take them through. 'Visitors for Tassel Glendower.'

Honey felt as though they were indeed visiting a human being, one with the benefit of private health insurance.

She wondered whether the receptionist might return to normal human behaviour once they were out of the way.

It didn't matter. They were on their way to Tassel Glendower's temporary accommodation, and although she wasn't expecting anything much, Honey decided to suspend disbelief — at least in the short-term.

Marion, their escort, vaguely resembled a beach ball on sticks. Her body was round, her legs thin and covered in crumpled jeans. Her face was round and amenable and her welcome ecstatic. 'For Tassel? How wonderful. She really needs to go home, you know. A queen of that breed needs the very best care and attention.'

'I expect a new home will need to be found.'

'Somewhere her breeding is appreciated,' Marion nodded. 'After all, one pays court to a Bengal queen. She's not just any old moggy from a back alley.'

'No,' said Honey. 'Of course not.'

'Will you be giving her a home?'

'No. I'm just investigating the death of her owner.'

Despite not really being a cat lover she was impressed. Tassel was beautiful. The sleek Bengal cat — its fur glossy and striped in similar fashion to the Bengal tiger it was meant to resemble, though on a much smaller scale and far from being a maneater — was housed in a narrow cage sandwiched between two others, which were wider but housed two cats rather than one. It occurred to Honey that the regally sleek Tassel was in solitary confinement.

The cat turned her blue eyes on them chillingly as they appeared at the end of her cage.

They gazed in and she gazed back at them unflinching.

'She's a lovely cat. Someone will be sure to give her a loving home if there's nobody else wanting her,' Marion said somewhat hopefully, it seemed to Honey. 'Do you know if the legal side has been sorted and arrangements made for Tassel?'

Honey had to disappoint her. 'We're not sure what's happening. There is a daughter and a chance that some provision has been made in the will.'

'Oh. Well, that's something, I suppose.'

'You are right, though. She does look like a queen,' said Mary Jane.

'She is. In a manner of speaking. Queen of all she surveys, so very demanding — not overly, of course,' she suddenly added as though wishing she hadn't said that. 'What I mean is that she deserves someone who will appreciate her.'

'A pampered puss,' Honey added, poking her finger through the tough wiring.

'You can say that again,' said Marion. 'She was wearing a glitzy collar when we took her in. We've taken it off her so she could have a good scratch. It's in a little bag of personal items and with everything else in her locker.' Marion indicated the wooden box set into the door of the cage above a top-of-the-range carrying basket. 'No need to worry. All valuables are taken care of and returned on departure and please be assured that it's not the first time we've housed cats wearing sparkly collars.'

'I was wondering why she's housed alone,' said Honey. 'Doesn't she get on with other cats?'

'She's not that sociable. A bit of a loner. Bengals tend to be a bit like that. Very valuable cats, you know. Are you sure you can't give her a home yourself?' Her face visibly brightened at the prospect.

Mary Jane got in first. 'No. As already mentioned, we're here to question her on a police matter.'

Marion blinked as Mary Jane's words sunk in.

'She's a witness to a murder,' said Mary Jane.

'But . . . does that mean she'll have to give evidence?' Her look was one of disbelief leading to outright confusion.

'I have a method,' Mary Jane began, keen to describe her special skills to someone — anyone — who would listen. 'Tassel cannot write a statement, but I can. I read her mind and I write the statement.'

Honey felt the breath knocked out of her. Mary Jane had succeeded in making their mission sound a bit mad. She needed to elucidate and get back to basics — and sanity.

'The cat raised the alarm about its owner. It was wandering around for a while before anyone noticed that she couldn't get into the house and hadn't been fed.'

Marion's expression dropped. 'Oh. Poor thing! Can you answer me how much longer she's likely to be here with us?'

There was something pleading about the look in her eyes.

'I don't think it will be too much longer. The daughter has turned up and will probably want her back.'

From what Steve had said and from what Honey had seen of Gabriella Glendower, she was far from being a cat woman — more of a trophy waiting to be snatched up by a ludicrously wealthy man. Keeping a cat wouldn't rate too high on her agenda.

Marion smiled with her lips, but it had trouble getting to her eyes. 'Oh. I'll leave you to it, then. Bring her back whenever you like. It doesn't matter to us. Will the money to keep her here at Wellspring continue?'

The cattery lady looked hopeful, eyes wide open and looking at Honey in anticipation that the answer she gave would be just what she wanted to hear.

Honey told her that she saw no reason why it wouldn't continue. 'Now, is there anything we should know about Tassel and her habits?'

Marion's lips did a sideways chewing action. It was as though she wanted to say something but was not sure whether she should.

Honey fixed her with a questioning look. Something was going on here.

'I think I should warn you — she does yowl a lot. Never a miaow. Just a lot of yowling.' She sounded apologetic.

'She's been quiet so far,' Honey pointed out, feeling quite relieved that it wasn't something worse, like the cat suddenly leaping at her and clawing her eyes out. Or, worse still, not being toilet trained. Or keen to bring home a feline version of a takeaway meal — a captured mouse with its head bitten off.

Marion was slow to respond but did get round to it. She gave a silly little laugh. 'Tassel is quite a character. She likes to think about making a racket before she does so. That type of cat thinks about it before yowling for no apparent reason. They're very intelligent you know — but demanding.'

'Can we have her out of there so I can do some preliminary studies?' Mary Jane asked. If she'd noticed Marion's odd behaviour she didn't say so.

Marion laughed as though the cat was a great source of amusement and enjoyment. A little treasure to have around the home. 'I don't see why not. She can't escape from the compound.'

'I mean home. With us. I can keep her in my room,' said Mary Jane. Not once did she look at Honey. Her attention was focused on the cat.

No sign of surprise showed on Marion's amiable round features. Honey decided she was a real feline enthusiast. Gladys Faversham probably would have christened her Cat Woman. Michelle Pfeiffer she was not. More Bagpuss, round and floppy.

The moment she was placed into Honey's arms, the cat let out an enormous yowl that took her by surprise.

'Am I holding it wrong?' she asked nervously.

'No. That's what she normally does when someone picks her up. Or doesn't. Or when she wakes up, or . . . well, anytime really. But you will get used to it.'

'Would it be all right if we took her away for a time so I can better evaluate what's going on in her mind?' Honey asked. 'Psychotherapy is best once practitioner and subject spend some time together.'

'Of course.' Marion's face shone like a full moon on a dark night. 'You're welcome. I'm sure she'll love being the centre of attention.'

'Can we have the carrying basket? It would make the journey that much easier.'

Tassel's personal carrying basket was taken from beneath the locker, the wire door opened, and the comfy cushion within patted and prodded so the little darling would be comfortable.

'Shall I leave her other things here or do you want to take them too?'

'We might as well take them. The daughter might want to keep her so it makes sense to take everything.'

'Splendid. Quite splendid! You could take her in the meantime,' said Marion. 'If the daughter wants the cat, then no harm done and all she has to do is pay the bill for Tassel's bed and board. If she doesn't want her, we won't bill you until you decide to give her a home. That's fair enough, isn't it?'

Marion showed unbounded delight, which led to Honey experiencing nervous misgivings. The woman's movements seemed to have sped up. 'If you could sign for her and said effects on the way out . . . I'll bring everything through for you to take with you.'

'Thank you. It's much appreciated.'

'Let me get her into the basket for you.'

Honey felt oddly relieved that it was Marion who was stuffing the cat into the carrying basket and not her. Somehow she didn't think her efforts would be that successful and had every intention of avoiding some bloodletting from a set of cat's claws.

Although her legs were skinny and her body rotund, Marion skipped ahead of them like Humpty Dumpty prancing with glee because he'd at last been put back together.

By the time they caught up with her in reception, the paperwork was spread out on the counter awaiting signature.

Although everything had seemed to go well, Honey's apprehension was strengthening into a premonition. What was it about this cat that Marion, and the receptionist, weren't telling them? She was sure from their behaviour that something was amiss. She just didn't know what.

It was as if they'd crossed the Rubicon — if leaving the cattery and entering the reception area could be termed that way — but suddenly the air was rent by what sounded like an air raid siren.

It went on and on during the signing of the paperwork consigning Tassel to their care. No amount of peering through the wires of the cage and offering calming, kind words and soothingly daft sounds cut any ice with Queen Tassel.

'Now, now, pussy,' said Mary Jane into the cage.

Honey assured herself that the cat would settle down.

It didn't. It was not just a low, growly yowl, it was a full-on one that pierced the brain and made Honey's eyes water.

'We'll see you out,' said Marion.

She guided them out, the receptionist following behind. It seemed to Honey that they were being marched from the premises. They escorted them as far as the door at the front of the cattery adjacent to the car park.

The faces of Marion and her colleague beamed, and their eyes sparkled with what Honey could only describe as excitement — or relief.

Once out and more than a little suspicious of what the two owners were up to, Honey placed the cat basket onto the bonnet of the car.

By the time that was done and they'd turned round, the two members of staff of the Wellspring Cattery had slammed the door of the portacabin and turned the open sign to closed.

'Ever felt you're not wanted somewhere?' said Mary Jane. 'Those gals seemed dead keen to get rid of us.'

Honey agreed, her voice barely audible above the yowling Tassel.

'Oh well,' Mary Jane said. 'They're probably glad she's out of there and on her way to somewhere more comfortable.'

'I'm sensing there's another reason.' *And you didn't need a sixth sense to pick up on it, either*, Honey thought as the cat continued its incessant wail.

'Hmm. Do you think they know something that we don't?'

'It's a noisy cat. That's what I think they know.'

There were times when Honey had felt taken for a ride — and this was one of them.

'Now what?'

Mary Jane was adopting her trance state, normal for when she was laying on hands to read someone's head bumps or getting the feel of an object inherited from a long-dead ancestor so she could give the heirs a message from the grave.

'Take the cat out of its carrier. Hold it in your arms while I give it the once-over.'

Honey wanted to suggest they get going but knew from experience that Mary Jane didn't like being interrupted when she was going into a trance.

'OK.'

The cat seemed to appreciate being lifted out of its carrier. At least, it didn't seem to be protesting.

The peace and tranquillity didn't last for long.

It occurred to her that they weren't going to get any words from this sleek feline, only more yowls — which proved about right.

Mary Jane's long fingers probed the cat's head and slowly travelled around her neck.

'Her collar's been stolen.'

The sudden pronouncement was unexpected.

'Marion said it's in the bag of personal effects.'

'So she did. A very expensive one.'

'How do you know that?' She expected her to say something like she'd been told this by a feline spirit, something that couldn't be proved one way or the other. She didn't.

'There's a furrow of short fur around her neck from where it used to be.'

'And how do you know it was expensive?'

Mary Jane's fingers retreated from the yowling cat's neck. A long fingernail of one finger dug out something stuck behind the fingernail of her thumb.

Honey took the item from her and held it up to the light. 'A diamanté. Can you put that somewhere safe?'

'I'll put it in my purse. It's got a small side pocket where I keep car parking receipts.'

She wrapped the tiny stone up in one of the flimsy receipts then turned her attention to the bag containing Tassel's effects.

A little rummaging inside the solidly made bag brought forth what she was looking for. The collar was folded up inside a muslin bag. The bag felt quite heavy. The collar was black velvet and studded with diamanté. Depending on size, Honey could imagine wearing it herself.

'Lucky pussycat,' she murmured while admiring how much the stones sparkled in the light. 'Well, what a grand moggy you are,' she said, looking into its wide blue eyes. The cat yowled.

'Is there anything else we can find out?' she asked Mary Jane. 'Would you like to take this in your hands and see if you get any vibes from this?'

Mary Jane held up a warning finger. Her eyes were still closed.

'The physical act of laying my hands on her head worked out well — now let's see about the spiritual.'

Honey clamped her mouth shut as Mary Jane closed her hooded eyes and attempted a trip into the subconscious of the well-bred and rather noisy cat.

'Her grandfather used to belong to a rajah,' she finally said.

Honey didn't ask whether it was Jaipur, Delhi or some other place she'd never heard of up towards the Northwest Frontier. It belonged to history and was all part of the process. Mary Jane was a dab hand at plunging into the historical world. No doubt she would likely come up with all manner of stuff that might or might not be true.

Diamanté. It wasn't that unusual to adorn one's favourite pet with jewellery. She'd heard of some who'd bought their pet dog a tiara, their parrot a gold cage, their pet pig a neck ruff dotted with pearls. Pearls before swine and all that. She couldn't work it out. All she did know was that there was nowt so queer as folk.

Her imagination ran riot before she dragged it back under control and thought about their next move. Gabriella Glendower had a part to play, of course. By right the cat now belonged to her, but would she want the burden of looking after the animal, of having to settle into a house or flat for the sake of a Bengal queen?

Mary Jane resumed her inspection of the cat, pinching an ear between finger and thumb, gazing into her eyes, running her hands along her back all the way to the tip of her tail. Closing in on her yet again and laying on her hands, she splayed her fingers in an attempt to pick up as much of the pussycat's mental vibes as possible.

Once she'd gone as far as she could with that particular plan, she opened her eyes and began examining the cat all over again. She picked up her paws, investigating the soft, warm pads and sharply curving claws.

'Her claws are due for a manicure.'

'A cat? A manicure?' Honey couldn't believe it.

'Yep,' said Mary Jane. 'I get the impression she has a regular manicure, no common scratching post for this queenly feline.'

'The cat has manicures?' Still disbelieving, Honey's eyebrows arched in surprise. She rarely had a manicure herself, but to hear a cat took a regular trip to the beauty parlour made her jealous. She only wished she got the same pampering.

Thinking it might yield something, she took a closer look. 'Good grief. They're gold-tipped. She's had a manicure and a spot of gold varnish applied. How long ago, do you reckon?'

'Judging by the few times I've had mine done, I would suggest her claws have grown out, and at a guess I would think it was last done about six weeks ago.'

Honey frowned thoughtfully. 'Before Norman Glendower was found dead.'

'So we can assume that your victim pampered her?'

'It would seem that way.'

'Now, who would give the cat a manicure and paint its nails?'

'A beauty parlour for cats.'

'That does seem the most likely.'

Honey frowned. 'I do know a place called Pampered Pooches but that only caters for dogs. Cats and dogs don't mix.'

She said it too quietly for Mary Jane to hear and anyway she was again standing there with her eyes closed, her hands laid on the yowling Tassel's queenly head.

Still, it might be worth checking, she thought, and made a vow to trot along to Pampered Pooches, but first another call to the owners of Wellspring Cattery. Perhaps they would know of a beauty salon specialising in cats that might have lacquered the cat's claws.

She went over to the door and knocked. A head appeared when the door opened. Marion held the door open about six inches and asked her what she wanted. Honey asked her about Tassel's claws and where she might have got them painted.

'Not a clue,' said Marion, and immediately shut the door. The sound of a bolt could be heard from behind it.

'They don't want to know,' murmured Honey, letting herself back into the car. 'But why?'

The cat let out another series of resounding yowls.

That, she decided, was the reason. She had inadvertently taken a cat on board that, if it were human, would be in receipt of an ASBO.

At that moment Mary Jane's cat-focused trance lifted enough for her to comment, 'I get the impression that this cat led two separate lives.'

'Believable, I suppose. Aren't they supposed to have nine lives anyway?'

A deep frown permeated Mary Jane's brow. She opened one eye. 'Cats walk alone. The lives thing is no more than an old wives' tale.'

That, thought Honey, is truly something coming from Mary Jane, who tended to believe in all things supernatural.

'What I mean is that this cat had divided loyalties,' Mary Jane continued.

'It yowled a lot when it wasn't fed. That's how the neighbours came to find out that something was wrong. It hassled them because it was hungry. So its loyalties were divided between whoever fed it.'

Mary Jane's eyes flashed open. 'Not necessarily, though those roused to its predicament might have had some bearing, but I'm getting the impression of Tassel's loyalties being divided. There wasn't just one person feeding and spoiling her. Look at her. She needs petting.'

Honey began stroking her fine fur. The cat yowled even more, which led to Honey having a change of thought. 'We'd better put her back in her cage.'

The moment she attempted to do exactly that, the cat's claws dug deeply into her sweater.

'Ouch!'

'Looks like she doesn't want to go back into the cage. Poor creature. I sense she wants something like the level of accommodation she used to have.' Mary Jane fluttered her eyelashes at Honey. 'I think she wants to stay with you.'

As though understanding what Mary Jane had said, the cat's yowls turned to profound purrs of appreciation.

When Honey stroked the creature's scalp, it buried itself in her hand.

'Poor thing. I understand how it feels. I know what it's like to suddenly find oneself homeless.'

She thought of the boat, the carefree lifestyle, watching the sun set below a distant horizon, sailing through a night full of stars and watching the sun rise again in the morning. Such a tragic loss and so quick. Such is life, she thought.

'Sorry, Tassel, but you have to go back into your cage . . .'

Seeing Mary Jane open the cage door, the cat clung on even more fiercely and its forceful yowl turned to a pitiful miaow as if she was crying.

'It won't let go,' said Honey. Much as she tried to disentangle herself from its claws, the more it clung on.

'She has chosen you,' said Mary Jane.

'I'm not sure about that and, besides, she does officially belong to Norman Glendower's daughter.'

Mary Jane reminded Honey of why they were taking the cat. 'While things are being sorted, we might learn something of what happened that night. You can take her around to the neighbours and see if she was at home with them rather than with Norman. It might lead to something. You never know.'

Honey had no idea what more could possibly be gleaned from the presence of a cat, but she had begun to feel sorry for the creature.

'All right,' she said, convinced she would regret this decision but resigned to some kind of plan and the hope that the cat might prove useful. 'One way or the other it might work out.'

The cat began to purr.

'Does this cat understand English?'

'It understands humans,' said Mary Jane. 'I think she's picked up on your energy. She knows you'll care for her.'

The clock was ticking towards five. The sun was going down but the bonnet of the Cadillac was still warm.

Across the car park, from the single-storey building that housed reception and the entrance to the cattery, Marion came out and gave them a little wave.

'Off home now?' asked Honey.

'Yes. Not far to go. I live in the bungalow next door.'

'Very close, so you can keep an eye on things.'

'Dead right,' said Marion with a heartfelt sigh. 'But all should be peaceful tonight. No problems expected.'

No, thought Honey. *That problem is now mine.*

'Drive carefully,' Honey said to Mary Jane once she was in the passenger seat. 'I've a feeling this cat is oversensitive — either that or dead crafty.'

'I would be too if I was holed up in that place,' said Mary Jane. 'San Quentin for cats. It's a wonder she didn't dig her way out before this.'

* * *

Marion Little breathed a sigh of relief, kicked off her shoes and locked the front door of her modest bungalow behind her.

Her partner Agnes was there waiting for her. 'I've poured you a glass of Pinot Grigio. I presumed you'd want one.'

'You bet,' said Marion. 'A celebration is in order. Someone connected with the police has taken the dreaded Tassel away. We're in for a peaceful night.'

She raised her glass. Agnes joined her. They both found the clinking of wine glasses extremely reassuring.

'Thank goodness for that. One more night of that awful yowling and I would have burned the whole place down and headed for the Australian Outback. Peace and quiet at last.'

'For us. Let's just hope she doesn't dump her back here too quickly. That yowling could get on anyone's nerves.'

'As long as it's not ours,' said Agnes, refilling their empty glasses.

CHAPTER NINETEEN

'I can't sleep like this,' Steve said drowsily. 'Can you do something with that cat?'

'Norman used to take it to bed with him.'

'Well, it shouldn't be in our bed,' Steve growled. 'It's a cat.'

'Correction. A spoilt cat. Did you notice it has its claws buffed and varnished? And it used to have a beauty treatment once a month. Washed and brushed. There was even a special talcum powder among the things the cattery gave us. Did you know that?'

'Oh, for goodness' sake! I need my sleep — do something with it before I drown it in the bath!'

Honey sighed and got out of bed. The cat had made itself comfortable between them, though it wasn't exactly still. It was clawing the bedclothes, supposedly in an attempt to make it more comfortable. It was annoying.

Without bothering to put on her dressing gown, she picked it up and took it out into the living room. The moment she shoved it into the cat carrier it began yowling.

Honey buried her head in her hands and groaned. No matter how much she tried to placate the animal, it just wouldn't stop.

She stared through the wire grating at its bright blue eyes. 'Please,' she pleaded. 'Won't you go to sleep? For me? So all of us can get some sleep?'

She was rewarded with yet another long yowl.

Her head slumped back on her arms. She opened one eye above her clasped hands.

'If you won't do it for me, how about doing it for somebody else?'

* * *

Mary Jane didn't look the slightest surprised to see her.

'I can't get her to sleep — well, not in her carrier. She wants to lie on the bed between me and Steve and Steve is complaining that he can't sleep. Do you think . . . ?'

'Sure. Give her here.'

Mary Jane took the carrier over to the bed and let the cat out. It seemed to immediately realise what was going on. For a moment it stared up at Mary Jane, its eyes big and blue.

'Time to sleep,' said Mary Jane, pointing at it with a finger as long as a magic wand.

The cat curled into a ball, did a bit of clawing of the bedclothes, then settled down.

'Leave it with me,' said Mary Jane. 'I'm good with cats.'

So are witches, thought Honey as she set off back down the stairs.

She paused halfway across the yard to the coach house and shook her head. No. Mary Jane wasn't a witch. Not a real one. Was she?

* * *

Honey's mother came swanning in on Sunday afternoon without her latest husband and looking good in a grey silk suit that had 'expensive' written all over it.

Steve Doherty had gone to his flat to read the riot act to the tenant renting it on account that said tenant was subletting

192

it to two musician friends. Not only was he taking rent from them but their claim to be musicians was disputed by the neighbours. Comments had been made about where one of them could stick his clarinet and that both were tone deaf if their rendering of 'House of the Rising Sun' was anything to go by.

Gloria Cross gestured for her daughter to join her around a low table in the conservatory. She was wearing a secretive look, and her voice was barely above a whisper. 'Did you find it?'

'Yes. We found Gladys's body, if that's what you mean, but then I've already told you that.'

'Not her,' Gloria exclaimed. 'The journal. Did you find the journal?'

'I don't know where it is. The police and fire brigade are still sifting through everything.'

Gloria gasped and sat back in the pale blue tub chair, one hand wafting before her face as though she was in danger of fainting. 'You really need to find it.'

This was given as a direct order. Honey suspected it held secrets about her mother that she'd prefer not disclosed. All the same, it was a tall order to snatch it from under the nose of the police or even to ask them if they had it.

'Mother, I can't just barge in there and have a shufti around. Police, mother. Police and fire brigade have priority.'

She stressed the words 'police' and 'priority' — not that her mother took much notice.

'You have to find it. A lot of reputations will be ruined if you don't.'

'You mean yours?'

Her mother had the effrontery to blush. 'It's nothing that scandalous, but I wouldn't want Claude to know.'

Claude was the name of her mother's latest husband. Sometimes it was hard to keep up, especially since the advent of dating sites for the over sixties. She understood some of the seniors were having a ball — and that included her mother.

What had her mother done that might cause speculation and gossip, stuff she didn't want to go public?

There was no alternative but to ask her. 'Why the urgency, Mother? What is it you're not telling me?'

Drawing in her chin, her mother eyed her as if she'd just slapped her chops. 'My dear girl. You are being presumptuous as though my concern is purely for myself, when all that concerns me is you. Finding it is advantageous to both of us. That man Glendower stole your money with his insurance scam. Has it not occurred to you that she may have noted the goings-on in Norman Glendower's house? You know from what I told you that Gladys didn't miss a thing. She was good at spying on people — not surprising really. She did work for the Ministry of Defence, listening to phone calls and suchlike at that place in Cheltenham.'

'GCHQ? Gladys worked at GCHQ?' Honey was seriously impressed. 'So she was a very good nosy parker.'

'Yes. That's about it,' said her mother, her manicured nails like blood-red dots as she slammed her hands down on her silk-covered thighs. 'I sometimes think that retirement bored her, so she watched everyone else instead. The trouble was she could be quite cruel in her observations. She enjoyed having people wriggle like worms on the end of a fishing line. It amused her.' Her mother grimaced. Elegant as she was, she could scowl with the best of them.

Honey let all this sink in but somehow it all lay a bit heavy. Her mother sympathising so totally with the loss of the boat and the surprising fact that they hadn't been insured when they'd thought they were was one thing and appreciated. However, it was obvious that she had ulterior motives — just what they were, she was keeping to herself.

'This is all very interesting.'

'Yes. I knew you'd think so. Is there any way you can get in there and look round?'

'It's a bit of a mess.'

Honey considered what had been said. One particular word — besides allusions to Gladys's interesting career — stood out.

'You mentioned that Norman Glendower was running an insurance scam. It could be that it was a Lone Ranger operation — no assistant.'

'The Lone Ranger had Tonto.'

Honey wasn't sure having a Native American sidekick was quite the same in the world of insurance scams, but let it slide.

'It's possible he wasn't the only one involved in the scheme.'

'How about other people who've lost their money? Have you spoken to them?'

Honey's brow furrowed in thought. 'Funnily enough, no, or at least no one else has come forward. It seems he only stole from us. I wonder why. It's as though something happened, and that was when he siphoned off our money and nobody else's. What could it be?'

'Do you think Gladys knew what he was up to?'

'Possibly. It seems a bit strange though that he only scammed me and Steve. And we insured the boat just after we bought it and before we set off.'

'And sailed away into the sunset,' her mother said, her lips curling with disgust. 'I always said it was a bad idea to leave what you know behind. You get out of touch with things.'

Gloria Cross often spoke disparagingly of things her daughter did that she didn't approve of. Which was most things. But in this instance, she'd hit on a prevailing truth. She and Steve had bought a boat and declared their intention to sail around the world for a few years. What were the chances of them claiming on their insurance? They would have no idea that their insurance policy document was just a worthless piece of paper. Anyone could create an official-looking document nowadays, and as for the insurance company itself — well, they already knew it didn't exist.

It was indeed a bitter pill to swallow, but her mother had a point.

'Mother, you've hit the nail on the head with a great big mallet! We were sailing away from home shores. People stick around when they've insured their houses or cars. We didn't.'

She held her head in her hands and groaned. 'And that's why nobody else has come forward. Their insurance policies were legit. Norman dared not scam them because he would be easily found out. But us . . .'

'It's still a scam,' her mother responded hotly. 'Or at least in my understanding it is.'

Honey fixed a steely stare on her mother's face. She noticed her flushed cheeks and the fluttering of her eyelids. Something was going on here. It was easily read that she didn't like the fact that Gladys's journal had not been found. Still, she had to give credit where credit was due. Her mother had led her to the reason why she and Steve were the only ones to have lost money. The question was what Norman Glendower had done with it. After all, it wasn't a huge amount, less than two thousand pounds, in fact. So why hadn't he passed it on?

Honey declared her intention to do her utmost to trace the journal.

'I think it would be to both our advantages,' she added.

'I'm glad I was of some help. Just because I'm of mature years, doesn't mean to say I'm completely gaga. At least what I had to say didn't fall on deaf ears as it usually does . . . and talking about deaf ears, what's that ghastly howling sound I can hear?'

'Ah. That's the cat. Norman Glendower's cat. Mary Jane persuaded me to bring it here. We're going to ask Norman's neighbours about its habits. Mary Jane seems to think that it has divided loyalties. What she means by that and what we're likely to learn, I've no idea. But it's worth a try.'

Her mother leaned forward in a conspiratorial fashion and whispered, 'And you can rummage about in Gladys's place while you're at it.'

'Not allowed,' said Honey, shaking her finger. 'The police would have grim words to say if she and I crossed the incident tape. Her house is still a terrible mess.'

'Get her to do her shape-shifting thing. She reckons she can make people think they're seeing a bear or a polecat if she waves her magic wand — or whatever it is she does.'

'I think the residents of Regency Gardens would be more than a bit surprised to see a bear or a polecat in their street. I think anyone in Bath would be, for that matter.'

'Do your best, Hannah.' Her mother's tone was firm, its seriousness emphasised by her using Honey's given name. Her mother was the only one who called her that.

Her mother got to her feet with superb agility for a woman in her mid-seventies. 'I'm off. Tea with friends overlooking Pulteney Bridge beckons.'

'Don't eat too many macaroons. You know they give you wind.'

Her mother made a wordless sound before flouncing off, leaving a trail of Chanel No. 5 behind her.

Once she was out of sight, Honey took the crockery out to the kitchen, where Mariah Ling, their school-age washer-up, transferred them to the dishwasher in double-quick time. Mariah did everything in double-quick time. It was as if she was trying to break some kind of record.

'The sun's shining for the next seven days,' Mary Jane said to her. 'I saw the signs in my new telescope.'

'I look forward to it,' said Honey.

Mary Jane had bought the brass telescope from an antique shop out at Bradford on Avon. Both Honey and Steve had tried telling her that a pair of modern binoculars would do a far better job, but she'd been quite adamant.

'Sir Percival specifically asked for a brass telescope like the sort used by Mr Herschel. He lived in King Street, you know. Sir Percival studied with him and his wife for a time.'

Honey was beginning to lose count of the past occupants of Mary Jane's room and she for one had never clapped eyes on them. Still, if the thought of the ghosts of past relatives living in her room kept Mary Jane happy, then so be it.

Mary Jane was waffling on, unaware or uncaring of what Honey was thinking.

'Your mother's keen on the telescope too. This was before I went on vacation and before you got back from your sailing adventure. That Mrs Faversham was most impressed. She said it was as clear as anything the modern world has to offer.'

Honey had been rubbing her arms, hoping the grey skies would soon turn blue and she would feel warm again. She hadn't felt warm since coming back to England.

Mention of her mother being interested in Mary Jane's telescope suddenly cut through.

'What was that you said?'

'Mrs Faversham praised my telescope.'

'You took it up to her place before you went on holiday?'

The brightly coloured plastic parrot earrings Mary Jane wore jiggled when she nodded.

'That's right. Your mother and I took it up there. To Regency Gardens. Mrs Faversham wanted to borrow it, to see if it was as useful as her security system.'

Honey frowned. 'Why did she want you to do that, and what security system?'

'I only lent it to her. She said it was a fine instrument and would help her calibrate her security system. Damned heavy, it was. I set it up for them, went for a walk and loaded it into the car when they'd finished.'

'So, Mrs Faversham had a security system.' Honey frowned. She hadn't recalled seeing cameras at the property. 'It seems odd to bother with an antique telescope.'

Mary Jane shrugged. 'I thought so too and was in two minds about it, but seeing as it was your mother who asked, I thought, what harm can it do?'

'So it wasn't for studying the heavens, or the earth at their feet,' muttered Honey. 'I'm supposing it was more likely to be used for studying the neighbours.'

Her mother hadn't said a word about taking the telescope up there. She'd also given the distinct impression that she disliked Gladys intensely. Why go to all that trouble?

Honey glided between the dining tables set for this evening though without really concentrating. Much as she tried to prevent it, her thoughts were being dragged back to Regency Gardens, both Norman Glendower and Gladys Faversham.

As for her mother . . .

She stabbed in the familiar number.

'What's this about a telescope?'

'Telescope?'

'Mother, sounding innocent doesn't become you. Has this telescope got some connection with the journal?'

She was convinced she heard a grinding of teeth on the other end of the phone.

'Gladys told me she wanted to study the stars. I suggested she borrowed Mary Jane's telescope before investing in one.'

'And?'

'I had an assignation in Regency Gardens.'

'A lover? Mother, you've got married enough times to know the line about keeping only unto thee and all that "till death do us part" thing. By the sounds of it you're tempting fate, which could be divorce — again — or a deep parting down the centre of your scalp. What were you thinking?'

There was a pause before her mother said, 'I get bored.'

Honey took a deep breath before asking who her tryst had been with. 'You do realise you or this guy you were seeing have made yourselves suspects — at least in the case of Gladys. You had an axe to grind with her. Was she blackmailing you?'

Silence.

'Mother?'

'I have a lover. Arthur. He lives at number four.'

Honey groaned. Her mother and her ilk were worse than the younger generation. Her daughter Lindsey was in her twenties and behaved with more propriety. OK, she was a smartass on historical facts and a whizz with a computer, but she'd never been a serial philanderer. Her mother, however, a great-grandmother in her seventies, was a nightmare. What was happening to the older generation? Was it the fallout from the sixties, still carrying the flame of free love despite the infirmities that come with age? They were carrying on as though the Summer of Love had never ended, hedonists till the end of their days.

'Suddenly I feel old,' muttered Honey as she broke off the connection. The thought that she and Steve seemed quite bland in comparison to her mother's generation was hard to shake off. But she had to. Steve was working on this case, and she had every intention of helping him out.

'Mary Jane, tomorrow we're paying a visit to Regency Gardens.'

'With the cat. I think that's a great idea.'

Honey was about to say she had no intention of taking that yowling monster, but thought better of it.

'I think that's a good idea. Tassel could be an icebreaker. We could go round asking everyone if they would like to adopt her. I particularly want to drop in on Karen Turpin, or Turnip, as Gladys called her.'

'You mean you don't want to adopt her? How come?'

Mary Jane looked shocked beyond belief.

'She makes Steve sneeze. I think he could be allergic. That was why I brought her up to you. You don't mind, do you?'

'Not at all. Sir Cedric reckons she makes the place feel homely and, anyway, she warms my feet. Better than a hot water bottle. Does Steve know we're going to do a bit of sleuthing on our own account?'

'No. He told me to stay away. I got the impression there's something going on that he's not telling me about.'

'Not safe? OK. I'll take a bunch of Indian sage with me. A bit of holy smoke should keep us safe.'

'I'm not sure burning sage in a house that's already been gutted by fire is a good idea.'

'Nonsense. It'll cleanse the air — and make it smell better.'

'Of course. Why didn't I think of that?'

CHAPTER TWENTY

With the digital camera sitting comfortably on its stand, Gabriella Glendower took more photos. Pouting photos. Cleavage-revealing photos. More photos in different scenarios were uploaded. Some had been taken on a location shoot she'd arranged, where a willing boyfriend had taken shots of her in a long white dress, a white bikini, and white butt-skimming shorts that fabulously showed off her long, tanned legs.

She had so many followers that cosmetic and clothing firms were chasing her for endorsements. The money was rolling in — though not as quickly and not in the stellar amounts she would like, but that would soon be rectified. Probate had been given, so she could use the money in her father's bank accounts. There were three — one business account, one domestic and one savings account. He'd had more savings in ISAs and suchlike, though they had gradually diminished. But, hey, she'd needed top designer labels, the best make-up, cosmetic beauty procedures, Gucci handbags, Manolo Blahnik shoes, jewellery that didn't look as though it had come from a charity shop. Everything had been top-drawer. If you were going to be a trendsetter on social media and get the followers and resultant advertising deals, money had to be spent. Her father, who'd always doted on her, had willingly obliged — or at least at first he had. These last couple of years he'd been more reluctant, asked her to rein in her spending. She'd ranted and raged, thrown herself onto the sofa, burst into tears and screamed that he was letting her down. He had to help her. He simply had to. Tears and tantrums had always worked when she'd been a child, and had continued to do so now she was an adult. 'Come on, Dad. Don't be mean,' she had said. 'I started at the bottom in this game. I don't want to go back to that.'

Tristan Sheldon's number suddenly appeared on her phone.

'Darling. How are you?'

'In need of funds. You promised to pay me last week for taking you to Cephalonia.'

'Well, I could hardly afford to pay for everything.'

'You didn't pay for everything. Anyway, I thought you would have been rolling in it by now. You did say you were coming into funds once the probate was sorted. I take it it's come through?'

Her pink lips were plumper than they used to be. Her teeth were whiter than they used to be. She was something different from what she used to be. Both contributed to a winning smile, but she didn't have one for Tristan — not at the moment.

'I'll be selling the house.'

'Is it worth much?'

'Edging close to one million.'

'I don't need a million. Surely he left you some cash. I only want the one thousand you owe me.'

Gabriella grimaced. 'There's not as much in his bank accounts as I thought there was.'

The truth was she'd expected more and was unwilling to splash the funds that were there and leave just a few thousand behind. Yes, she'd have a good deal of money once the house was sold, but that could take time. She explained that to Tristan.

He seemed generally accepting, but then he was yet another man who she could twist around her little finger.

'I'm going to the bank tomorrow to sort through the paperwork.'

'Can't you do it online?'

She laughed. 'Tristan, darling, you're so naive. Not everything can be done over the internet. Leave it with me. I'll transfer what I owe you as soon as the paperwork is in order. All right, darling?'

It was a relief when he agreed. Just for once she was glad he was at a distance, still in London, kicking his heels, waiting for a call from her. Like a fish on a hook, she thought to herself. She had plans for that money. For a start she was considering hiring a professional photographer to help her become the online influencer she wanted to be. Top of the tree. She couldn't tell Tristan that, of course. He was madly in love with her. That's how come she'd managed to get him to pay for the trip — and dragged him around the island to beauty spots taking photographs that would make her look good. Making love in isolated places and letting him take a few more 'personal' photos she'd thought would suffice as payment. She knew damn well he was flogging them online, just as he knew she hadn't always been wearing fashion accessories on the videos she'd made.

Obviously, she'd been wrong. *But that money was my father's*, she told herself. *And he would have wanted me to have it. Of course he would.*

* * *

Steve Doherty had requested the deceased Norman Glendower's bank statements. Nobody had been that interested in getting them. After all, the account holder was dead and the only people who had queried whether his business dealings were honest were Steve and Honey. That was until the Metropolitan Police had come in on the act and sent on some information that shed an entirely different light on things.

Somebody placed a coffee on Steve's desk although he didn't recall asking for one. He took a sip or two before becoming engrossed in Norman Glendower's bank statements, especially his business account.

The insurance policies were paid for by direct debits through the broker to the insurers — the latter usually underwritten by Lloyd's of London. Steve had also been provided with a manifesto of payments to various insurance companies. All seemed to be in order. All were traceable. Except for the monthly direct debits to insure the good ship *SY Footloose*. The payments from Honey and Steve went in but didn't go out to the insurers. The premium was paid 'on the nail', as per the saying handed down from the eighteenth century from merchants paying for their corn on the nails in Corn Street Bristol. They went no further than Norman's own pocket. It wasn't huge as payments go — one hundred and twenty pounds per month — but the insurance being paid for was for all eventualities, including public liability. If anyone had come aboard *Footloose* and taken a tumble — or drowned — then a payout would have been due. It would have been down to the insurers to cover the millions that would have cost. Unfortunately, that wasn't the case. No premium paid, no payout.

Steve stared. It was blatant fraud, though not on such a big scale as the scam insuring 'valuables', some of which did not exist or had been flogged by the insured owners but not admitted to. Sell the stuff, claim on the insurance and, hey presto, double the profit. That's what the Met had told him and Norman had been complicit, the middle man who'd handled all the paperwork.

What had tempted Norman Glendower, insurance broker with a good track record? It seemed to him he wasn't one for spending on flash cars or antique furniture — that's if the aged Renault and the lack of fancy furnishings inside the house in Regency Gardens was anything to go by. If he hadn't been materialistic, where was the money going? For whose benefit?

He frowned at the domestic account. Norman's spending had been frugal.

'I printed these off for you.'

A young man in a crumpled shirt, tie slightly askew, offered him a batch of papers. Steve tried to remember his name before thanking him.

'Ah. Tony. Thank you.'

'Terry,' said the young man. 'But never mind. They both begin with T.'

Steve apologised and added, 'Are these the same as the ones I'm seeing here on the screen?'

'No. These are from savings accounts up to about two years ago. There were quite substantial sums in them until then. I've checked through the paperwork, but there's still a bit to do. The bank accounts themselves are closed now.'

Steve nodded thoughtfully as he began shuffling through the pile of bank statements.

Two years ago was when he and Honey had set sail. Two years ago, Norman's savings accounts had money in them, but the substantial amounts had gradually diminished, large amounts taken out and nothing going in.

In Steve's experience he was looking at a man who'd become a gambler, a man who'd needed money and got in with the wrong sort.

The Metropolitan Police had filled him in on what they thought had occurred. 'We think he'd already stopped doing straightforward brokerage when you ran into him.'

'But why bother to insure me at all?'

'Number one, he knew you would be living off-grid, sailing around and not being easily traceable. Number two, he didn't want to arouse your suspicions and say that he couldn't insure you. Something else was going on insurance wise, though not in the same manner as you — as far as we can tell, that is.'

The boys of the London Met had also informed him they'd got a few stolen items back, though not all. 'There were big-value items — really big, that we've yet to trace. I'll keep you informed of developments.'

Stolen money was quite often used to feed bad habits, perfectly ordinary people who had suddenly been caught in a downward spiral. Gambling was the prime reason. It was getting harder and harder to control the big-bucks industry because so much of it was now online.

Hopefully there might be a few local leads on the gambling front. He couldn't be sure until he'd had a rummage around. Now, where to begin? He decided on the Pink Elephant Club, a casino tucked away in a series of cellars fronting the river. In the distant past they'd been used as stabling for horses. Nowadays they were frequented by those who fancied their chances, few of whom regarded themselves as mugs but if they'd been more honest with themselves would have realised they were sheep ready to be shorn.

There was no entrance fee to the Pink Elephant. The management hoped to cover that from the punters' losses.

The place smelled like money. The sound of the ball rattling around the roulette wheel negated any musical accompaniment. That rattle was music to a gambler's ears, though not as much as it was to the casino. The house always won. It was geared that way.

Steve narrowed his eyes so he could better take in the clientele. There were the usual high rollers, the handsome men in smart suits, crisp white shirt collars accentuating their Costa Brava suntans. There were also the women, of course, some who were seasoned gamblers in their own right and others who were merely arm candy, pretty little things hanging onto men old enough to be their fathers — or grandfathers.

Fools and their money are soon parted. For this reason, those with vast amounts to spend were shadowed by those who were skilled at taking it off them. Gamblers and criminals; it was a well-seasoned combination.

Steve kept his eyes peeled for old acquaintances — grasses — who would sell their grandmother for a ton. Eventually his search alighted on a face he knew.

Charlie Brent, who preferred to be called Charles, was a classy-looking gent in his mid-forties. He told everyone that he was ex-army — SAS, no less — and sometimes called himself 'Major'. On a good day he promoted himself to Colonel.

One moved slowly through the crowds in a casino, sliding through without disturbing the stance or nerves of those sitting behind a pile of gambling chips.

'Colonel Brent. Long time, no see.'

Charlie didn't acknowledge him. He didn't even attempt to turn away from the action happening in front of his eyes.

'Doherty, I heard you were back.' He turned then and looked him up and down. 'Still that same old leather jacket and black gear? You could have made the effort, old boy, and put on a suit.'

'I'm on duty, so compelled to wear my uniform.'

Charlie's stance was unchanged. 'I heard you almost drowned at sea.'

'Almost. My urge to come back and see you helped me survive.'

'Me? What would you want with me?'

Steve leaned in closer. 'You keep your finger on the pulse in Bath, Charlie. You know where the rats are in the sewer.'

'Do I, indeed?' His voice was casual, totally unfazed.

Steve rifled in his pocket and found a fifty-pound note, which he slipped into Charlie's pocket. 'Fifty for a snippet about Norman Glendower. So-called insurance broker.'

He sensed Charlie's silky demeanour slipped a bit. 'Glendower?'

'Been to London lately, Charlie?'

To his great surprise, he felt the fifty-pound note being slipped back into his own pocket.

'I don't want nothing to do with that.' Charlie's voice sounded very final.

'Norman divided his time between here and London, so I hear.'

Charlie's lack of response told him quite a bit. Although the money had been refused, Steve decided to push a little. He would use the information from the Met to prise Charlie's trap open.

'I hear he was doing a bit of insurance business in London.' He slipped the note back into Charlie's pocket. 'Is that right?'

No response.

Steve tried again. 'Come on, Charlie. Give me something. Just for old times' sake.'

This time the fifty-pound note stayed put.

'I don't know anything in great detail, but one thing I do know is that you don't go messing about with the outfit he got himself involved with.'

'And he did mess them about?'

'You could say that.'

'Have you got a name?'

Charlie fingered his coat pocket as he thought about it.

Steve eyed him with interest. Charlie was a smooth-looking man who could have rivalled James Bond in looks. Obviously, his career hadn't gone in that direction.

'Standish. South London. Not a man you would like to cross.'

Steve thought quickly. How exactly had Norman messed them about? He took a wild guess.

'Not all the valuables got back to their owners — all of whom were part of the cartel. And they want whatever it is back. Is that about right, Charlie?'

Charlie said nothing but picked up his pile of plastic gambling chips and departed.

'What valuables?' he wanted to shout, but he knew Charlie was finished. Now it was down to his own deduction. He'd been told that the place had been done over and Norman had been lying in the middle of it, his head caved in.

Someone had searched the place before bludgeoning Norman over the head.

'Awoken in the middle of the night. A bit woozy perhaps. Not fully taking on board that they meant business. Not answering the questions that were asked.'

So, what was it they'd been looking for?

The next morning, he got the list of items the insurance company were suspicious about.

The police had almost broken the puzzle they'd been landed with, so the insurance company was holding out before making payment.

In front of him was a long list of valuables — no cash, just antiques, paintings and jewellery. The most expensive item of all was a bag containing eight rose-cut diamonds.

He was perusing a photograph of the missing gems when Honey phoned.

He groaned in response to the yowling in the background. 'Does that moggy never shut up?'

Honey's voice broke through the caterwauling. 'She's far from being a moggy. Quite a queen, in fact. I'd wear her collar on a night out. Velvet and scattered with sparkling stones. I've always liked chokers. A bit sixties, but all the same . . .'

CHAPTER TWENTY-ONE

Tassel the cat yowled like an air raid siren from within her carrying basket, which Mary Jane had plonked on the back seat of the Caddy.

Honey's idea was that the cat could act as a calling card, a catalyst that might encourage people to talk about her and in some kind of magical way get them admitting things they might not admit to otherwise. OK, it was far-fetched, but she expressed the plan to Mary Jane and waited gamely for a response.

Mary Jane's face lit up like a candle all of a sudden, bright and full of good cheer. 'Brilliant! Cats are clever creatures. They have a sixth sense, you know.'

'Of course they do.' Not so to Honey's mind, but it didn't hurt to give encouragement.

Mary Jane's eyes sparkled. 'Tell you what, we'll take the collar with us separate to the cat. It might jog someone's memory a bit better.'

She was unusually enthusiastic, and Honey had no intention of daunting her staunch ally. 'Let's hope it works.'

Mary Jane's eyes were round and big as golf balls. 'Honey,' she said, pinning her with the kind of look given by a schoolteacher to a pupil who was not paying attention.

'There's a reason a witch kept a cat. You can read people through cats. They respond to unseen forces. They react to different people in different ways. Mark my words, Tassel will do her job. In fact, I had a word with her before putting her in the carrier. She wasn't keen, you see.'

'I gathered that from the scratches on your hand.'

'It was just a temporary misunderstanding. She knows what we're about.'

'So I hear,' said Honey. 'And no doubt she'll be howling like a banshee all the way to Regency Gardens.'

'It's just her way,' replied Mary Jane. She jammed her foot on the gas, Honey's head jolted on her neck and away they went.

Traffic swerved in all directions.

'Damn,' snarled Mary Jane, no longer in Regency mode. 'I was thinking I was still in San Diego.'

Honey hung onto the seat belt. 'What's happened to Lady Caroline Lamb?' Her voice trembled. Her knuckles turned white.

'She married Lord Melbourne.'

What that had to do with anything, Honey hadn't a clue. But she did know that Mary Jane's responsible driving was no more. All she wanted was to get where they were going, get the answer to some questions and get back alive.

* * *

Gabriella Glendower's face glowed with the light from the computer screen. She'd finished posting fresh pictures of herself doing things that internet influencers do, such as striding across the road, a top-of-the-range handbag hanging from her arm, coquettish bending of her head to show off her bladed eyebrows and newly plumped lips. She looked good. Eat your heart out, Victoria Beckham!

An online magazine had asked her to write a feature on the best beauty treatment spas in the country. Her first task was to contact each spa, explain what she was doing and ask for a free two-day break. There were ten on her list and if half of them agreed to a free break in exchange for a glowing report on the website, then — hey presto — result!

Pleasure followed, the pleasure of searching out beach holidays in luxury locations, preferably within a short distance of upmarket marinas where she could wangle an invitation onto a millionaire's — or, preferably, billionaire's — superyacht. The sky was the limit now she had a bit of money behind her, or would do once she'd sold the house. The amount of cash her father had left was disappointing, but the money from the house would be fair compensation.

The downside was the stipulation in his will that she should take care of Tassel.

'I bought her for you,' he'd told her when the cat was just a fluffy bundle and quite cute. But that was years ago when her life had not been so demanding as it was now. She was no longer obsessed with fluffy pussycats. Her only obsession was with herself.

The ringing of the front doorbell brought forth a far-from-elegant expletive until she reminded herself that although it was early days, it could be the estate agent.

'Bloody Warren,' she muttered. It was up to the security guard to inform her that she had a visitor. Too much of the hard stuff was muddling his brain, she thought grimly. Still, she thought, shutting down the laptop, he had his uses.

On the way to the front door, she fluffed up a couple of cushions and looked around the plainly decorated room, a businesslike expression planted firmly on her face.

Nylon eyelashes fluttered as she regarded the two women standing there. One she recognised as the woman accompanying the policeman who'd asked her annoying questions. The other was tall and skinny. The clothes she wore would have looked good on a scarecrow.

'Miss Glendower. We've brought your cat.'

Honey was instantly aware that her cheery smile cut no ice with the cool beauty standing in front of her. *My goodness,* she thought. *She looks like she's about to go clubbing. At this time of day?*

The expertly made-up eyebrows twitched along with one corner of her mouth. 'I could do without that.'

'The poor creature's missing her home comforts,' Mary Jane added helpfully. 'Would you like her back?'

The perfectly made-up face seemed to crack. 'I can't do that.'

Honey raised surprised eyebrows. 'Oh, really? I hear it's a term of the will that you take care of Tassel for the rest of her days. Is that so? Can we come in?'

With reluctance, Gabriella invited them over the doorstep. Once inside, she turned to face them, arms folded defensively in front of her. 'How do you know that? About the cat?'

Honey shrugged. 'The police have a copy and I'm being kept in the loop.'

It wasn't true. Honey had guessed that Gabriella was not the sort to share either her home or her lifestyle with a four-legged furry friend. She'd counted on it unnerving her — and it had.

Judging by the look on Gabriella's face, the cat's return was about as unwelcome as an overflowing litter tray on the dining table. She couldn't help feeling that Tassel's days might be numbered if that hard-eyed look was anything to go by.

Gabriella paced the room, fingernails tripping around her lips, the desire to bite them fed by her anxious predicament. 'I'll have to make arrangements.'

Honey peered up at her. 'Whether to find it another home or . . .'

Gabriella shrugged. 'Whatever is necessary.'

'But if the cat belonged to your father and it was a term of his will, you could get into a difficult position.'

'I'll take legal advice. I'm sure my father would have made arrangements if I had difficulty adhering to what he wanted. There are extenuating circumstances. I can't alter my lifestyle for the sake of a cat.'

If Gabriella were a cat she would be spitting by now, thought Honey.

'Did the cat originally belong to you or your father?'

'Me.' The single word was full of exasperation. 'My father bought her for me. I was only about thirteen at the time. I wanted a cat. I wanted a Bengal cat because it reminded me of a tiger. I had a favourite book about a tiger.'

Honey had to admit that the domesticated Bengal did have the looks of a small tiger. 'They're quite expensive.'

'I know that. My dad knew that too, but he'd do anything for me. It was his way of making up for the loss of my mother. He tried to be both mother and father to me. Daft as a brush and as soft as butter, that was my dad,' she said with a smug smile. 'Whatever I wanted, he went out of his way to get for me.'

'Lucky you that your father doted on you.'

'Yes, he did.' She tossed her head as though being spoiled was her right.

'I take it he also bought that smart car outside?'

'Yes. It was what I wanted.'

'Your father's car's not so posh, is it?'

'My father wasn't too fussed about material things. So long as I was happy, that was all that mattered.'

The wailing from the cat carrier reminded Honey that she was not alone.

'So, what do I do with Tassel?'

Hopes of persuading Gabriella to keep the cat were instantly dashed.

'Look, that cat was always a wanderer. Stalked through everyone's gardens. She made a nuisance of herself everywhere. She even tipped over a birdcage placed outside to air and ate the budgie inside.'

'You wouldn't want to turn her out now, would you? She might starve.'

Assuming the exploit with the budgie was true, starving wasn't likely.

Gabriella was adamant. 'She'll have to go back in the cattery for a few weeks or so. I'm going away on holiday, you see — what with everything that's happened. I'll decide what to do with her when I get back.'

There was a jerkiness to the resultant smile. Honey thought it insincere. She sought to exchange a look of mutual understanding with Mary Jane, but her look wasn't met.

Mary Jane didn't seem to be concentrating. Her ghostly grey eyes were darting around the room like damsel-flies, hovering in some places and flitting in others.

Honey carried on. 'That's a shame. She makes a lot of noise when she's lonely. I don't think she likes the cattery that much.'

Gabriella shrugged. 'It can't be helped. I have a career to think about without being burdened with an animal.'

'Did you know anything about your father's insurance business?'

'Nothing. He tried to get me interested but, quite frankly, it's too dry for me.'

'But surely you benefited from that "dry" income, as you put it.'

She threw Honey an accusing look. 'I wasn't entirely dependent on him. I do make my own money, you know.'

'As an influencer.'

'Of course.'

'There are a lot of people trying to break through on that particular scene. The market must be getting crowded.'

Was it her imagination, or was Gabriella's complexion turning from sun-kissed bronze to pink?

'I hold my own. I'm doing quite well, in fact. I've got the looks. You have to have the looks.'

The look she threw Honey was full of contempt, as though nobody of her age or looks was ever likely to make it in the plastic world of selfies, reels and trivial information on make-up, clothes and cosmetic surgery.

'Well, that's another career closed to me,' said Honey nodding her head in such a way that Gabriella couldn't read her thoughts — which were disparaging. Instead, she carried on pleasantly, 'I fully understand that a girl's looks have to be at the centre of everything. You're quite right insinuating that I wouldn't get to first base. Done some modelling jobs too, have you?'

'I have. It can be very well paid.'

'And how many followers do you have on social media?'

Her face glowed with pride, chin high, hands languorously posed on her silky brown knees. 'I have close to half a million followers.'

'But a long way to go before it really hits the big time,' said Mary Jane.

Honey looked at Mary Jane in surprise. Since when had she taken an interest in social media, not to mention the internet in general?

'I applied myself to the subject while you were away sailing the seven seas,' Mary Jane said in response to that look. 'I missed you. Had to find something to occupy my time.'

Honey's mouth dropped open. 'Hardly seven.' She reined in the vision of a blue sea and matching sky so she could properly phrase the next question. 'Has being an influencer had much of an effect on your social life?'

A disconcerting frown creased Gabriella's smooth brow. 'I fit it in when I can. I'm in demand. That's why I cannot be lumbered with a cat or any other dependent creature.'

'Including men?' Honey smiled disarmingly, feeling that an injection of humour was needed.

Gabriella's expression lightened. 'They can be burdensome.'

'You don't have a boyfriend at present?'

'I'm busy.' Gabriella's face clouded over again.

For her part, Gabriella didn't mention Tristan because she didn't regard him as a boyfriend. He was just somebody she could make use of, but she was fed up with the questions. With an air of finality, she picked up her mobile phone. 'I'm sorry, I must ask you to leave. I have a Zoom meeting to attend.'

'What would you like us to do about the cat?' asked Mary Jane. 'At least in the interim.'

'Take her back to the cattery for now. I'll foot the bill. Dad made provision so I wouldn't have to worry about a thing. Find your own way out.'

Parting was abrupt and certainly not deep sorrow.

'Did you see a tear trickling down that dolly-girl face?'

'No.'

'Neither did I. It strikes me she's hardly the grieving daughter. I get the impression she wants to get her hands on the money asap.'

'That make-up is a bit on the heavy side — even for a top-ranked internet cowgirl.'

'Cowgirl? What do you mean?'

Mary Jane's thin eyebrows were like two sharp needles above her deep-set eyes. 'I felt something more. That girl is riding two broncos.'

'She's the centre of her own little world, if that's what you mean.'

'She's that too and I get the impression that her father led a lonely life.' Mary Jane frowned. 'I've never been in such a cold house.'

'Is it haunted?'

Mary Jane was good at picking up atmospheres. New or old, any house could be haunted by its past.

'No. Just cold. No pictures on the wall. No things that make a place a home.'

'Perhaps he was just a skinflint and didn't like ornamentation.'

Mary Jane shook her head. 'It used to have nice things. I could see the traces of them here and there. Feel them too. It strikes me that things excess to requirements are gone.'

'Sold off?'

'Possibly. All I know is that the Glendower house has a chilly atmosphere. It has no warmth, nothing to make it a home.'

'And what did you mean about her riding two broncos? She doesn't have a horse, does she?' Honey laughed.

Mary Jane didn't. Her frown deepened. 'It takes money to make yourself a social media influencer. Top-of-the-range merchandise can only come with success. It costs money up until then. Influencers must spend their own money to be noticed. I don't think she made that much from it. Fashion houses only give to those who don't need — famous people, celebrities who are household names, or at least internet names — which makes me think she's making money by some other means.'

Mary Jane had triggered interesting thoughts.

'She admitted that being an influencer was her career choice. But how can she do that if she has no income? I can't believe it's that good. There are thousands out there like her. Then again, there are rumours of how she got her money.'

'Certainly, if she's got no other profession, then Daddy provided?'

'Hmm. That's what I was thinking. She admitted that he doted on her.'

'Perhaps giving her his last cent?'

'His last farthing even.' Honey took a big and thoughtful sigh. 'And clients' money too — or at least mine and Steve's money. I think I need another look at Mr Glendower's bank statements.'

'Elementary, Mrs Driver.'

'Quite so, Professor.'

'Where do we start?'

'Here.' Honey came to a halt outside the house on the opposite side of the road to Norman's. There was a nondescript car in the drive and a child's bicycle propped against the front wall. Karen Turpin was first stop — and right at the top of Honey's list.

A yowl of protest came from within the cat carrier. 'Right,' said Honey. 'Let's see if this noisy cat jogs anyone's memory.'

Karen's cheeks were pink, her hair unruly and her clothes had the faded look of items washed and dried many times over the years.

'Yes?' She looked surprised to see them, nervous even.

Almost as if she recognised the voice, Tassel let out an extraordinary yowl.

'Hi, Karen — Honey Driver, we met at the Green River Hotel? I'm a police liaison officer. I've collected this cat from the cattery where it was placed by the police. I'm now trying to work out its last movements in the time before Mr Glendower's body was found.'

'The cat's movements?'

'That's right,' interrupted Mary Jane.

'I understand it used to wander.'

Karen looked a bit nonplussed.

Mary Jane stepped in. 'The poor creature's a bit disturbed by all that happened. I'm Mary Jane, a practising professor of the paranormal and this cat is one of my patients. Tell you what, I'll put its collar on in case it jogs your memory that much better.'

She pulled a wailing Tassel out of the wicker cage and put the sparkly collar back round her neck.

Honey jumped in before Mary Jane's discourse got even more incredible. 'You live here with your family?'

'My children — and my husband. He's away working.' She said it in a defensive manner, offering the information although they hadn't asked her about him.

It began to rain. Honey felt the first raindrops trickling down inside her collar. 'Can we come in?'

A pensive-looking Karen Turpin stepped back to let them enter.

The living room typified a family residence. Family photos and kids' paintings of what were loosely recognisable as animals, trees, a house and what looked like Mum and Dad were on the walls. A pile of books sat on the coffee table. So did half a bottle of white wine and a nearly empty glass.

'The cat,' said Honey. 'Am I right in saying that it was you who noticed it was starving and called the police?'

She nodded. 'Yes. Poor thing. It was making such a racket but shut up when I gave it some fish fingers my children had left on their plates. Once I did that it kept coming back for more.'

'How well did you know Mr Glendower?'

She flushed slightly. 'Only as a neighbour. He was older than us. My husband and I, that is. We didn't have much in common.'

'Did you see him on the day he died?'

'No.'

'And you didn't hear anything that night that might have made you think there was an intruder?'

'Nothing.'

Tassel continued to yowl.

'Did you have anything to do with Gladys Faversham?'

Another shake of her head. 'No. She was even older than Mr Glendower.'

'What about the daughter, Mr Glendower's daughter, Gabriella? Did you have anything to do with her?'

'Years ago, I did. We went to the same school.'

Honey's eyebrows rose. 'Did you indeed? Was she a friend?'

Karen shook her head and gave a slightly strangled laugh. 'Gabriella loved being the centre of attention but only mixed with girls she thought worthy of her. I wasn't one of them.'

'Lots of boyfriends?'

'Yes. Girlfriends too, until they realised what a cow she was.'

'Would it be truthful to say that her father doted on her?'

'And then some!' Again, that mocking laugh. 'I remember seeing her hit him once. The poor man.'

'Really? Why was that?'

'It was something about him refusing to take her to London with him because it was to do with business. I heard him say that he'd shower her with diamonds when he got back. It seemed laughable, but he really seemed to mean it.'

'Did anyone else overhear this?'

Karen tilted her head to one side as she considered the question. 'Mrs Faversham might have. She used to walk aimlessly around the place. I think she was bored with being retired.'

'Hmm,' said Honey. 'Did you know that Mrs Faversham kept a record of everything that happened in the street? That she gave her neighbours nicknames and noted their private lives?'

Karen's eyes widened when she shook her head. 'No.'

There was little else they could ask so they thanked her for her help and left. Honey was disappointed.

'Your impressions?' Honey asked Mary Jane as they sat in the car considering what to do next.

'She was at the Green River tea party with her children but not her husband and there's no smell of man in the house — only her and the children. I'm guessing he's not away working. I'm guessing he's left for good.'

* * *

Karen tipped the last of the wine into her glass. A rumbling of footsteps preceded the appearance of her two children above the banister on the landing. It was daytime but she'd sent them to bed because she was feeling down.

'Can we come down now, Mum?'

Her son's voice was plaintive. Her daughter's voice followed. Neither cut any ice.

'Get out of the house. Go out to play.'

They didn't wait for a second but hurtled down the stairs and out of the door.

Her thoughts were still on her husband. 'Is there another woman?' That's what she'd shouted at him. Until everything had come out — the lies, the company he kept, the news that he'd been arrested and thrown in prison.

Jealousy, and even their rows, helped her cope. It was better to believe he was having an affair rather than being in prison. It was just too embarrassing. That wicked old cow, Gladys, had turned the knife once too often.

The look in her visitors' eyes had made her nervous — especially the tall, angular one who had professed skill in the paranormal. Was it possible she could read her mind? The very thought of it made her tremble.

Angry beyond belief, she'd gone in there to get that journal early in the morning. The door had been unlocked. Gladys relied too much on her security system. Just out of bed, making tea and starting the day, she hadn't been as alert as she usually was. But then, that was only to be expected. She was getting on in years, more vulnerable than she'd thought.

Visions of her husband and arguments kept getting jumbled up with Karen's memories of that day.

'What if there is?' he'd shouted at her.

'What's sauce for the goose is sauce for the gander,' she'd screamed.

It had seemed that she'd overstepped the mark. 'You wouldn't dare.'

But she had. She still wasn't sure whether it had been love or sheer lust. All she'd known was that she'd craved affection, the deep urge to be wanted — by anyone. She hadn't really cared who knew, until Gladys Faversham had whispered, 'I know what you've done.'

'So what,' she'd shouted. 'So bloody what?'

'I've written it all down. I keep a journal.'

She did indeed.

Karen stared at the drawer of the coffee table. She still wasn't sure what she was supposed to do with the journal. Her husband had called from Wormwood Scrubs and told her to get hold of it by hook or by crook. Panic stricken, she'd suggested burning it.

'Listen, you silly bitch. Do as I say.'

She'd been given a time. Someone from London would be collecting it. That's what he said.

She'd been on tenterhooks waiting for her two visitors to go. She hadn't wanted any awkward questions. She didn't like questions of any sort. However, at least she'd had enough time to tear out the references to her playing the field while her husband was inside. There'd be hell to pay if he ever found out.

She sat there waiting with the journal on her lap, ready to jump up the moment the doorbell rang.

* * *

Still sitting outside in the car, Honey and Mary Jane were undecided as to what to do next.

Gladys's place? Honey was just wondering where the idea had come from, when Steve phoned.

'Forensics have just confirmed that it was being hit over the head with the funeral urn that killed Gladys. Her sister-in-law identified it as the one containing her husband's ashes.'

Honey pulled a face. 'Both cremated and together for all eternity.'

Two children ran out across the back of the car just as a Mercedes E-Class pulled in behind them and two people got out.

Honey passed the information on to Steve. 'I recognise her. It's the woman who owns Pampered Pooches. I saw her photo there. As for the other, let's put it this way, a Mercedes does not a gentleman make.'

'He's the devil not disguised,' proclaimed Mary Jane, her eyes bulging, something that tended to happen when immersed in vibes nobody else was aware of.

Steve's response was immediate. 'I'm on my way with backup. Hold tight.'

The other person was a bulky man she did not know, his fine clothes ruined by the brutish look on his face. At first, she thought he was wearing a collection of gold rings on his fingers, but then realised it was knuckledusters.

'We've got visitors,' she whispered to Mary Jane. 'Dangerous visitors.'

A high-pitched yowl sounded from the cat carrier on the back seat. Resplendent but unimpressed by her sparkly collar, Tassel was expressing very vocal protests that she was not being allowed to wander out and about.

'Where are they going?' asked Mary Jane, her eyes engaged and her voice as soft as butter.

'Into Karen Turpin's house.'

'Who are they?'

'I don't know who the man is, but I recognise the woman.' She sucked in her breath. She remembered the photograph of the blonde woman and matching dog at Pampered Pooches. Mrs Hildegard Hunter.

* * *

Karen was incredibly scared. The man and the woman towered over her.

'I've got it here,' she said, her voice trembling, her arms folded around the journal she'd taken from the house of Gladys Faversham.

Her arms shook as she held it out to them.

Hildegard frowned at her. 'So what's in here?'

'Everything she wrote down.'

'What sort of things?'

Karen shrugged. 'People's secrets and things that interested her.'

Hildegard passed the journal to her male companion, who had not said a single word.

'I did take a look. She gave people nicknames. She called Mr Glendower "Mr Slippery".'

The man and woman exchanged looks of mutual interest. The man began to flip through. The woman sat down on a chair, one leg crossed over the other. She was wearing jeans and trainers, but all the same she looked well groomed. White blouse. Yellow sweater.

The man had a bullish face, the sort that looked as though it wouldn't feel a thing if you dared land a punch on its hard, unforgiving expression. He pointed at a page in the journal.

Gilt-ringed knuckles caught the light as he passed it to the woman.

The woman looked at the page and gasped. 'Well. Now we know.' She raised her eyes and looked directly at Karen. 'Where's the cat?'

'The cat?'

'Yes. The cat. The one that belonged to Norman Glendower.'

Karen's jaw dropped. This wasn't at all what she'd been expecting. 'They've just left.' Her voice wobbled slightly.

'They?'

She nodded. 'Only just.'

The man and woman exchanged looks of sheer panic. 'What colour car did they have?'

'Um.' Karen tried to think. 'A yellow one. I don't know what model.'

She didn't need to know. The two of them were up and out of the room in a flash. Halfway down the garden path, they met Honey and Mary Jane coming the other way.

Before she had a chance to say anything, the man grabbed Honey by the throat.

'Where's the cat?'

'Gone.'

His eyes almost burst from his head. It took a few seconds before he regained the impetus of his action and the strength of his grip.

'You let the cat go?'

She nodded. 'Why not? It's a cat and she hated being in that cage. Wouldn't you feel the same?'

'Search her,' he said suddenly, deflecting Honey's attention from worrying about the cat.

Hildegard Hunter looked confused. 'What? Why?'

'The collar. She might have let the cat go but could still have the collar.'

'The cat's wearing her collar,' Honey managed to exclaim even though he was holding her throat rather tightly. 'It's just a cat collar.'

Even as she said it, she knew that the stones in the collar were not diamanté. They were the real McCoy. They were diamonds.

She suddenly realised that they were not alone. A man wearing black had wandered down the road whistling as though he hadn't a care in the world. Warren Hart, the security guard, walked behind him, looking a bit scared but resolute.

It was odd also to see people spilling out of the houses, though Honey couldn't quite understand the reason why — until Mary Jane laughed and pointed.

Tassel was running through the front gardens, up and down garden paths from the fronts of the houses to the backs, yowling for all she was worth.

Steve had seen the mugshot of the guy standing in front of him.

'Let her go, Standish. Now.'

The big man, who had driven all the way from London to regain what he thought was his, gave Honey a little push when he let her go.

'I haven't done anything.' Hildegard Hunter tried to make herself small, a totally useless enterprise. 'It was him.' She pointed.

'I didn't do anything!' The man looked flabbergasted. 'I just came to give the cat a home.'

Honey frowned. 'How did you know where the diamonds were? Blast,' she said, suddenly slapping her forehead. 'You run a dog grooming parlour, so you obviously know the owners of the cattery. They mentioned the cat's collar, I take it.'

'You can't prove anything,' shouted Hildegard, her colour rising.

'So how do you two know each other?' Honey's curiosity was well and truly roused.

Standish stood glowering, hands in pockets. He was the archetypal London gangster, a bruiser from south of the river. Bullish, sparse sandy hair carefully combed over his scalp.

Almost the same colour, thought Honey, as Hildegard. The penny dropped.

'Oh! I see. You came down here to visit your sister? Blood thicker than water and all that.'

'Sister?'

Standish and Hildegard exchanged tight-faced looks, and clamped their mouths tightly to prevent any more disclosures creeping out.

Nobody denied anything.

'I doubt this visit had anything to do with brotherly love. More likely the diamonds,' said Steve, unable to keep the smile from his face.

'Unless you're going to arrest me,' continued the man identified as Standish, 'I'll be going, thank you.'

'Oh, I'm going to arrest you, all right. Disturbing the peace should do for starters — this is a respectable neighbourhood, Standish! After that you can tell me about how many of the owners of the insured valuables were in on the scam. Blow the jewellery, just give us the money! Nice little earner in anyone's language!'

* * *

Relaxing at each end of a shared bathtub, Honey sipped champagne as Steve outlined the insurance scam that Glendower had been running.

'And our insurance money?'

'Gone for ever. Glendower was so blinded with the big money from the scams he was involved in that he simply forgot to pass our premiums on — at first, and then he couldn't stop gambling. Gabriella was the cause of that. She'd been spoiled all her life and expected to have everything she wanted. It seems that she spent the bulk of his money, both legal and ill-gotten gains. It was a downhill spiral he couldn't get out of. Once upon a time he was an honest broker, but his daughter's demands had him selling everything he owned and, once that was gone, he turned to crime. Gamekeeper turned poacher, you could say. By the way,' he said as a sudden thought came to him. 'Are you sure that cat will be fine living with Mary Jane?'

'Absolutely.' Her expression turned mischievous. 'Every witch should have a familiar — and it's almost always a cat.'

CHAPTER TWENTY-TWO

The outcome had been good. The culprits were apprehended
— Standish and Hildegard Hunter for the death of Norman
Glendower, Karen for the killing of Gladys Faversham.

Steve was well pleased. Honey had somewhat relaxed.

'Well, that's that, then. The money's gone, along with
your beloved *Footloose*.'

There. She'd said it. The truth had been spoken out
into the world.

She felt Steve's searching look but declined to meet his
eyes. Her thoughts were an odd mixture of relief and excitement. There was no moving on until she'd heard what he had
to say. Put the ball in his court. Wait for him to take a swing,
to express his innermost thoughts.

'You said *your* beloved *Footloose*. Not ours.'

'Well. It was ours but let's face it, you loved her much
more than I did. She was your dream. I was just a passenger.
Sorry,' she added, glancing at his expression and wishing the
ground could swallow her up. She hated confrontation, hated
not fully agreeing with him, but in the circumstances . . .

'Don't you think I didn't know that? I've told everyone
it was a sabbatical. Although I entertained living the life for

a time yet, circumstances — fate, as Mary Jane would say — intervened.'

'It certainly did. The container was there, and we hit it. Gone was the carefree life.' Honey sighed. 'It looks like it's gone for ever — thanks to Norman Glendower.'

She caught Steve pursing his lips, a sure sign that he was thinking deeply. A slight shiver ran down her back. Was he considering buying another boat? They didn't have the money. His flat was mortgaged and rented out to cover the monthly clawback. The only other means of financing another sailing venture was to sell the Green River Hotel and, somehow, she just couldn't do that. Especially now that Lindsey had been in touch and given her the news that she was expecting another baby and was coming home.

That was it. This was the time to tell him of feeling broody — not as a mother but as a grandmother. She'd hardly had a chance to hold Minnie, Lindsey's little one, in her arms before they'd sailed away. It had been hard to let go. She'd been torn between her family and Steve. She loved them all.

Then there was Mary Jane and all the other characters who had made their homes in the city of Bath and couldn't see themselves living in any other part of the world. She bit her bottom lip as she remembered how much she'd missed them. Steve might think her mad if she voiced what she was thinking, but, goodness me, it was hard to keep it in.

Steve broke the silence. 'I've enjoyed working this case.' He looked down at the untouched drink, which was going flat. 'I didn't realise just how much I missed being a copper.'

Lips parted, Honey looked at him. Was there a small chance he too was contemplating staying put, going back to base and embracing the old life they'd had here?

She dived in. 'Lindsey's pregnant again. She's coming home. I wasn't here when Minnie was born, not for long, anyway. Even grandmas like to see a baby take its first steps. I've missed so much. I want to be here for this one. I want to play at being the best granny in the world. I want them to love me. I want to love them, cuddle and kiss them, and set them on the right path in life.'

Eyes unblinking, a surprised smile flickered on his lips. Turning towards her, he grabbed her hands between his. 'That doesn't seem a bad plan. Any chance of you doing the same for me? Although you don't need to set me on the right path. I'm fine being a copper.'

Honey could hardly believe her ears. At the same time, she felt an inner glow that in no time could become a Roman candle, a celebration that perhaps they knew where they truly wanted to be. With each other.

'Home is where the heart is and all that.'

'Suits me.'

'We'll move permanently into the coach house.'

'We'll play happy families — literally.'

'And Cluedo. Literally.'

They hardly noticed how flat and tasteless their drinks had become. They were laughing, happy, because it didn't matter where you lived — it was who you were with and what you were doing that mattered.

They clinked glasses. 'To being a grandmother.'

'To being a landlubber.'

She reached into her purse to count what change she had — and discovered the stone that had fallen out of Tassel's collar.

For a moment its luminosity filled her eyes. A diamond, not diamanté, and worth enough to buy another boat.

But it's not yours, she told herself. *And, anyway, I think I'm going to like being a landlubber again.*

She fought hard to pretend she hadn't seen the way Steve was looking at her. It was a look that was easily read. Sad, intense and clinging onto the dream that had ended so abruptly, wishing and hoping that she would change her mind.

THE END

ACKNOWLEDGEMENTS

To what used to be the Zodiac Club and all the people I met in Bath, some still here and some gone, including Betty Jane — Mary Jane in this book. She really was a professor of the paranormal — that's what she said. Also to Darleene Rixey who persuaded me that I was a writer. And to the sunshine of California, Betty Jane's pink Cadillac and John Rixey's forbearance for our madness when we drove down into Tijuana. Plus the life that came after, living on *Sarabande Serene*, who in this story I've named *Footloose*, because that's what we were. Footloose and fancy-free. And to my late husband Dennis, who was determined to live the dream and sometimes scared the life out of me!

THE JOFFE BOOKS STORY

We began in 2014 when Jasper agreed to publish his mum's much-rejected romance novel and it became a bestseller.

Since then we've grown into the largest independent publisher in the UK. We're extremely proud to publish some of the very best writers in the world, including Joy Ellis, Faith Martin, Caro Ramsay, Helen Forrester, Simon Brett and Robert Goddard. Everyone at Joffe Books loves reading and we never forget that it all begins with the magic of an author telling a story.

We are proud to publish talented first-time authors, as well as established writers whose books we love introducing to a new generation of readers.

We won Trade Publisher of the Year at the Independent Publishing Awards in 2023 and Best Publisher Award in 2024 at the People's Book Prize. We have been shortlisted for Independent Publisher of the Year at the British Book Awards for the last five years, and were shortlisted for the Diversity and Inclusivity Award at the 2022 Independent Publishing Awards. In 2023 we were shortlisted for Publisher of the Year at the RNA Industry Awards, and in 2024 we were shortlisted at the CWA Daggers for the Best Crime and Mystery Publisher.

We built this company with your help, and we love to hear from you, so please email us about absolutely anything bookish at feedback@joffebooks.com.

If you want to receive free books every Friday and hear about all our new releases, join our mailing list here: www.joffebooks.com/freebooks.

And when you tell your friends about us, just remember: it's pronounced Joffe as in coffee or toffee!

www.ingramcontent.com/pod-product-compliance
Ingram Content Group UK Ltd.
Pitfield, Milton Keynes, MK11 3LW, UK
UKHW020026050825
7227UKWH00004B/245